THE OTHER

SISTER

pabfi
HILL

POR

Hill, Donna (Donna O.)
The other sister
33410016660880   07/16/20

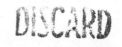

Also by Donna Hill

If I Could

Say Yes

A House Divided

Heat Wave (with Niobia Bryant and Zuri Day)

The One That I Want (with Zuri Day and Cheris Hodges)

Published by Kensington Publishing Corp.

THE OTHER SISTER

DONNA HILL

KENSINGTON PUBLISHING CORP.
www.kensingtonbooks.com

DAFINA BOOKS are published by

Kensington Publishing Corp.
119 West 40th Street
New York, NY 10018

All Kensington titles, imprints, and distributed lines are available at special quantity discounts for bulk purchases for sales promotion, premiums, fundraising, and educational or institutional use.

Special book excerpts or customized printings can also be created to fit specific needs. For details, write or phone the office of the Kensington Sales Manager: Kensington Publishing Corp., 119 West 40th Street, New York, NY 10018. Attn. Sales Department. Phone: 1-800-221-2647.

Dafina and the Dafina logo Reg. U.S. Pat. & TM Off.

ISBN-13: 978-1-4967-2380-2
ISBN-10: 1-4967-2380-5
First Kensington Trade Paperback Printing: July 2020

ISBN-13: 978-1-4967-2381-9 (ebook)
ISBN-10: 1-4967-2381-3 (ebook)
First Kensington Electronic Edition: July 2020

10 9 8 7 6 5 4 3 2 1

Printed in the United States of America

This novel is dedicated in loving memory to my mom, Dorothy Hill, who was my cheerleader and champion. She taught me how to love and instilled in me the importance of family. I miss you every day.

ACKNOWLEDGMENTS

I have to send a big thanks to my editor, Selena James, for her patience and guidance with this novel and through the years with all the projects that we have worked on together.

Without my readers, where would I be? Since 1990, when my first novel, *Rooms of the Heart*, was published, the most dedicated readers anywhere, romance readers, took me in and gave me a new family. Through the years, they have continued reading my work, sharing the good news of the stories that I write, and sending me uplifting letters (back in the day). To your posts on social media supporting all my "babies," I thank each and every one of you from the bottom of my heart!

PROLOGUE

Zoie Crawford opened the cover of her laptop. She had her story to write. Not the one that her editor, Marc, was expecting, but her version.

Her cell phone rang. She picked it up from the desk and was surprised to see it was Kimberly Maitland-Graham. The long-lost half-sister she was just thinking about. She pressed the talk icon.

"Hello, Mrs. Graham."

"Hello. I've thought about . . . our conversation," Kimberly said.

"And?"

"I need you to understand that no matter what threats you make to expose my family, no matter how I feel or what I want or believe, I can't tell my family. It would destroy my marriage, ruin my children. My children!"

Zoie shut her eyes, heard the passionate plea in Kimberly's voice. "Don't you even want to know your real mother, *our* mother—me? Don't your children deserve to know their grandmother, their roots?"

"I can't. Please . . . if you have any compassion, you won't do this. They can't find out this way." She paused. "At least let me do it my way in my own time. Do you have children, Zoie?"

"No."

"Then you can never understand that a mother will do anything, anything to protect her children."

Zoie thought about her great-grandmother, her grandmother, her own mother, and the sacrifices they'd made, the losses they'd endured, the deals and secrets they'd kept, hoping for a better life for their children.

"I think I do," she said softly. "Good luck with whatever you decide to do, Kimberly. Maybe one day we'll see each other again—as sisters."

Zoie pressed the call end icon and slowly set the phone down. She turned to her laptop, opened her Word program to a blank page and began to write her article on Kimberly Maitland-Graham.

She wrote nonstop for a steady three hours before she was satisfied with the piece. After a last spell check, she hit send, and off it went to Marc. He would be disappointed to put it mildly. It wasn't the story they'd discussed. It wasn't even close. But it was the story seen through her new eyes. At least she would be able to sleep at night.

She went to look for her mother. They had a lot more talking to do.

⸻

The ringing phone stirred her from sleep. With one eye open, she groped for the phone on the nightstand.

"Hello?" she mumbled.

"Turn on the television. Not that local mess, a national channel," Marc barked into the phone.

Zoie fumbled, bleary-eyed, and located the remote and turned to MSNBC. There was a Breaking News banner running across the screen.

"It was just announced at Graham campaign headquarters that Kimberly Maitland-Graham has withdrawn from the race for State Senator, citing family concerns as a reason. Graham was considered a shoo-in for the nomination and all the polls indicated that she would win by a large margin over her Democratic opponent," the announcer said.

Zoie still held the phone as she watched in stunned silence.

"Are you hearing this?" Marc said, snapping her to attention.

"Yes. I'm watching."

"So much for your series. Not much point now."

"I suppose not," she said absently.

"And what was that crap fluff piece that you sent me on Graham?"

Zoie drew her knees to her chest. "A change of heart. All that other shit isn't as important as I thought it was."

"I see." He pushed out a breath. "When are you coming back to work?"

"That's another thing, Marc. I don't know when I'll be coming back . . ."

CHAPTER 1

"Have you lost your mind, Kimberly?"

The fury in Rowan's words struck her harder than a shove.

He paced the off-white carpeted bedroom floor, running his hand across his face as if he could wipe away the absurdity of what he'd heard. He whirled toward her, the ocean blue of his eyes turned dark and ominous. "You need to tell me what the hell is going on."

Kimberly drew in a breath, tucked her strawberry blond hair behind her diamond studded ears. "I should have told you first before I made the announcement."

"You think!" he snapped.

Kimberly inwardly flinched. "I've been . . . struggling with this decision for weeks."

Rowan started to speak.

"Please let me finish." She closed her eyes for a moment. "Running for office. Having a higher calling. It all sounds so wonderful. Altruistic." She forced a half smile. "But it's not what I want. The life of a politician . . . what that kind of life that would mean for the girls." She crossed the room and stood right in front of him. She clasped his shoulders. "Our lives would be turned upside down," she pleaded.

Rowan's sleek brows drew together, cinching his eyes into

stormy slits. "Kim. We talked about this for nearly a year before you announced that you were running for State Senate." He pulled away from her and threaded his fingers through his sandy brown hair. "What about the staff, the lease on the campaign office, the donors! I put my fucking name on the line to get them to dig in their pockets." He jabbed his finger in her direction. "For you! What do you plan to tell them? What am *I* supposed to tell them?" He shook his head and resumed his pacing.

The knot in Kimberly's throat grew. "I'll find a way to handle it. I will."

Rowan peered at her as if seeing her through a veil of fog. "Oh . . . you will. Like how you handled it by sending out a fucking press release instead of talking to me! That's what you mean by you'll handle it?" He snorted a laugh of disgust then blew out a breath. He snatched up his jacket from the chaise where he'd tossed it. "I'm going out."

The bedroom door slammed shut, vibrating through her veins. Her heart thudded. She dropped down to the side of the king-sized bed and lowered her face into her hands. Tears squeezed out from between her fingers. She sucked in air. In all their years of marriage she'd never seen Rowan that angry. He had every right. She should have talked to him first, but she knew that she couldn't. He would have used every logical and emotional tool in his toolbox to get her to stay in the race. Worse, he may have gotten her to admit the real truth and she was not ready for that. Not yet, maybe never, which is why she had no choice except to pull out.

Slowly she pushed herself to her feet, crossed the room, and stood in front of her dressing table mirror. Same soft pale skin that tanned perfectly in the sun, thick hair that tumbled in waves to her shoulders, dissolving into a riot of strawberry blond curls in damp weather, and gray-green eyes that changed color with the season. What stared back at her was the same reflection she'd seen for her entire thirty-eight years. But she wasn't the same. All the little quirks about her complexion, her hair, even the slight flare of her nose looked different now. Made sense now.

If Rowan lost his mind over her dropping out of the race, what would he do if she told him the real reason?

She turned away from the damning image.

"Mom?"

Kimberly blinked, turned toward the door.

Her twin daughters, Alexis and Alexandra, stood in the threshold. Their identical doe-brown eyes were wide with concern.

Kimberly forced a smile. Sniffed. "Hey. My girls."

"I heard you and Daddy yelling," Alexis said softly.

"Oh, sweetheart." She crossed the room, bent down and put her arms around her daughters. "Grown people argue. Just like you two do," she added, looking from one to the other.

"You and Daddy *never* yell," Alexandria insisted.

Kimberly tucked her lips in before she spoke. "After you and your sister fuss and fight don't things always go back to the way they were? You make up. You forgive. Right?"

They nodded, their chestnut ponytails bobbing.

She kissed each one in turn on the cheek. "Everything is fine. You'll see. Now, who wants pizza?"

"I do!" they chorused in perfect harmony.

"Great." She rose to her feet. "You ladies go wash up and I'll put in the order."

"Extra pepperoni!" Alexis called out as the sisters darted out of the room.

Kimberly sighed heavily, turned around, and crossed to her nightstand and picked up the phone. She opened the drawer and took out the small collection of menus, found the one for their local pizzeria, called and placed her order. *Forty minutes.* Maybe Rowan would be back by then. She tossed he phone aside.

This was all Zoie Crawford's fault. Every damned bit of it! She'd made a name for herself for her investigative series following the World Trade Center attack a year earlier. Now she'd set her sights on digging through *her* life with the same tenacity.

When she'd been approached with a phone call from Zoie months earlier to do an feature piece on her run for senate, she'd been very hesitant. But Zoie had insisted that it would highlight her career as an attorney, while also being the wife of one of New York's biggest tech giants, and a mother to twin girls. A story of a young girl from the south, growing up to become a New York powerhouse. Women everywhere would love an empowerment story like hers, she'd said. Ironically, it was Rowan who ultimately convinced her to agree to the profile, insisting that it would be great publicity.

Kimberly had looked up Zoie's writing credits to discover that she'd done an extensive series on the World Trade Center disaster. The writing was vivid, insightful, and compassionate, but a stark reminder of a day, the remnants of which were still visible and visceral a year later. So, she'd finally agreed, thinking at the time "little paper, little coverage," but every negative thing that she'd ever heard about journalists, Zoie proved to be true.

It was no wonder that those in politics had such an adversarial relationship with the press. Zoie Crawford epitomized all that was reviled in journalists; the unshakeable tenacity to shovel up every ugliness, misstep, secret, and pain, without regard for their prey or the upheaval that it may cause in their lives.

Perhaps Zoie felt that she was being magnanimous by sending her an early copy of the story that she'd intended to send to her newspaper publisher.

She still experienced the visceral shock that accelerated her heart and swirled her thoughts, the morning the draft of the article popped up on her computer screen. The words were knife-like, stabbed her with precision, and opened wounds she didn't know she had. All those months of "friendly" phone calls and follow-up visits, even showing up at her campaign gala, was all part of Zoie's ruse to seep into her life and infect every aspect of it.

What choice did she have? She did the only thing she could to protect her marriage and her family. Family! She didn't even know what that meant anymore. Whatever she'd believed family to be had been shattered. Her parents weren't her parents. Her father was not her father. And her real mother had been the housekeeper's daughter. She couldn't wrap her own mind around it. How could she ever tell that to Rowan? Rowan Graham was the poster child for nouveau money and east coast elitism, who quietly embraced the ideologies of white privilege, from which she'd passively benefited. Until now.

The printing of Zoie's proposed story "The Rise of Kimberly Maitland-Graham—The Other Side of Politics," would have exposed innocent people to the Maitland family secret that had remained hidden for decades, and the inevitable fallout that would come with its unearthing. She couldn't let that happen, especially to her children.

That last phone call between her and Zoie, she'd practically begged Zoie not to go through with submitting the exposé. *"I need you to understand that no matter what threats you make to expose my family, no matter how I feel, or what I want or believe, I can't tell my family. It would destroy my marriage, ruin my children. My children!"*

"Don't you even want to know your real mother, our mother— me? Don't your children deserve to know their grandmother, their roots?"

"I can't. Please . . . if you have any compassion, you won't do this. They can't find out this way." She paused. "At least let me do it my way in my own time. Do you have children, Zoie?"

"No."

"Then you can never understand that a mother will do anything, anything to protect her children."

The very idea that she and Zoie Crawford were related by blood sickened her to her stomach.

It was after midnight when she heard the front door open and close. Her body stiffened beneath the soft, pale peach sheets. She heard her own heartbeat thump against the pillow that she gripped against her body. Minutes passed, but Rowan didn't come into the bedroom. She strained her ears for any sounds coming from the front of the penthouse apartment.

Tossing the covers aside, she got out of bed, grabbed her robe, and slipped it on. When she opened the bedroom door, she was taken aback to see the entire front of the apartment was settled in darkness. Goosebumps rose along her arms. Was she going to be like one of those women from television that walks into the dark room while the audience screams for her not to go in there?

She eased out into the hallway that led to the living room. She was certain she'd heard Rowan come in. With a flick of the switch, the room was bathed in soft light. She was alone.

"I am not going crazy," she muttered. "Rowan," she called out, barely above a whisper. She walked in the opposite direction toward the formal dining room that led to their respective home offices.

A sliver of light peeked out from under Rowan's office door. The thudding of her heart slowed. She walked toward the office, knocked once and opened the door.

Rowan's back was to her. He stood facing the window that looked out onto the Manhattan skyline. His silhouette cut an impressive sight against the dark sky and twinkling lights. That was Rowan—impressive. So much about who he was as a person was tied to creating impressions. She remembered how awestruck she'd been by him that very first time they'd met.

It was a fundraising event for the rehabilitation of the famed James Theater. She couldn't remember why she was even there. Those kinds of events she generally steered clear of. She'd been groomed and nurtured on fundraisers, attended more than she could count. As an adult, she avoided them as often as she could. As an attorney whose client roster resembled the who's who of the marginalized, her work didn't lend itself to fancy galas. But she'd gone to that one. She was seated at the table with one of her colleagues from the legal clinic where she worked. Something drew her attention to the door, and there he was—standing there, framed in the archway. She remembered that she couldn't breathe. Her throat had grown dry and her heart raced as if she'd been chased. She watched him cross the room and the waves of well-heeled guests parted like the Red Sea then closed in around him.

"Who is that?" she'd whispered to her friend Gwynne.

"Rowan Graham. Big tech guy. Has his money in all the right places from what I hear," she said over the top of her champagne flute.

Kimberly couldn't look away.

"I can introduce you," she said after a while with a knowing grin.

Kimberly felt her cheeks heat. She shook her head in an unconvincing no.

Gwynne got up. Pushed her seat back and grabbed Kimberly's wrist. "Come on."

"Gwynne," she weakly protested, yet the flow of excitement propelled her across the room.

Gwynne, always the outgoing one, smiled and made quick small talk as she guided Kimberly around the mingling guests until they reached the bar where Rowan was getting a drink.

"Rowan Graham," Gwynne said as if she'd run into an old friend.

Rowan slowly turned around and the sea blue of his eyes settled somewhere down in her soul and she hadn't looked away since that night.

Now, Kimberly steeled herself against the anger she feared she would find in those eyes.

"I thought you would be asleep," Rowan said without turning around.

Hesitantly she walked over and stood beside him. "I couldn't sleep. Waiting for you." She glanced toward him only getting his profile.

Rowan brought the tumbler of bourbon to his lips. "I think I'll sleep in the guest room."

Her stomach knotted. She wouldn't cry. She swallowed over the dryness in her throat, started to speak but changed her mind. She knew her husband. When Rowan was in that mental space, he didn't allow room for anything other than his own feelings and opinions until he'd worked through whatever the issue was. Then he would talk. He always did. They'd work through it. She drew in a breath and slowly exhaled.

"Good night," she whispered, then walked out, closing the door softly behind her. It was only then that she let the tears fall.

———————

It had been over two weeks since she'd withdrawn from the race. Just as long since Rowan had slept in their bed. In front of their girls they played the role of loving parents. But when they were alone, between the time the girls left for school and they left for work, utter and complete silence or one-word answers were all that passed between them.

Once again, Rowan left for the office without a backward glance at her. This was going on longer than usual. By now, they would have been talking, laughing, making love, making plans.

The morning copy of *The New York Times* was on the counter next to her cup of coffee. It had been opened, folded back to the politics page that featured a short article about how she suddenly pulled out of the New York State Senate race and the fallout as a result. She rolled her eyes in frustration. This was clearly another dig by Rowan, leaving the paper for her to see. However, it was good news for her competitor for the primary that she was no longer in line for. The words blurred in front of her.

She picked up her purse and briefcase from the kitchen counter, tossed the paper in the trash, checked for her keys, and walked out. There were clients to see, an office to run. Kimberly Maitland-Graham, Esq. At least she still had her practice and the girls to keep her mind occupied. She checked the time. Her taxi should be there in about five minutes.

"Good morning, Mrs. Graham," Howard the doorman greeted. He pulled open the glass and chrome-plated door.

"'Morning, Howard." She crossed the threshold. "Oh no, rain," she bemoaned. "I left my umbrella upstairs."

"Wait right here." He went behind the desk, took out an umbrella, and handed it to Kimberly. "Don't want you to get wet."

Kimberly smiled. "Thanks. And I promise to bring it back." She stepped out beneath the building's awning just as her taxicab pulled up in front.

Settled in the back seat she mindlessly peered out at the pale gray morning, the cityscape obscured by the rain. If only she could pull a pale gray veil around her current situation, shield her spirit from it. She was exhausted, and not because she'd worked endless hours and stayed up overnight to prepare for a case. She was exhausted trying to walk the tightrope that her marriage had suddenly become, fielding and dodging phone calls from friends, frenemies, her campaign staff, and the press. Rowan insisted that he would deal with the donors, but he acted as if it was the gauntlet to hell and the attitude of it wafted around him like cheap cologne.

The rain beat and slapped the windows, splashed pedestrians and limited visibility. From her spot in the back seat, the Big Apple resembled the moors of London. By the time she arrived at her downtown office, the heavens had fully opened, complete with thunder and lightning, and as she made a mad dash from the cab to the office building, she was immensely grateful to Howard for the umbrella.

She pushed through the revolving door and shook her hair as she walked toward the security check in.

"Good morning, Lenny," she said to the security officer. She inserted her ID card into the scanner.

"Real mess out there today, Mrs. Graham," he said as he verified her information on the computer screen that projected a picture of her face. "Sorry to hear you pulled out of the race," he said in a conciliatory voice.

The card scanner beeped and she extracted her card. "Thanks," she murmured, took the card, and put it back in her purse. "Have a good day, Lenny," she said over a tight smile.

She strutted toward the elevators and wished that she could hide behind her tumble of hair and avoid the questioning glances, or bold 'why did you do it' questions. Then of course there were those who gave her sympathetic puppy dog looks and sad smiles. She entered the elevator, happy to be the sole occupant, stepped to the back, and wished all the floors between the lobby and tenth, where her office was, would speed by nonstop. At least that wish came true and she didn't have to be subjected to being enclosed with the curious.

The doors slid soundlessly open and she crossed the short hall to her office door. Seeing her name on the door, emblazoned on the gold plate, slightly lifted her spirit. This was something that all the news stories in the world couldn't take away from her. She'd worked her ass off to get to where she was. Maybe she wasn't the high-priced Wall Street corporate lawyer that her husband and his associates thought she should be, but what she did mattered to her, and to all the people that didn't matter to anyone else.

She drew in a deep breath of resolve, prepared to be greeted by her assistant with her handful of messages from news outlets that wanted to interview her, and clients worried that her personal life had affected their cases. She mentally checked her taut expression and fixed a smile on her face.

"Good morning, Gail."

"Good morning, Mrs. Graham. How was the weekend?"

"Too short," she quipped.

Gail's freckled face tightened in concentration. "You look tired. I hope you're not letting all the political noise get to you."

"It can be a bit much. But I'm getting through it day by day."

"It will ease up as soon as they find something more interesting. I put coffee on."

"Thanks."

"Messages are on your desk."

"Hmm."

Kimberly walked into her office and closed the door behind her. When she lowered herself into the chair she felt as if someone had stuck a pin in her, deflating her of any motivation or energy. She hadn't done a thing but was already exhausted by the day ahead of her.

Mindlessly she flipped through the half dozen or so messages. Most were, as she'd expected, calls from reporters that wanted to talk with her. The rest were from two of her clients. But the last message stopped her cold. The paper in her hand rattled. The message was from Zoie Crawford.

Her breath heaved in and out. How dare she? Zoie Crawford was at the center of the nightmare that had become her life!

She spun her chair so that she faced the window. Ten floors up wasn't high enough to make everything below small and insignificant. That's what she needed for her soul right now, to feel big, towering, invincible. She blinked back the sudden burn in her eyes, then swung her chair back around.

What did she want now? Hadn't she done enough damage? She stared at the slip of paper with Zoie's name and number, snatched it up in her fist and crushed it, then tossed it in the trash. If only it could be that easy to toss in the trash the shitstorm that had swept through her existence.

Her intercom buzzed.

"Yes, Gail."

"Your eleven o'clock is here."

"Thank you. Give me a minute and then send him in."

She opened the side file drawer and pulled out the manila folder with Jerome Washington's name on it. She did a quick scan of the case notes and the details of what had taken place so far, the briefs that had been filed, and the upcoming court date. Jerome Washington was nineteen years old, picked up in a drug sweep, and through a series of procedural screw-ups, he wound up in a lineup for robbery suspects. The witness picked Jerome out of the lineup. He was charged with robbery and assault and sent to the infamous Rikers Island, where he'd languished for the last six months. When Mr. Washington came to her office two months earlier, he was at the end of his rope. Desperate. She'd taken the case because she believed that justice had been perverted in Jerome's case and she could easily see him spending decades in jail without intervention. She pressed the intercom and instructed Gail to have Mr. Washington come in.

Kimberly rose from her seat, extended her hand. "Mr. Washington. Good morning. Please. Have a seat."

He shook her hand in a less than firm grip and lowered his hefty body into the padded seat. "Mornin'." He swept his cap from his head.

"I've gone over all the details of your grandson's case, Mr. Washington, and I'm confident that we'll be able to get him out on bail until his trial." She smiled with confidence. "Things look much better for your grandson, Mr. Washington."

He squeezed his damp hat in his hand. "See, I'm worried that you not gonna be able to give it your best. And my grandson deserves the best. He's a good kid."

Kimberly sat straighter, blinked back her surprise. "I don't understand."

"I had my doubts when you were running for office and handling clients."

She swallowed. "That's over now." She felt her cheeks heat.

He lowered his head. "I done found another lawyer. That's what I come to tell you."

"Oh. I see. When did this happen?"

"Couple of weeks."

Her brows rose. She pushed out a breath. "I'm sorry that you found it necessary to seek other counsel."

He pushed to his feet, slid his cap back on his head. "I want to thank you for your time."

Kimberly stood up and extended her hand. "Thank you for coming in, Mr. Washington. I wish the best for you and your grandson."

He shook her hand, gave a short nod, turned and walked out.

Kimberly plopped down in her seat. Under normal circumstances she would have put up a fight. She would have pulled all the stops to assure her client they'd made the right decision in choosing her, and that to leave would be a mistake because no one would fight as hard as she would. But the reality was, she didn't care. In a way, she was mildly relieved. The only thing on her mind was this 'new person' she'd become, and how she would explain to Rowan that she was not the woman he married.

The light knock on the door barely drew her attention. How long had she been sitting there staring at her framed degrees on the wall? Gail poked her head in. Kimberly blinked the room back into focus.

"Everything okay? Mr. Washington kept saying he was sorry on his way out."

Kimberly glanced away. "He has decided to find other counsel," she said on a breath.

"Oh . . ."

"It's fine." She ran her tongue along her bottom lip. She linked her fingers together and looked up at Gail. "I have some follow-up calls to make. I think I'll do them from home." She swallowed over the tight knot in her throat. "If you need to reach me, call me on my cell."

"Is there anything we need to talk about?"

Kimberly made busywork of looking for something on her desk, anything not to look into Gail's all-knowing eyes.

Gail sat down in the chair that Mr. Washington had vacated. "I know we aren't best friends or anything, but if you want to talk . . . I'm here to listen. I know things aren't easy right now, but this will pass." She offered a tight-lipped smile.

"Thanks." She opened her desk drawer and took out her purse then sat it on top of the desk. She looked Gail in the eyes. "I appreciate the offer. I really do." Her throat clenched and her eyes were beginning to burn. If she sat there for a moment longer she knew she'd burst into tears. She pushed back from the desk and stood. "If anything comes up, you can reach me on my cell." She walked past Gail.

"Sure. No problem. Have some wine and put your feet up."

Kimberly glanced at Gail over her shoulder and smiled.

"Works for me," Gail added.

"I'll keep that in mind." She left the door open on her way out.

On the ride home, Gail's words of comfort replayed in her head. If only a glass of wine and putting up her feet could fix all that was broken.

CHAPTER 2

Zoie Crawford checked her voicemail. Still no response from
Kimberly. It was going on two weeks since she'd swallowed her
pride and made the first of several calls. She'd been doubtful that
Kimberly would respond, but there was an inkling of hope. She
totally understood why Kimberly wouldn't want to have anything
to do with her, but now that she knew who she really was and who
her family was . . . Anyway, it was in Kimberly's ballpark now.
She'd done all she could to mitigate the emotional damage that
she'd inflicted on Kimberly by unearthing the dark family secret.
The entire family was still navigating the repercussions.

She tossed the cell phone on the bed and walked over to her
closet to find something to wear. She had her own set of issues to
deal with, which seemed to mount by the day.

When she'd returned to Louisiana for her Nana Claudia's
homegoing, she had no intention of staying in the toxic household from which she'd fled to New York years earlier. But she
had; first because of the stipulations in her Nana's will, and then
because she'd truly wanted to. The fractured road between her
and her mother Rose was slowly on the mend. She'd also discovered that not only was she an outstanding journalist, but she had
a head for business, which had helped her to grow her grandmother's small enterprise exponentially in the time since she'd

taken over. And she'd stayed for Jackson. Now she wasn't sure what would happen between them. Jackson was going to be a father—and not the father of *their* child, but the father of a child he'd conceived with his ex, Lena. How fucked up was that?

She pulled on a bright white blouse and watched her reflection button the tiny white buttons. It was the same blouse she'd worn that afternoon two weeks ago when Jackson came over to tell her about Lena. Déjà vu? Freudian slip? Who knew? What she did know was that she still loved Jackson. As crazy as that may seem under the circumstances. What she was unsure of was whether she was cut out to be the woman that had to deal with baby mama drama. Lena insisted to Jackson that she could handle it, that she was going through with the pregnancy not because she wanted him back but because she wanted to have her baby. She wasn't looking for him to come back to her.

That all sounded good, but Zoie knew of too many relationships that went down the drain because reality seeped into everyone's life. After Jackson's heartfelt confession, she told him that she needed some time to think things through. Today was the day and she still wasn't sure if she could separate what was on her mind from what was in her heart. But before that she had to meet with the distributors for her grandmother's fruits and vegetables.

※━●━※

Rose glanced over her shoulder at the sound of footsteps. "Hey." She dried her hands on a red-and-white striped hand towel and turned off the faucets.

Zoie walked over to the sink and gave her mother a soft kiss on the cheek.

Rose tenderly stroked Zoie's back. "Hungry? There's some fresh biscuits until dinner."

Zoie flashed a sheepish grin. "Starving, as usual. I swear Mama, since I've been back here, I musta gained at least ten pounds."

Rose waved off Zoie's complaint. "Chile, it's the air, *and* the genes."

If it was the air, she was going to have to start holding her breath. Genes on the other hand—there wasn't much to be done about that. The Bennett women were endowed with cat-calling hips and thighs, and bosoms that you wanted to sink your hopes and dreams into. The kids would call the Bennett women 'thick.'

Zoie poured a cup of coffee and plucked a fresh-baked biscuit from the wicker basket on the table. "This right here," she mumbled as she chewed on the heavenly soft, buttered biscuit, "is the reason. If you and my aunties would stop with all this baking, I could get my figure back."

Rose smothered a chuckle. She turned from the sink and faced her daughter. "I'm really glad you're here," she said, her voice slightly wobbly. She blinked rapidly, pressed her lips together, and turned back to the sink.

Zoie froze before taking another bite of her biscuit. Her heart beat faster. To say that she and her mother had a rocky relationship would be a world class understatement. Years of miscommunication, accusations, and emotional wounds had done decades of damage that they were both working to heal. Finding out the truth about her grandmother Claudia, who'd been the keeper of the family secret, and then locating that secret—Kimberly, who turned out to be her half-sister—had been major turning points for mother and daughter, a point where they could move forward together. But twenty plus years of animosity and misunderstandings didn't vanish in a matter of months. They were still a work in progress. Her mother was the one moving fast, and as much as she wanted to keep pace with her mother, she wasn't there yet and she knew it affected her mother.

"I have a meeting with the distributors," she said, sidestepping her mother's comment. "Then I'm going to have dinner . . . with Jackson." She watched her mother nod her head. Her tummy tightened. "See you later this evening. Do you need me to bring anything?"

"No, but you might want to check with your aunts. I think they're sitting out back on the porch."

Zoie wiped her mouth with a napkin, tossed it in the garbage, then gave her mother's shoulder a slight squeeze. "Thanks." She turned to leave.

"Zoie . . ."

"Yes, Mama?"

"Have you heard anything from Kimberly?"

The flickering light of hope in her mother's eyes was a stab of guilt to her heart. "No, I haven't. I'm sorry," she added gently.

Rose looked away, nodded.

Zoie wanted to offer some reassurance, some words of comfort but it was still something she struggled with. "I'll see you later, okay." She headed out.

She shouldn't feel guilty about anything. All that she'd done was dig for the truth, what she'd been trained to do as a journalist. How was she to know that what she discovered would upend her entire family and Kimberly Maitland's as well? Kimberly, when presented with the choice, made a conscious decision to dismiss what she knew to be true. That wasn't Zoie's fault. It wasn't her fault that Kimberly didn't want to have anything to do with them. It wasn't. Then why did she feel so guilty?

She turned the key in the ignition of her Honda Accord and pulled out of the short driveway onto the main road. What she needed to concentrate on now was negotiating a solid deal with the distributors, and keeping her grandmother's business thriving. At least for the next few hours she could keep her mind off 'the talk' with Jackson. It was a conversation that she'd been avoiding for weeks, and couldn't any longer. They were going to meet for an early dinner in town at their favorite spot, and by the time dessert was served, they would either be together for the long haul or it would be over for good.

One of Kimberly's favorite places in Manhattan was the main branch of the library on Forty-second Street. The majestic pink Tennessee marble lions—known as Patience and Fortitude—that guarded the vaulted entrance were iconic symbols of New York. At the time of its opening in 1911, it was the largest marble building ever built in the United States. Every room, every nook, was sprinkled in elegance, from the soaring arches, sweeping marble staircases, and dazzling chandeliers, to the unrivaled massive collections that scholars and researchers traveled from across the globe to study.

Her favorite spot was the third floor—the Rose Main Reading Room—that was nearly the length of a football field. The enormous space was stocked with manuscripts, archival ephemera and rare books. She could spend hours tucked away in one of the many comfy alcoves devouring one of the classics.

Most often, she came to the library for research and of course to find that treasure of a book. Then there were the times she came simply to immerse herself in something larger than herself, unwind and become inspired. Today was one of those days. The library was her oasis where she came to replenish her soul, and if there was ever a time she needed replenishing, it was now.

She slipped out of her lightweight trench coat, draped it over her arm and began the slow perusal of the shelves in hopes of finding something to take her mind away from herself. After more than a half hour of picking up and putting down, she finally settled on nothing at all and instead, found a cozy corner to tuck herself into, and closed her eyes.

For a time, the soft whisper of turning pages fluttered like wings of a butterfly. She smiled at the comforting sound and if she listened really closely, she could hear the pens pressing against paper, carving out new ideas for posterity.

The sounds lulled her, not to sleep, but rather into a place of clarity. The history that was hers *she* needed to write. She must decide how the rest of her life was going to play out. For the past year, her life had been the purview of the media, formed by her PR team that crafted her image, her speech writer that outlined what she should say and when, and her donors who supported the well-crafted image. In order to take control of her life, she was going to have to tell the truth to her husband. Yet the very idea was more frightening than the truth itself.

Since she'd been confronted with the darkness of her family's past, literally and figuratively, she saw the world and the people in it through new eyes. There were the shaded comments from Rowan's associates and even their friends about 'thugs' and foreigners, and how they were sick of walking the streets of New York City and not hearing English. The comments were filled with veiled bigotry and until recently she thought nothing of them, until she realized that now she was one of 'them' an 'other,' the very person that her friends and associates disparaged. That is what gave her pause. Her husband, the man that vowed to love her, expressed the same sentiments as their friends. Would he still be able to love her when he knew the truth—that she was not the pristine, white southern belle he'd married, but was the product of a black mother, and had black blood running through her veins? And if not, what would become of them and their family? Would it matter that she'd been lied to all her life as well?

Her lids fluttered open and she gazed around at the depth and breadth of history, and knew that going forward whatever story was told about her, it would be the one she wanted to tell. Rowan loved her. She had to believe that above all else, and their love would see them through—for their sakes and for the sakes of their daughters.

When she walked outside from the sanctuary of the library, and into the late afternoon, it was still a couple of hours before she was expected at home. She decided to stop at Whole Foods and pick up everything she needed to prepare Rowan's favorite meal of braised New York strip steak, mushroom risotto, and grilled asparagus. She selected all the main ingredients and the fresh seasonings, along with two bottles of wine. She'd put the girls to bed early so that she and Rowan could talk undisturbed.

Zoie left her meeting with Lee Harding, the owner of Homestead Distributions. It was a relatively small operation, and at the time that her grandmother partnered with them, the partnership worked well. But although her grandmother's fruit and vegetable business began as a local endeavor, it had begun to spread to the surrounding parishes, and Harding was no longer sure if he could adequately provide the service that the growing business needed. Even Zoie had to hire three college students to help with the picking and packing.

Harding agreed to continue to work with Zoie as he wanted the business, and because of the boom in business he planned to bring in an additional driver. But she knew that if the business continued to prosper, she would soon have to look for another trucking service. One more thing to worry about. At least for now, business would continue as usual.

She sat behind the wheel of her car staring at nothing in particular. When she'd returned to Louisiana for her grandmother's funeral, she would have never thought in a million years that not only would she wind up staying, but that she'd be running a business. There were days when she desperately missed the rush, the exhilaration of living and working in New York City. Her job as an investigative journalist for the *Recorder* was her passion. She lived for the next big story, to dig beneath the surface and unearth the truth no matter how ugly. That searing need had led her to Kimberly and all the fallout as a result. The irony was not lost on her.

She turned the key in the ignition, put the car in gear and headed off to her meeting with Jackson. She was still torn, and Jackson was going to have to do a lot more than look like dessert, touch her in that way that made her lose her mind, and smooth talk her with his voice of silk. He was going to have to bring his A-plus game and then some, and she was going to need to resist falling under his spell, and listen to reason and not her heart.

However, making reservations at her favorite restaurant did earn him some points.

She pulled to a stop at a red light. Things between her and Jackson had always fluctuated between raging passion and searing tempers—mostly hers, she had to admit. Jackson was the one that wanted tradition, stability. He brought balance to her life, even as she sought constant challenges, wanted to pull open every door, and look under every rock, no matter the consequences. Jackson may have gone along with that part of her that could not be contained, but he never liked it. Combined with, at least for him, the fracture between her and her mother that led to arguments too numerous to count. Jackson could never get behind or support her ongoing battle with her mother. It was antithetical to everything he believed about family. He was the eldest of three, and although his married sister and world-traveling brother didn't live in Louisiana, family holiday gatherings were must-attend, major events for the Fullers; birthdays and anniversaries were celebrated with cards and flowers and FedEx'd gifts. Jackson, religiously, drove down to Baton Rouge where his parents lived at least three or four times a month for dinner, and would return filled with anecdotes about his mother's 'mother wit' on everything from adding just the right seasoning to her famous crawfish, to how many times she peeked out her window and saw her neighbor Stella's secret lover sneaking away before her husband got home from the overnight shift. All the while, his dad would pretend not to care by muffling his chuckles behind the sports page of the *Baton Rouge Centennial*.

"Be the bigger person, Z. That's your mother," he'd said as they'd sat together on his couch watching their favorite show, *Criminal Minds*. "The only one you'll ever have."

"Lucky me."

"You *are* lucky. You have a family. You know how many people wished they had what you do?"

"You don't get it! *Your* family actually loves you. *Your* mother doesn't try to suffocate you, wring the life out of you. And your dad is your biggest supporter. I haven't seen or heard from *mine* since I was a kid. That's *my* life, Jax. I have all the reasons in the world to feel the way I do."

"At some point, you gotta let all that go. 'Cause one of these days your stubborn stance is going to backfire, Z, but hopefully you'll see that chasing after someone else's truth won't stop you from crashing right into yours."

That was the last major conversation they'd had before she'd packed up and moved to New York, still fuming through the entire flight to JFK airport that he should say those things to her. In those ensuing years between her leaving Louisiana and coming back home she'd done what she'd set out to do, and much as Jackson had predicted, her tenacity for the truth led her right back to where she'd started. Jackson had been right about so many things. She'd spent years being 'the martyr' and never realizing or wanting to actually know the real truth that lived beneath the surface of her family. She'd wasted so much time gnawing on the bitter rinds of her perceived injustices and shutting out her family—time that she could never gain back. But now she was home and although the fence was still broken in many places, the family was mending the pieces. She wasn't the same woman who'd left years earlier, but had she changed enough to accept what Jackson was offering?

She cruised down the narrow street, hoping to locate a parking spot within walking distance of the restaurant. Finally, after her third spin around the block she found one a door down from the restaurant. She chuckled at the irony of the situation that mirrored her life—what she was looking for was always right there waiting.

The sun had just begun to set. Rooftops and church spires cut into the waves of orange, gold and white that lay like a blanket above them. She'd always loved this time of day. Back in New

York to get this view you'd often have to look out from the window of a skyscraper.

Zoie shut off the engine, grabbed her purse and got out. Chez Oskar was a true Louisiana-style restaurant from crayfish to po' boys to spicy gumbo, and they made the best Hurricanes this side of the Mississippi. Her tummy smiled the instant she crossed the threshold.

"Welcome to Chez Oskar," the hostess greeted. "Bar or table?"

"I'm actually meeting someone."

"Did they make a reservation?"

"Yes. It should be Jackson Fuller."

"And you would be right," a voice deep as the ocean said from behind her.

Zoie felt the heat start at the base of her spine and inch its way up her neck to explode in her head. She slowly turned with as much nonchalance as she could summon. "Hey," she managed over the thundering of her heart.

Jackson tenderly clasped her shoulder, leaned down and placed a light kiss on her cheek, but it may as well have been a lighted match. Her cheek was on fire.

"Hey, yourself."

His Hershey chocolate-brown eyes held her momentarily mesmerized. She blinked away the trance.

"Your waitress will seat you," the hostess said, took two menus from the rack and handed them to a young Nia Long look-alike.

"Right this way," 'Nia' said.

They were shown to a table, passing a horseshoe-shaped bar that dominated the space with its mirrored backdrop and rows of top shelf spirits, and lined from end to end with thirsty customers. The restaurant, though known for its down-home cuisine, could rival the five-star restaurants in décor. The soft lighting, nooked-in 'kiss me corner' seating for privacy, bright-white linen-topped tables and crystal and flatware that glistened beneath the lighting, offered an ambiance of luxury. What also set Chez Oskar apart was that it offered live entertainment and somehow Jackson had secured them a table with an excellent view of the small stage. Jackson, always the gentleman, helped her into her seat.

"I'm Toni and I'll be your server tonight," the Nia look-alike said. She placed the menus in front of them. "Can I start you with something to drink?"

"Apple martini," Zoie said.

"Bourbon, neat."

"Be right back." She whirled away.

"So . . . how are you?" Jackson began. He linked his long fingers together on top of the table.

Zoie drew in a breath and slowly exhaled. She placed her purse on the seat beside her. "Having a successful business is not a walk in the park. It's growing faster than I can keep up. I already have three helpers and I may need to hire more. My distributor is barely keeping up as well. That's what my meeting was about earlier."

"How can I help?"

Zoie stopped mid-thought and looked at Jackson. "This isn't your problem, Jax. 'Preciate the offer, though."

"Z. I promised your grandmother that I would do whatever I could."

"That was then. Things are different now. I'm here," she flung at him like an old shoe.

Jackson pursed his lips. "I see."

She licked her bottom lip. "I'm sorry. I didn't mean for it to come out that way. What I meant was that Nana Claudia left the business to me to run."

The waitress returned with their drinks and took dinner orders. They both ordered their favorite, Louisiana-style gumbo with just enough heat to flush the cheeks.

Jackson gave a slight shrug of his right shoulder. "Fine, Zoie. But my offer is always open."

"Nana's business is my responsibility. I'll work it out. I owe it to my grandmother. But that's not what we're here to talk about."

Jackson reached for his drink and took a short sip before set-ting the glass down. "No, it's not."

She wrapped her hands around her glass, but let it sit on the table.

Jackson cleared his throat. "I know finding out about Lena and the baby was not anything that you wanted to hear. But other than being a father to my child, there is no relationship between me and Lena. It's mutual. It was over between us before she told me."

Zoie pushed out a breath, glanced away, then slid her gaze to-ward Jackson. "I get that you had a life while I was gone, and I'm not faulting anyone in this Lifetime television scenario. But I have to be honest, Jackson," she said, her voice softening, "I don't think I can do the whole baby mama thing. I don't feel good about it. And to be perfectly honest, when your child arrives, there is no telling how you will feel or how Lena will feel about being a single mother. Babies have a way of changing people." She stared into her glass. "I think we should . . ."

"Should what, Z?"

"I think we should take a break until after . . . and see how we feel then." She swallowed over the hard knot in her throat. This was the second time she found herself walking away from Jack-son. Their relationship was fraught with breakups and passionate makeups. Her years away from him only served as a finger in the dam of her feelings for him. When she'd returned, and saw him again after so many years, she realized how much she still loved him, wanted him, needed him. She'd let down her guard and he'd stepped right in. And now this . . .

"Z." He stretched his hand across the table. His finger stroked her knuckle. "I don't want to lose you. Not again. We can make it work. Together." He unwrapped her fingers from the glass and held her hand. "We can do this. I love you, Z, and I know you love me."

How many times had they shared those exact words with each other over the years? Jackson Fuller was her Achilles heel, her weakness. He'd always been able to find a way over and around all the guardrails she'd constructed around her, weakening her resistance. She could never put her finger on exactly what was in his magic formula. Was it the corny way he'd introduced himself to her that very first time, on the campus of Tulane; asking her if she believed in love at first sight or should he pass by again. It was so ridiculously corny that she broke out laughing.

"I have a million of them," he'd said, grinning at her with a smile that seemed to settle the rush that constantly propelled her. "Jackson Fuller."

She'd told him her name and before she fully grasped what was happening, he'd gotten her number and they'd set up their first date that very weekend. When he'd come to pick her up, she felt that same sense of peace mixed with a tingling every time he touched her, looked at her as if she were the most incredible thing he'd ever seen, listened to every word she'd said, and laughed at her jokes. Making love with Jackson was the most natural thing in the world. That first time was surreal. It unmoored her, dismantled any emotional barriers, even as they had to temper their moans and cries of passion from the prying ears of her family a bedroom away. "We can do this," he'd whispered in her ear. "I want you totally in my life, whatever it takes." Jackson had wrapped her in the strength of his arms and promised to always be there for her, to listen to and support her dreams, to love her for as long as she'd let him. What choice did she have but to tumble headlong into love and lust with Jackson? Yet, it was all the reasons that she fell for him that caused the constant combustible episodes between them. Jackson's devout, often blind loyalty, and his unwavering central pillar of family always, and his non-confrontational personality continually reared its head. He could not wrap his mind or heart around her dysfunctional relationship with her mother, no matter the issue, no matter how many times she tried to explain it. He admired her tenacity when it came to her love for journalism and digging up the details of a story, but he couldn't condone her 'at any cost' mantra. They argued, they loved, they argued, they made up, *we can do this*, and round and round it went, until finally she knew that the only way to flush her soul and get off the merry-go-round was to leave Louisiana, and Jackson.

Her throat clenched and her eyes burned. "I can't risk," her voice broke, "falling any harder for you, investing in you, in us and then . . ."

He squeezed her hand. "That's not going to happen."

"You don't know that!" Tears spilled from her eyes. She snatched her hand away and swiped at her wet cheeks.

The waitress appeared with their dinner.

Jackson glanced up, whispered his thanks.

For several moments they avoided eye contact, focusing instead on the steamy bowls of gumbo in front of them.

Zoie pushed the spoon around in her bowl. She'd been through this emotional minefield before. She realized long ago that she would never 'get over' Jackson. Of that she was certain. She'd tried; other men, inhuman hours at work. But always in the back of her mind, sitting inside her soul, was Jackson, nudging her, reminding her of what could have been if she'd let it. Being away had dulled her need for him but didn't erase it. When he looked at her, she was putty, when he touched her she exploded inside, when he made love to her she lost her mind, body, and spirit and turned it all over to him. No one should have claim to that much control over another. She knew what it was like to have love turn on you. To want love so desperately that you were willing to snatch whatever crumbs fell from the table. She could not risk losing herself to him again only to find out six, seven months from now that he was going to be with his baby's mama. It would crush her and she wasn't sure if she would recover this time.

"Z . . . I'm not asking for you to commit yourself to me. But I am committing myself to you! No if, ands, or buts. You need to believe that. Baby, I wasn't the same man after you left." He drew in a long breath. "I tried to understand why you needed to leave, to do your thing to get away. I made my peace. And to be honest I wasn't sure if you were ever coming back. But I never, never stopped loving you." He reached across the table and held her hand. "Yeah, I got involved with Lena. She is an incredible woman. I cared about her. I still do, but I was never in love with her, and I think she always knew that. Lena is not a vindictive woman. She's as adamantly independent as you are. She doesn't need a man to make her whole. Not even the father of her child."

"I get all that, but—"

"No. I need you to hear me and not all the doubt that is running around in your head. I need you to put aside your investigative instincts and stop looking for a shoe to fall. This one time I'm asking you to trust your heart, Z." He squeezed her hand. "What is your heart telling you?" he quietly asked.

Zoie's lashes fluttered like butterfly wings over her eyes as she fought back tears. She dared to look at him and was immediately drawn into the dark warmth of his eyes, cocooned there in that secret place inside of him where she'd always sought solace. A tear slid down her cheek.

"I love you, baby. We can make this work. I know we can."

She bit down on her bottom lip to keep it from trembling. Her nostrils flared and she swore he could hear her heart hammering in her chest.

"I . . . I deal in facts, things I can prove," she said, her voice thready. She reached for her glass and took a swallow of her drink. "That's what scares me, Jackson. What's always scared me. Emotions, love, there is no explanation, no evidence, to prove that it's real or will last, or that it's the right person. It's all feelings."

"Whatever kind of proof you need to let you know that I'm all in when it comes to us, that you're the only woman I've ever loved, I'll find a way to prove it to you."

She sniffed hard. The ember of a smile flickered around her mouth.

"Your mother and your aunts are my secondary sources," he added.

Zoie chuckled at the journalism reference. "Hmm, they're all biased when it comes to you. Don't know if I can trust their judgment."

He leaned forward and brought her hand to his lips and kissed the inside of her palm.

A jolt shot up her arm. The air hitched in her throat.

"They're biased toward the truth. They know how much I love you. Always did. Nana Claudia especially."

She heaved a sigh and puckered her lips. "If we do this . . . and you hurt me—"

"I won't."

Moments of pounding silence hung between them.

Slowly her gaze moved across his face. "All right," she finally whispered.

Jackson's warm brown complexion lit up from inside. His eyes widened along with his smile. He got up, came around the table and slid onto the leather bench seat next to her. He cupped her cheeks in his palm, leaned in and kissed her as if they were alone in his bedroom and not the middle of a busy restaurant at dinner hour.

With great reluctance, he eased back even as he held her face in his palms. Zoie's breath skipped and ran in circles in her chest. She tugged on her bottom lip with her teeth.

"All right," he murmured against her mouth, reconfirming her words.

***

"Thank you so much for doing this, Grace," Kimberly said to her friend and neighbor.

"I love having the girls over, and Samantha is in heaven." She laughed, then lowered her voice for only Kimberly to hear. "I know how it is when we need a little husband and wife time." She winked.

Kimberly forced a smile. "Absolutely." She looked down and placed her hands on the shoulders of her twins. "Remember your manners and you listen to Ms. Grace."

"We will," they chorused. Their slender young bodies vibrated with energy.

In the background, Samantha squealed and jumped up and down with delight.

"Thanks again, Grace. I'll be by to pick them up around noon."

"Whenever is fine. Enjoy yourself."

Kimberly walked down to the other end of the carpeted hallway and returned to her apartment. There were only two units on her floor: hers and Grace's. Grace's unit however was a coveted duplex. She and Rowan, and Edward and Grace Harrison, applied for occupancy at the same time. When Rowan saw the floor plan, he was set on having the duplex. It took Rowan quite some time to accept that someone had actually outbid him for a thing that he wanted. Eventually, Rowan and Grace's husband Edward became fast friends. Now after nearly five years of sharing the same floor, you couldn't tear the two men apart. Having Grace as a friend who was also a mother of a young girl was an added bonus.

Kimberly quietly closed the door behind her. Rowan should be home in about two hours. That gave her enough time to finish the meal, take a nice hot shower, and change. She needed everything to be perfect. The food, the atmosphere—*her*. Instead of feeling the ease of a wife making a special meal for her husband, she felt the uncertainty and jitters of a woman trying to impress a man with a home cooked dinner with her as dessert.

She wasn't a praying woman, or particularly religious, but she found herself saying little prayers that Rowan would understand, that he would forgive her, that they would make it through, that all the side comments and racial innuendos would be forgotten. He loved her.

It was well beyond the two hours when she heard the front door open and close and Rowan's steady footsteps crossing the glossy hardwood floors. She stood from her seat in the dining room and re-lit the candles. He stopped at the entrance, frowned for a moment as if he could not quite make out the scene in front of him.

"What's all this?"

"I wanted to make a special dinner for you. And . . . talk."

His cheeks flushed. His perfect mouth tightened.

"Talk about what, Kim?" He shrugged out of his dark blue jacket and hung it on the back of the chair and sat down. He loosened his maroon striped tie.

"Fixed your favorites," she said, her voice rising to a cheery octave. She hurried out of the dining room and returned shortly with the platters from the kitchen that had been on the warmers. She smiled hopefully while she set the platters down. She prepared his plate then hers.

Rowan poured himself some wine then took a long swallow, nearly finishing the glass before setting it down. "Talk about what?" he repeated.

Kimberly slowly lowered herself into her chair opposite Rowan. Her heart banged in her chest and seemed to rise and stick in her throat. She drew in a breath and slowly exhaled. "I know what I did . . . pulling out of the race without talking it over with you . . . was wrong. I know that. But I didn't have a choice."

"Oh, now it's you didn't have a choice? You told me it was because it would break down the family, that it wasn't worth it." He flung his cloth napkin across that table. "That was bullshit and now this 'other choice.' Okay explain. Let me hear it." He stared across the table at her, his blue eyes nearly black.

"I'm not who you think I am."

Rowan grumbled something under his breath. "What the hell is that supposed to mean?"

Her gaze drifted away. "My entire life has been a lie." Her eyes swung toward him. "It wasn't my fault, Rowan. You have to believe me." She pressed her fingertips into the table. "Everything my parents told me was all to hide their secret, a secret that could have ruined my family."

"You're not making sense, Kim," he said, his tone softening as he listened to real distress filter through her voice and register patches of red on her pale skin.

Tears slipped from her eyes. She sniffed and wiped the tears away. "You see . . . my parents," she swallowed, "aren't my real parents."

Rowan's sleek black brows drew together. His eyes cinched in the corners. "What? What are you saying? You were adopted? So what, baby? Big deal. Is that the ugly secret?" He rose and came around to her side of the table, and pulled her to her feet. He tilted her chin upward with the tip of his finger. "That's nothing. Your folks loved you enough to choose you." He smiled down at her. But his smile quickly dissolved.

Kim tucked her lips for a moment, looked at her husband, silently praying that the next words she spoke would not destroy them. "I need you to really listen, hear me out and not make any judgments until you've heard what I have to say." She took a step back, but held his hands, tightly, as she hesitantly revealed the decades-long secret of the Maitland family: how her parents were really her grandparents, that her biological mother was the black daughter of the Maitland's housekeeper who'd conceived her with Kyle Maitland, the man she'd grown up believing was her brother, who in fact was her father. "They forged my birth certificate," she whispered, her voice ragged with emotion. "They told Rose—my real mother—that I'd died at birth." She swiped at the tears running down her cheeks. "She . . . she was going to tell the world. Ruin everything. I couldn't let Zoie Crawford do that to us," she said her voice bordering on panic. Her eyes widened, pleading with Rowan to understand. "I had no choice. Don't you see that?" She reached out to him.

Rowan's body tensed. His expression morphed from its initial empathy, to confusion, horror, then outrage. He nearly pushed her to the floor with the force of his retreat.

"You're lying! Why are you trying to hurt me like this? Haven't I been a good husband and father, provider?"

She made another move toward him. He recoiled.

He threw his hands up. "Don't touch me!" He looked wildly around the room like one awakened from a nightmare only to discover that it was real. "Everything between us . . . has been tainted. I . . . I made love to you," he said with revulsion. "My god, the girls!" He tore at his hair. "What have you done!" He came storming toward her with such ferocity that he pinned her against the wall. "What have you done!" His own eyes filled with tears.

"Rowan! Please!" she wept. "I didn't know. I swear to you." Her body shook with the force of her sobs even as his fury gripped her.

One last scathing look scorched her face before he whirled away and stormed out. The apartment vibrated in the aftermath of the slammed door and seemed to echo forever in Kimberly's ears.

She slid to the floor in a heap of debilitating sobs—for how long, she was not sure. When she was finally able to get to her feet, her entire body ached and her eyes were nearly swollen shut. Her temples throbbed. She glanced around, dazed. The antique clock atop the china cabinet showed that it was after two.

She moved through each room, ghostlike, hoping to find that Rowan had returned. She was alone. Finally, she collapsed across the bed—spent.

⟶◆⟵

At some point, she drifted off and only realized that when she was roughly shaken from a troubled sleep.

She blinked rapidly against the light and brought her husband into focus. She pushed to a sitting position. "Rowan. . . ."

"I'm taking the girls away for the rest of the weekend. When we get back I want you gone. I want you out of my house and out of my life. Take your things with you. You are not to contact me or try to contact the girls. If I have to get the courts involved to keep you away I will and you know that I will. Don't test me."

"No! Rowan. Please. You can't do this. They are my children, too!"

His stare stopped her words and froze her in place. "I've packed their bags and I'm picking them up from Grace. We'll be back Sunday night. Don't be here, Kimberly. I'm warning you."

Without another word, he spun away.

Kim jumped up and ran behind him, catching him at the door. She gripped the back of his jacket. "Rowan," she pleaded. "Please. Not my babies. Not my babies!"

He didn't even turn around. He opened the door and keeping his back to her said, "Don't make this any uglier than it already is. If you think you're miserable now, try to imagine what I will do to you if you cross me." He pulled the door open and walked out with a small suitcase in each hand.

CHAPTER 3

"So, we're going to do this?" Jackson stated more than asked, as they finished off their meal with a cocktail—his usual bourbon and her martini.

Zoie slowly turned the glass on the table by its stem. She tugged in a breath and rested in the cocoon of his eyes. "We're going to do this. Cautiously. I need you to really understand that no matter what, I am not coming between you and your child or what Lena may eventually want. That has to be clear."

He tipped the shot glass to his lips. "In the words of Jack Nicholson in *A Few Good Men*, 'crystal.' "

Zoie snorted a laugh. "Now that we have that moderately settled, what's been going on with you and your development project?"

His eyes widened with excitement. "It's going extremely well, actually. With the added funding from the Maitlands, we're right on target for completion this fall."

The housing development project was close to his heart. The plight of the 9th Ward residents living in substandard housing was an environmental issue that he was determined to tackle. The development was a gated community with three low-rise buildings that housed ten apartments each, along with a half-dozen single family bungalows, a supermarket, and a recreation center—all for low-income families. An added perk was that the residents of the bungalows—in partnership with Habitat for Humanities— helped to build their own homes, ensuring a true sense of ownership. Along with his own team of construction workers, he made it a point to hire as many able-bodied residents as possible. Not only was he bringing housing, but also jobs, and boosting the local economy as well.

Zoie's smile radiated pride. "That is absolutely amazing, babe. I am so happy for you, *and* for the folks in Louisiana."

"Yeah," he said on a sigh. "It's been a long hard fight, but we made it." He finished off his drink just as the waitress approached.

"Can I get you anything else?" she asked looking from one to the other.

Jackson gave Zoie a quick, questioning look. "No. We're good. If you could bring the check, please."

"Sure. I'll get it prepared right away."

"Speaking of the Maitlands," Jackson began, "have you heard anything from Kimberly?"

Zoie slowly shook her head. "Not a word. I've called several times and left messages." She sighed and linked her fingers together. "I feel so guilty."

"The truth was sure to come out at some point," he offered.

"I only wished it hadn't been me. I mean, in hindsight, I should have done things differently. I shouldn't have been so hellbent and determined to prove my point."

He gave her a half smile. "That's what makes you a fantastic journalist. Kimberly is a big girl. I'm sure that once she accepts the truth she will find a way to deal with it and you'll hear from her again."

"I wonder if she's been in touch with the Maitlands since she dropped out of the race."

His brows quirked. "No idea."

The waitress returned and showed Jackson the electronic bill. Jackson nodded and handed over his credit card. She tapped a few keys then swiped his card. Moments later she handed it back and asked for his signature. "Would you like a printed receipt or email?"

"Email is fine." He added his email address and handed back the electronic card reader.

"Hope you enjoyed the service. Please come again."

"Thank you," they murmured in unison.

"I've only seen all that electronic restaurant stuff in New York. And only in very few places. Guess the twenty-first century is pushing south," Zoie said with a grin.

"We's got runnin' water right out da tap and paved sidewalks, too," he joked in an exaggerated drawl and bugged eyes.

———※◆※———

Zoie tossed her head back and laughed. "Okay, okay. Very funny."

Jackson chuckled. "It's still kinda early," he said after checking the time on his phone. "Want to take a walk, drive, go someplace for a nightcap?"

"A drive sounds nice. I'd love to see the progress on the development."

"Sure." He stood and helped her to her feet. "The horse and buggy is right this way, ma'am," he whispered in her ear.

Zoie playfully swatted his arm and rolled her eyes.

"Jackson," Zoie said, the awe radiating in her voice. "This is amazing." She took in the array of structures in various stages of completion and could easily imagine the final product.

"Right down that road is where the supermarket will be located," he said, pointing to his right. "It's always been difficult getting fresh food at reasonable prices down in this area. Folks often had to travel on buses just to get fresh groceries." He shook his head in disgust.

"Hmm, I'm thinking that since this development will primarily be run by the residents and they have a stake in its success—

maybe they would be interested in a community garden. They could grow their own produce, run it like a co-op."

The right corner of his mouth lifted. "I like it. Love it," he said nodding his head as he spoke. "And I know the perfect person to get it started and run it." He gave her a pointed look.

"Jack—son." She pushed out a breath. "I wasn't putting in a job application, just making a suggestion."

"And a damned good one. Think about it. You grew your grandmother's business leaps and bounds in less than a year. Imagine what you could do here, on a wider scale. Think of all the families you would help." He paused a moment, watched her expression go from 'no way' to 'hmmm.'

"I don't know," she hedged. She looked around.

"At least think about it."

"I'll think about."

He leaned down and kissed her forehead. "That's all I ask." He took her hand. "Come on. I'm in the mood for some dessert. How 'bout you?"

A slow grin moved across her mouth. Her right brow lifted seductively. "I prefer something covered in chocolate."

Jackson chuckled deep in his throat. "I may be able to help you with that."

"Perfect. Let's stroll over to the harbor, walk off the rest of that dinner before driving back," Zoie suggested as she slipped her arm through the bend of Jackson's.

"Cool." He eased her close enough for their thighs and hips to bump as they walked.

"Remember that time when we left Chez Oskar . . . after the Luther Vandross concert?"

"Of course. How could I forget. First time we made love in the house with all the aunts and your mama steps away in their beds."

She glanced up at him and giggled, hugged his arm tighter. "Thrilling. The idea that we might get caught."

"You always were ready to cross the invisible line. Dance on the edge. It's what I've always loved about you."

"And I thought it was my winning smile." She tightened her fingers around his bicep. "I'm feeling very tempted to be very bad . . . with you."

Jackson stopped in his tracks, scooped his arm around her waist and pulled her flush against him. Her breath hung in her chest. Her lips parted ever so slightly. He lowered his head and tenderly covered her mouth with his. She sighed, leaned into him, gave herself over to the sweetness of the tip of his tongue, suckled it as late night strollers parted and flowed around them. He tightened his hold on her, but reluctantly eased back to the sound of clapping, coming from a group of four teens out for the night.

Zoie lowered her head against Jackson's chest and laughed. "Guess we're causing a scene," she said over her laughter.

"At least we got applause," he chuckled, kissed her forehead. "Come on. I don't want an audience for the rest of our evening."

<hr />

Zoie crossed Jackson's threshold first, took two, maybe three steps into the entryway before turning to him. He pushed the door closed and slid his arm around her waist pulling her tight against him. No words were needed, just hands, lips, and bodies that melded perfectly together, finding all the dips and curves.

Jackson tugged off her jacket and tossed it aside. She yanked his shirt up from the waistband of his slacks and snaked her fingers along his chest. His large hands tangled in her wild curls, sealing her mouth to his. In harmony, they inched further into the house, discarding clothing along the way, nearly naked by the time they reached his bedroom door. The hot frenzy of need too long denied, sizzled in the air and snapped like live wires.

Zoie suddenly pulled away, stepped back, her eyes dark and tempting. She smiled, slow and seductive, as she slipped the strap of her bra from her right shoulder. Jackson grinned, stroked his chin as if contemplating his next move. She slipped off the other

strap, spun around and turned her back to him. Jackson stepped
out of his slacks and shorts, came up behind her and unhooked
her, then moved closer, pressing his erection firmly against her.
She sighed, sliding out of her panties as she swayed her hips,
much to Jackson's delight.

She turned, presented herself in all her warm chocolate glory,
draped her arms around his neck, and puckered her lips.

"Damn, you're beautiful. You know that?" he said from deep
in his gut before sealing his mouth to hers.

"Hmm, umm," she murmured against his lips before they tumbled onto his king-sized bed.

Like a song that has been sung over and again, they knew the
words of each other's bodies, the high notes, the low notes, the
changes in tempo. And as he moved slow and deep within her, re-
moving them both from their ordinary world to one of their own
making, she silently prayed that she'd made the right decision to
stay, and that her staying wouldn't ruin another life.

⸺⧫⸺

Kimberly moved through the apartment that she'd lived in for
years, bumping into furniture, turning over figurines that had sat
in the same place since their purchase. Nothing was familiar. She
stumbled from room to room, feeling her way along the walls and
door frames, beds and couches, tables and chairs. Nothing was
familiar. Everything had changed. Yet was painfully the same.

I want you out. The words, drum-like, banged in her head. She
lowered herself to the edge of her bed and sat, looked, unseeing,
around the room. What was she going to do? How could he expect her to leave her home, her children? Yet even through the
fog of her thoughts, there was one thing that she knew to be clear
and true: Rowan never said anything that he didn't mean. It was a
trait that had secured his rise in corporate America, lauded by his
colleagues, friends and adversaries. Rowan was a man of his
word. He didn't make promises that he didn't keep. Ever.

For as much as she wished that he didn't really mean what he said, that it was said in the heat of the moment, she knew that if she was still there when he returned he would have her physically removed. She couldn't allow her daughters to see that happen.

The vision of her daughters seeing her disheveled, begging, and tossed out of their home spurred her to move from one drawer to the next, to the closet. She filled a small suitcase and an overnight bag, checked her Kate Spade tote for her wallet, keys and phone. Draping her trench coat over her arm, she took a final look around then walked out.

"Mrs. Graham."

Kimberly blinked the lobby into focus. How long had she stood there?

"Are you all right, Mrs. Graham?"

It was Howard, the doorman, she realized. Her thoughts turned over. She must look a mess. She ran her hand over her hair and felt the web of tangles, saw her wrinkled clothes that she'd slept in, and could only imagine how mottled her face must look and how swollen her eyes must be. She forced a smile. "Yes," she rasped in a voice she barely recognized.

He came from behind the desk, took her arm, moved her to sit on the sofa on the far side of the lobby. "Can I get you anything, Mrs. Graham?"

She looked up into his kind face and eyes of concern. Her lips tightened. She blinked rapidly to keep a fresh set of tears at bay. "A cab," she managed.

"Of course, right away." He paused. "Are you sure I can't help you?"

She touched his hand. "No one can."

The cab pulled up in front of the Hilton on Sixth Avenue. Of all the hotels she'd stayed in, it was the only name she could remember. When she entered the sprawling lobby with its hush of luxury and hum of voices, she knew why she'd found her way here, the same way she and Rowan had made a split decision to spend the night at the hotel rather than at home—anonymity. They were both exhausted after a grueling week at work, but refused to break their Friday date night. Rowan's last meeting for the day had been in midtown and they'd agreed to meet in this very lobby and dine at the hotel restaurant. Of the hundreds of guests that filled the rooms, she would simply be one of many. She could vanish into the ambiance, and still benefit from the amenities. She needed someone to take care of her now.

The clerk behind the desk gave her a one eyebrow raised look, but quickly schooled her expression to one of practiced welcome. "How may I help you?" she asked with a slight accent, maybe Scandinavian.

"I need a room. A suite if one is available." *She should have worn dark glasses.*

The young blond woman turned her attention to the screen. "We have two suites available ma'am, on the seventeenth and the twenty-first floors."

"Either is fine."

"Is the room for one or two guests?"

She swallowed, lifted her chin. "One."

"I'll need a credit card."

Kimberly dug in her purse, took out her American Express black card, with her maiden name Maitland embedded, rather than risk exposure with her married name. When the card successfully processed the shadow of skepticism on the clerk's face moved away like clouds after a storm.

"How long will you be staying with us, Ms. Maitland?" the clerk asked with a sudden bright smile.

"I'm not sure, but make it for the week."

"Not a problem." She clicked away on the keyboard. The hum of the printer spewed out the itinerary. "You are booked in Suite

1701, with a wonderful view of the Manhattan skyline. The suite comes fully stocked, but if there is anything that you need simply call the concierge. Housekeeping comes each morning at ten and again in the evening by eight." She slid the small envelope across the marble desk that held the room card keys along with her credit card.

"Thank you," Kimberly murmured.

"I'll have someone take up your bags." She signaled for a red cap. "Enjoy your stay, Ms. Maitland," she said cheerily.

A bellhop decked in a red jacket, snow white shirt, and black slacks appeared at her side. "I'll take your bags, ma'am."

Kimberly brought him into focus as the controlled bustle of the five-star hotel receded into the background. "Thank you," she said as he placed her suitcase and carry-on onto a luggage cart. "Right this way, ma'am." He headed off toward the elevator.

Her heels clicked in an uneven rhythm across the gleaming black marble floors, streaked with hair-thin lines of white, passing towering white pillars, soundless escalators, and strategic lighting that cast everything in a flattering glow. They reached the bank of elevators. The doors slid open. A laughing couple stepped off. The bellhop stood in the doorway, letting Kimberly on before allowing the doors to close.

"First time to the Hilton, ma'am?"

Her thoughts spun backward. "No."

The elevator stopped and a man stepped on, looking so much like Rowan that Kimberly's breath caught in her chest. It took a second for the blank look on his expression to register with her that it was not Rowan. He offered a halo of a smile, turned to face the door as it slid silently closed.

Kimberly squeezed her eyes shut, focused on slowing her heart. Mercifully, the bell tinged for the seventeenth floor.

The bellhop waited while Kimberly walked off.

"This way, ma'am." He led her down to the end of the carpeted hallway.

The room number gleamed in polished gold letters. The bellhop opened the door and stepped to the side as Kimberly entered.

The bellhop rambled on about the suite of rooms and its amenities. Kimberly barely heard him and was immensely thankful when she finally heard the door close behind him. She kicked off her shoes and tugged off her coat as she walked through the front of the suite that was divided into two sprawling areas. The dining room easily sat six around a circular smoked glass table perched on crisscrossed black wrought iron legs, embraced by high-back calf soft leather seating, all of which opened to the step down living room. A massive sectional couch in a butterscotch leather complemented the highly-polished wood floors, buttressed by a matching chaise lounge and easily accessible footstools. The off-white walls were graced with strategically placed artwork, that both drew the eye and at the same time seamlessly blended with the decor. The focal point, however, was the floor to ceiling windows that overlooked the twinkling Manhattan skyline.

Kimberly barely registered her surroundings. She drew the dramatic off-white drapes closed, cutting off her vision of the outside world, then turned and opened the double doors to the bedroom.

The king-sized bed commanded the room, flanked by onyx nightstands and shaded lamps, a walk-in closet and a six-dresser drawer. Within the bedroom was an enormous Jacuzzi tub, steps before the *en suite* that boasted double sinks, dressing table, shower and tub and state of the art toilet complete with heated seat and all the bells and whistles.

The effort that it had taken to pack her bags, take a cab, and wind up where she was, standing in front of a mirror, took the last vestiges of energy that she had left. She barely got out of her clothing before falling across the bed and into an unsettled sleep.

——⋙◆⋘——

Kimberly awoke the following morning, grainy-eyed and achy. She pushed her tousled hair away from her face, blinked the room into focus, and was momentarily confused. Then the overwhelming sinking sensation took hold and dragged her down to her new reality. She ran her hand across her face then levered to a sitting position. Stiff-legged, she walked to the bathroom, relieved her bladder, then turned on the tub and added lavender scented bath beads.

Moments later, she was neck deep in soothing water and relaxing aromas. She leaned her head back against the lip of the tub, closed her eyes and let her body succumb to the experience.

Mildly refreshed and the cobwebs somewhat cleared, she made a decision. Sure, Rowan said he wanted her out and would give her the weekend to leave, but deep in her heart she needed to believe that once the enormity of what he was asking set in, he would see things differently. For now, she would give him some space. Give him the rest of the weekend. She was banking on her girls asking for her, demanding to know where their mommy was.

———≫◆≪———

Monday morning, the yellow cab pulled in front of her Sutton Place apartment. Not having any cash on hand, she was grateful the cab was a newer version with a credit card machine. She collected her receipt and pushed through the glass and chrome door into the lobby.

"Mrs. Graham . . . ?" The quickly came from around the horse-shoe-shaped desk to stand in front of her.

Kimberly stopped short. "Howard . . . What in the world . . . ?"

"I'm sorry, Mrs. Graham, but . . . I can't let you up."

"What do you mean you *can't* let me up?"

His cheeks flushed. "Mr. Graham made it very clear that you were not to be let upstairs." His eyes registered his internal angst. "I'm sorry."

The lobby shifted. There were two Howards.

"Mrs. Graham!" He caught her as her knees weakened. "Come. Sit down." He ushered her to the lounge chair.

The air hitched, released and hitched again in her chest. It was so hot. Her temple throbbed. "I don't understand," she said in a halting voice.

"Mr. Graham came last evening, gave clear instructions, and indicated that if his instructions weren't followed we would be out of a job. He brought a locksmith."

Kimberly's gaze rose from the spot on the floor that she'd ze-roed in on and landed haphazardly on Howard's stricken face.

She wouldn't humiliate herself any further by collapsing in a pool of tears. She dragged in a long deep breath and pushed to her feet. "Thank you, Howard." Without another word or a back-ward glance, she walked out.

———⋙•⋘———

Kimberly glanced at her reflection in the hotel mirror again.

Who was she now, this false self, her reflection unrecognizable when viewed through new eyes. Ghostlike, she moved, unaccus-tomed to this discovery of this other self, this black woman coated in white skin—a fake. She felt like a character from *Passing*, a Nella Larsen novel, tricking the outside world of her truth. But unlike Irene Redfield and Clare Kendry, her subterfuge was not of her own making. Those who professed to love and care for her had deceived her, created a world of privilege to which she had no true claims. *Her parents were her grandparents, her brother was her father*. Her husband had banned her from her home and their children.

The slow burn of bile churned in the pit of her stomach. Her eyes stung as the eruption rose, choking her, before spewing the ugliness of her existence into the sink. Waves of despair expelled itself until she was weak, huddled on the cold tiles of a bathroom floor that was not hers.

She wasn't sure how long she sat, curled fetal-style and soiled. At some point in the swirl of her thoughts she knew what she must do. Crawling to her hands and knees she slowly stood. Her mirrored reflection damned her. This new face, this new person stared back at her with vacant gray-green eyes. Eyes like her half-sister—the epicenter of her ruin. She would make Zoie pay, make all of them pay for what they had done to her and to her children.

Kimberly stood in front of the towering windows, watching the spring rain pelt against the pane. She tried to wrap her mind around the fact that her husband had barred her from returning to the home they'd shared for nearly fifteen years. He'd changed the locks, threatened employees. As much as she struggled with her new reality, her new self, she had to now take a very close look at the man she thought she knew. Who was Rowan Graham? The place that she found herself in was not of her own doing. She never set out to deceive anyone—especially not the man she loved. Yet, her husband acted as if *he* were the victim. Not once did he consider what all this was doing to her, or how he could help. What happened to their vows; *for better or for worse*?

She tugged out of her clothes, pulled back the sheets and crawled into bed. Maybe, if she could sleep, when she awoke this would be some horrible dream, even though she knew it wasn't. She stared up at the ceiling. She would have to put a plan in place.

CHAPTER 4

When she awoke, hours later, the sun was beginning to set. Apparently she'd slept, yet she felt as if she'd tumbled down a flight of stairs. Moaning softly, she sat up, looked around, reached for her cell phone on the nightstand. She squinted at the face. *Five-thirty*. She swiped to her messages. There were three from her office, and four voicemails from Gail.

"Dammit," she muttered. She pushed her hair away from her eyes and lifted her puffy face toward the ceiling. Her private life was falling apart, but she couldn't let her public life, her livelihood, fall apart as well. She had Gail and clients who depended on her. Her eyes stung. She would not cry. Tears couldn't wash away the quicksand of ugliness that had begun to suck her under.

She needed to contact Gail. Her messages had escalated from questioning, to mildly concerned to very upset. She took a deep breath and tapped 'call back' on the phone. Part of her wanted the call to go to voicemail, but knowing how diligent Gail was, she knew Gail was still at her desk even as the hour drew closer to six.

The call was answered on the second ring.

"Mrs. Graham. Thank god, I was so worried."

"I'm sorry, Gail. I should have called."

"Are you alright, the kids okay?"

"The kids are fine." She squeezed her eyes shut for a moment. "Gail, I . . . am going to need to take some time off. I don't know for how long."

"I don't understand. We have clients."

"I know." She cleared her throat. "I can't explain everything now, but I will." Her voice cracked.

"Mrs. Graham, you can talk to me. Maybe I can help," she softly pleaded.

"There are some things you can help me with."

"Anything."

"I need you to request a postponement on the two cases that are pending. Then contact Leslie Hall's office and see if she would be willing to take them on. If not, reach out to Meredith Horowitz's office. I'm sure she will do it. She's always looking for new clients. But I'd really prefer Leslie."

The silence from Gail magnified Kimberly's request, bringing the reality of what had become her life into stark relief.

"Whatever you need," Gail finally said.

"Thank you. I'll call you . . ."

"What about regular office operations?"

Kimberly squeezed her eyes shut against the sudden pounding in her temples. "Um, set up a voice mail message that the office is temporarily closed." She swallowed. "There's no reason for you to have to deal with the calls and questions. Return any calls that are urgent." She listened to the muffled sigh.

"All right. Whatever you need, but if you would just tell me—"

"I . . . will. I promise. And I don't want you to worry about your salary, Gail. I'll make sure that you're paid."

"How long do you think the office will be closed?"

Kimberly dragged in a breath. "I'm not sure."

"Please, I'm here if you need me. To talk, listen . . . whatever."

"Thanks. Listen, I really need to go. I'll be in touch." She paused a beat, knowing that she was severing a lifeline. "Goodbye, Gail." She disconnected the call before Gail could ply her with any more questions, or inadvertently make her feel any worse than she already did. She tossed the phone aside and flopped back on the bed.

Fully fed, Zoie's lioness purr vibrated from her center and settled in her chest. She curled closer to Jackson, needing to feel his heartbeat against her. He draped his arm across her and kissed her forehead. They'd been virtually one person for the past two days, putting all distractions aside and only focusing on each other.

"I could get used to this," Jackson said.

"Me, too," she said, feeling that swell of vulnerability rush through her, but maybe this time she could simply ride the tide to shore and the safety of Jackson's love.

He drew in a long breath, stretched hard muscles before tossing the comforter and sheet aside and rolling to his feet.

Zoie ogled his milk-chocolate physique, the ripple of hard muscle when he moved. She sighed in delight. *He was all hers*. Almost. She flinched at the idle thought that jabbed her like a hot pin. This time she trained her carnal observation to what rested beneath the surface of that edible skin.

Jackson was a complex man. It would be easy to simply paint him as handsome, sexy, a good businessman and friend. But the one trait that put Jackson in his own lane was his unwavering loyalty. Once he committed, neither hell nor high water nor dynamite would shake him loose. He valued friendships, and anyone that was lucky enough to get swept into his orbit was assured that their friendship would be nurtured and protected. Loyalty was his great strength, and at the same time his big weakness. Loyalty bound him to Lena. It would bind him even more to the child they'd created.

As much as Jackson assured her that he could stand on the outside looking in when it came to Lena and the baby, she knew deep

in her soul, in that part of her that totally understood Jackson
Fuller the man, that he was not the stand-on-the-outside kinda
guy. This time around she wanted things to work between her and
Jackson. For that to happen, she needed to be confident that the
loyalty that would inevitably bind him to Lena and the baby
would not jeopardize what they were trying to build. If she was
truly honest with herself, she didn't see how that was possible. He
would have to cut himself in half. Was she willing to settle for half
of a relationship?

Jackson reentered the bedroom with a towel tied around his
waist. He walked over to his dresser and pulled out a pair of gray
sweatpants, dropped the towel and slipped the pants on. "I'm
going to whip us up some breakfast," he said over his shoulder.
"Don't know about you, but I'm starving." He winked and walked
off to the kitchen.

Zoie sat up then pulled herself out of bed, went to the bathroom and took a quick shower. She wrapped herself up in Jackson's much-too-big-for-her robe and went to the kitchen.

"Need some help?"

He peeked out from the side of the refrigerator door. "I got
this. Coffee is hot. Help yourself."

Zoie poured herself a mug full of coffee, splashed some vanilla
flavored cream to lighten it to a soft taupe, then sat at the circular
table.

"J . . ."

"Yeah, babe." He cracked eggs into a bowl.

"Tell me about Lena."

Jackson froze for an instant then turned to look at her. He
drew in a long breath, pursed his lips then whipped the eggs.
"What do you want to know that I haven't told you?"

"How did you meet?"

"Why are you doing this, Z?"

"I need to know. I need to know everything if this is going to
work."

He lined up a row of thick bacon strips into the frying pan that sizzled on contact. "We met at a party, well more of a fundraiser. My company hosted a gathering for community leaders to raise awareness *and* donations," he added with a chuckle, "about the housing crisis in the wards. Lena came on behalf of the college and as a concerned citizen."

Zoie waited for more. Several moments passed. The tantalizing aroma of frying bacon reminded her how hungry she was. "And?" she finally prompted.

His right eyebrow arched. He gave a slight shrug. "We talked after the event. She told me she wanted to find a way to get involved." He knew from the moment they first spoke that Lena was as interested in him as she was in getting involved in the project that he'd proposed. She was the one that suggested they 'get together' and talk. With Zoie out of his life and a beautiful, accomplished woman eager to get to know him better, of course he was flattered and interested. That first night led to others. Lena filled that void that Zoie's leaving had left. Sometimes, she almost made him forget.

"Did you love her? Do you . . . love her?"

The question stung. Was this how she pried information out of her sources, by locating soft tissue and pinching? His jaw tightened. "What Lena and I had is over now, Zoie. I told you before I will always care about Lena." He braced his hands on the table and stared her hard in the eyes, his voice coming from that deep place in his soul. "I love you. I always have." He took a breath and slowly shook his head. "But I won't do this with you. You can't be with me if you want Lena to be the third person in our relationship. I know it's going to be fucking hard, but," he took her hands, "if you want to be with me the way I want to be with you we can make it work." He took a step back. "So, once and for all, is it me and you or not?"

She tugged on her bottom lip with her teeth. "It's the journalist in me. Gotta check and double check." She lowered her gaze then looked right at him. "It's me and you, babe."

He half smiled, leaned down and lightly kissed her lips. "Good. Now, you wanna help get us fed or just sit there looking cute and sexy."

She crossed her bare legs. "I'll take cute and sexy for five hundred, Alex."

Jackson laughed, waved the spatula at her. "Very funny, just the way I like you."

CHAPTER 5

It was only a phone call but she was exhausted. The life had been sucked out of her simply getting through the charade that she was setting up—the pretense that things were semi normal. She wanted to confide in Gail, in someone. The reality of her aloneness rushed up and against her with tsunami force. She clutched the phone in her hand. Gail had offered her a lifeline, an ear to listen, but she hadn't taken it. She didn't know how.

Sitting alone in a hotel. How pitiful was that? It was a reflection of her life. Outside of her children and her husband she didn't have a true girlfriend, someone to share something more than complaints with. She'd never had that. Her circle of so-called friends were mere associates that sat together during fundraisers, shared nothing personal beyond the best places to vacation, investments, and the newest spas.

Her parents never encouraged friendships. To the Maitlands, relationships were results based. What could this person do for you? If she showed an interest in a friend from school, her mother would insist that the girl or her parents only wanted to get close to Kim because of who her parents were. She grew to believe that no one cared for her for who she was. She was suspicious of anyone that showed an interest in her in any way. The exception had been Rowan. He had his own portfolio of success and thus the blessing of her parents. He'd been able to chip away at the brick fortress she'd constructed around herself. How ironic that he chipped away only to discover that she wasn't who he thought she was underneath. The one person she'd finally opened herself to and trusted had tossed her aside, which in her mind reinforced her parents' mantra. She no longer provided the image that Rowan needed to project to the world. Vows meant nothing. She'd become disposable.

She squeezed her eyes shut. Blinding images of Zoie Crawford, her parents, and Rowan flashed behind her lids. By degrees, her sadness morphed into anger, and her anger into purpose. If there was one thing she'd learned from her parents, it was never to get knocked down and stay down. Get up. Never let anyone see you defeated no matter how badly you've been injured.

Her lids fluttered open. She blinked the hotel room into focus. This would not be her life. Where she was right at this moment— a woman cast aside—was not of her doing. She would not remain a victim.

She picked up her phone.

———◆———

Zoie walked into the kitchen. Her mother, Rose, sat at the table absently stirring a cup of tea.

"You okay, Mom?"

Rose glanced up. "Thinking about my mother is all," she said. "Missing her a little extra today for some reason."

Zoie pulled out a chair and sat opposite her. "I think about her all the time." She smiled wistfully. "She wouldn't want you to be sad." She covered her mother's hand with her own.

Rose offered a tight-lipped smile. "No. She would be blasting me out about sitting here when there was work to be done."

"She *did* keep busy. I'm still amazed at all she accomplished with the business. Keeps me on my toes. I don't know how she did it."

Rose fixed a hopeful gaze on her daughter. "Have you heard anything from Kimberly?"

"Not a word. I'm sorry."

Rose looked off into the distance. "Can't blame her really. Imagine finding out that everything you believed to be true about your life was a lie."

Zoie lowered her head. Her mother's words, though true, stung. The guilt of what she'd done, the lies she'd unearthed had altered the reality of two families. She'd done that. When she could have stopped, she didn't. She pressed and dug and pressed until the foundation upon which they all rested crumbled, while she stood atop her convictions. She was certain that her revelations were the impetus as to why Kimberly dropped out of the race. How had it affected her family—her daughters?

"I wish I would have done things differently," she admitted.

Rose pursed her lips and slowly pushed back from the table. "No sense in wishing on things you can't change. What's done is done." She stood, took her cup and brought it to the sink. "Sometimes we have to look beyond our own wants and think about how what we want will affect others." Her sputtered laugh held no humor. "Found that out for myself."

Zoie flinched at the barb. "I'm sorry, Mom. I really am."

Rose dried her hands on a red and white dishtowel then slowly turned to face her daughter. "I believe that. I can even accept that, but it won't change what's been done. Maybe it's a lesson for you, Zoie. There's a part of you that can't stand the idea of being slighted or not given every single thing you think you deserve— whether right or wrong. You go after what you want. It's an admirable quality, but you have to find a way to balance what you want with how it impacts others. All we can do is move on."

Zoie linked her fingers together, studied them. These same fingers had flown across the computer keys pounding out words, shaping opinions, changing lives. If only these same magical fingers could, with a keystroke, go back and hit delete and make what she had done go away, she would do it. She would do it all differently. One thing that was drummed into students in journalism school was that to be a good journalist you must put your opinions and biases aside and search for truth—objectively. She didn't do that. When she went after Kimberly—sure, part of it was to get the story—but the other part was that she wanted to see Kimberly pay for some crime Zoie believed she'd committed. The crime of denying her identity, denying her family. She glanced at the slight stoop of her mother's shoulders as she turned her attention back to cleaning the countertop. How would she ever be able to move on from what she had done to her mother, Kimberly, and two families?

A murmur of voices drifted toward the kitchen, growing louder.

"I told you that today is Tuesday," Sage Bennett admonished. She held onto the arm of her sister Hyacinth as they shuffled their way into the kitchen. "Told you three times."

"Don't make sense that today is Tuesday, if yesterday was Sunday."

"You two fussing already so early in the morning," Rose said with a threat of laughter in her voice.

Sage sucked her teeth in dismissal then helped Hyacinth onto a chair at the kitchen table. "Chile fix me a cup of tea, would ya?" she said to Zoie.

"Yes, Auntie. Can I get you anything, Aunt Hy?"

Hyacinth peered at Zoie as if trying to get her in focus then a sudden smile and a flash of off-white teeth lit her face. She pointed a thin finger at her. "Rose's little girl. Zoie."

"Yes, Auntie, it's me, Zoie." She patted Hyacinth's hand. "Mama's fixing breakfast. Do you want some tea or fruit while she's cooking?"

She gripped Zoie's hand with sudden surprising strength, pulled her so close Zoie could see the specks of light in her gray-green eyes from the overhead florescent light. "Someone was outside last night," she said in a hard whisper. "Watching the house. I saw them from my window."

Zoie scrunched her face. "I'm sure it was just someone passing by, Auntie." She gently pulled her hand out of Hyacinth's grip.

"She still talking that craziness," Sage grumbled into her teacup.

"What craziness?" Rose set down a platter of fluffy scrambled eggs and thin slices of Virginia ham on the center of the rectangular table.

"Her ramblings," Sage said with a wave of her hand.

"Don't listen to them," Hyacinth insisted, once again grabbing Zoie's hand. "They think I'm crazy."

"No they don't, Auntie," Zoie assured her with a conciliatory smile. "Want some eggs?"

Hyacinth pursed her lips. "Those eggs look mighty pale."

"Those are egg whites, Hy. We all need to watch our cholesterol. Remember. That's what the doctor said."

"I'll try some if it will make you happy."

Zoie snickered. She ladled eggs onto a blue and white patterned plate and added a slice of ham and placed it in front of Hyacinth. "Can I fix your plate, Auntie Sage."

Sage screwed up her face. "Do I look helpless to you, chile? I can damn well fix my own plate."

"Yes, ma'am," Zoie acquiesced, having grown to accept that Sage's sharp tongue was only a cover for her soft heart. She pushed the platter closer to her aunt. She finished her cup of coffee and took it to the sink. She pecked her mother on the cheek. "Have some errands to run. I'll be back in a couple of hours."

"Sure. Oh, would you take the box that's on the dining room table to the post office for me?"

"No problem." She turned to her aunts. "You two try to stay out of trouble today."

"What's the fun in that," Hyacinth quipped with a twinkle in her eyes.

"You're probably right, Auntie."

"Where's that Jackson fella? I sure do like him." Hyacinth chuckled.

"You are too old and wrinkled for that young boy," Sage scolded.

"Says who?"

Zoie shook her head in amusement.

"They'll still be at it when you get back," Rose said. "You won't miss a thing."

"I'm sure." Zoie finger waved. "See you all later."

Zoie tucked the box under her arm and adjusted her canvas tote bag over her shoulder. When she stepped out onto the front porch and caught sight of the patches of gray clouds hovering in the sky she considered going back for an umbrella, but a white car idling in front of the house caught her attention. She took a step down to get a closer look, just as the car pulled away. She frowned, then shrugged it off and walked the short path to her car.

If there was one thing that she hated more than liver it was standing in line at the post office. No matter what city or state she was in, there was always a line at the post office, which is why she opted to do damn near everything she could online. She inched along, sighed, fumed, shuffled with the rest of all humanity it seemed. Since 9/11 the days of dropping off anything larger than a slice of an envelope into a mailbox was out of the question. Finally, she reached the front, lifted the Plexiglas door and placed her box on the metal scale. The whole exercise took a full forty minutes out of her day, but she was glad to be able to do something for her mother, even something as insignificant and mind-numbing as a trip to the post office.

The strain of her relationship with her mother dated back to her preteen years, and continued to escalate until she finally left her New Orleans home and moved to New York. She stepped out onto the marble steps of the post office. A light mist dampened the air. Great for the complexion, lousy for the hair, at least it used to be for her. Since she'd detoxed from perms, and gone back her natural wild curls, days like this no longer mattered.

She reached the landing and stopped short. "Lena. Hello." Her gaze instantly dropped to the rounded protrusion beneath the aqua-blue swing dress.

Lena's polished pink lips flattened into a thin glossy line. She cupped her stomach and for an instant Zoie wondered if it was maternal instinct or protection from her.

"Hello," she finally said.

"I uh, never got to tell you congratulations. You look wonderful. Glowing."

Lena looked at her for so long that Zoie shifted her feet and averted her eyes.

"Thank you." She walked passed Zoie toward a car parked at the curb.

Becoming unnerved was not an emotion that Zoie was accustomed to feeling. She'd been stripped bare on the steps of the post office for all the world to see what a bitch she really was. She fought against the burn that stung her eyes. The remnants of her debris were everywhere. She watched Lena open the driver's side door and get in before turning in the opposite direction. The sensation of being totally rattled remained as she walked toward her car.

Her errand was a meeting with Mr. White, the attorney that handled her grandmother's will. According to the terms of her grandmother's will, she'd met the requirement. Now it was only a matter of paperwork.

The mist evolved into a light spray. Along the downtown streets umbrellas popped open like buds in a blooming garden. Now she wished she'd gone back for her umbrella—natural hair or not. She quickened her step then slowed by degrees. She spun back around in the direction she'd come from, trying to spot

Lena's white car. Her heart thumped. Had it been Lena parked in front of her house? Was that who Aunt Hyacinth saw?

She ducked into the doorway of a coffee shop as the wind suddenly whipped and the skies opened up in a deluge of chilling rain. Water splashed against her feet and turned the hem of her jeans an inky blue. She peeked out from around the protection of the doorway. It was silly to think that Lena would be sitting outside of her house. For what? If anything, she could imagine her sitting in front of Jackson's house. She supposed it was the suddenness of running into her on the street and then seeing a car that looked like the one in front of the house that got all twisted in her wild imagination. That and her cloudy conscience. It was easier to cast Lena as the boogey woman than to fully acknowledge her role in the demise of Lena and Jackson's relationship.

She pulled her phone from her purse and checked the time. Her meeting was scheduled to start in ten minutes, and she was fifteen minutes away by car. She looked skyward. Her car was parked on the next block. She decided to make a dash for it and hope for the best.

Zoie eased down the lane to her house. Her conversation with Mr. White continued to replay in her head. Yes, she fulfilled the terms of her grandmother's will by staying at the house for one year, but according to a clause in the will, if the business was successful Zoie would turn it over to her aunts and her mother and then she would be free to return to New York.

She turned off the car, stared at the house—her childhood home. The first chance she'd gotten, she'd run from this place and stayed away for years. Returning for her grandmother's funeral brought back all the memories, both good and bad. For months after, she fumed at the trick her grandmother had played on her. But as time passed, she'd eased into her new life and the business grew like weeds. Then, after getting back together with Jackson, going back to New York no longer held the same appeal. Her relationship with her mother was not perfect, but it was something—more than she'd had in years. Now she was essentially free. It was what she thought she wanted from the instant she set foot on Louisiana soil a year earlier. She rested her chin on the steering wheel and the realization that had been taking shape inside her materialized. She no longer wanted to leave, and she didn't want to turn over the business. She sighed. Even from the grave, Nana Claudia was still running things.

The ornate iron gate that separated the Maitlands from the rest of the world loomed in front of Kimberly. Beyond those gates was the mansion she'd grown up in, intimidating in its grandeur, plucked right out of *Gone with the Wind.* She rolled down the car window and pressed the intercom. It was almost a badge of honor to say that the place she called home had once been a plantation that enslaved hundreds. The irony was not lost on her.

A disembodied voice asked who was calling. She gave her name and the gates soundlessly opened. She drove down the winding path to the front of the house, and as always, she was awestruck by the towering pillars and sweeping wraparound balconies.

Kimberly slowed to a stop and turned off the car. For several moments she sat there contemplating how this would all play out. She tried to wrap her mind around a scenario that ended civilly, but couldn't. She walked up the stone steps to her parents' grand front entrance. She gripped her purse against her churning stomach. Finally, she rang the bell and cringed at the barely audible melodic chiming that gently echoed through the house, much like everything and everyone in the Maitland household. Loud voices, running, even too much laughter were 'not civilized,' 'young ladies didn't behave that way.' How many nights did she lay in bed praying that she would wake up and no longer be a young lady?

She hadn't been home in nearly five years, and had it not been for Rowan she would not have come then. The twins were three when he insisted that they bring their daughters to visit their grandparents. Who knew how long they would be around, he'd said while he stroked her bare hip. He only wished his parents were still around. He'd kissed the butterfly pulse at the base of her throat. We owe it to our children for them to understand and appreciate their heritage, he'd whispered deep in her ear while he'd spread her thighs. It will be good for all of us to take a trip, he'd groaned and pushed deep inside her. As a family.

So she'd given in. She'd said yes, over and again until her mind and body spun the way it always did when Rowan made love to her. It was surreal. It made her forget everything that hurt her, the loneliness, the feeling of being unloved by the people who should love her most. Rowan made her believe that in their bed being a lady was not an option. He wanted her loud and giddy and kinky. With him, she was the self she always wanted to be. With them she was the child that could do nothing quite right. Being a wife and mother, successful attorney, having her own law office, running for Senate—none of it mattered and she never knew why, until Zoie Crawford bulldozed her life to bits.

She dragged in a breath of resolve as the door was pulled open.

"Margaret." She actually felt herself smile for the first time in weeks. After Ms. Claudia left, Margaret had taken her place and had been the one friend she had in the massive home.

"Ms. Kimberly. Oh my goodness." She wrapped Kimberly in a tight embrace then stepped back to hold her at arm's length. "Pretty as ever." She peeked around her. "Did you bring those beautiful girls?"

Kimberly's cheeks flushed. "No. School. They're at home with Rowan."

Margaret studied her for a moment. "Look at us standing in the door like strangers. Come in. Come in. Did your folks know you were coming? They didn't say anything."

"Uh, no they didn't. It was a last-minute decision."

"Oh. Well I know they'll be happy to see you. Your mother hasn't come down for the morning yet and your dad was off early this morning for a meeting with one of his boards. I tell you, for a man his age and in a wheelchair, he sure gets around." She chuckled, flashing deep dimples in her warm brown face. "Let me just go let her know that you're here."

"Thank you, Margaret."

"Before I do that is there anything I can get for you?"

"No. I'm fine, thank you."

"You just make yourself at home."

Kimberly watched her amble away and wondered how much longer Margaret would work for her family. She must be almost as old as her mother.

The sound of her heels snapping against the marble floor had her envisioning the firing squad she was about to face with her mother. How many shots would her mother fire to try to put her down? She slid open the patio door and stepped out onto the enclosed veranda. So many nights she'd come here to sit alone and gaze up to the heavens to wish on the stars—wish for a friend, someone to share secrets with. Sometimes she would wish for her freedom.

"Well, the prodigal daughter has returned."

Kimberly's entire body tensed as if seized by a spasm. She steeled her resolve and slowly turned to face her mother. Shock hit her first. She felt the hitch of air in her chest. Lou Ellen Maitland was still stately, regal almost in her gray silk blouse and pleated pants with the requisite string of pearls around her thin neck. Her winter-white hair was more sparse, a bit receded, but expertly coiffed as if she'd just returned from the salon. But that was not what struck Kimberly. What parted her lips was that her mother had visibly aged. In was the blue veins visible beneath the pale, paper-thin skin. It was the deep lines around those damning blue eyes, the sag around her jaw, and the slight tremor in her hand that she tried to hide when Kimberly noticed. Her shoulders were not quite as erect as they once were, and her step had slowed. Individually, these were minor things, but collectively they gave Kimberly pause, and perhaps for the first time in her life she saw her mother as human, vulnerable, and not the invincible, unbreakable woman of steel whom she'd loved and feared all her life.

"Mother. You look well." She walked over to where her mother stood.

"You look like you lost weight." Her gaze rode over Kimberly in waves. "And you could use some sleep."

Kimberly's jaw tightened. She lowered herself onto the thickly padded cushion of the chair.

Margaret surreptitiously appeared on the veranda carrying a silver tray with a carafe of lemon water and two crystal glasses. She placed the tray on the white wrought iron table, poured water into each glass and with the same level of stealth that belied her advanced years she was gone as if she'd never been there.

Lou Ellen lifted the glass toward her pinched lips. "Why are you here? I do hope it's not to get any sympathy from me after what you've done." Her cheeks flushed in manufactured agitation. "After all the sacrifices everyone made to support your run for Senate. The time, the money. Total embarrassment. But I'm sure you never thought of anyone else other than yourself."

Kimberly's insides twisted so tightly she could barely breathe. She gripped the arms of the chair. She was that little girl again, chastised into silence. She turned her face away. Her eyes stung with the burden of tears that pooled in them. She would not cry. Not in front of her. And she would not be shoved into ladylike silence.

"Since you're in the mood to talk about embarrassment to the family, why don't you tell me who my real father is, for starters." She lifted her chin and turned her head to look at her mother. The stark white of her mother's face was so alarming she had a momentary flash of panic that Lou Ellen would keel over dead.

The blue eyes darkened and stood in stark relief against her sheet-white face. Her thin nostrils flared and a tiny vein fluttered at her temple.

Lou Ellen reached for her glass of water and for an instant, Kimberly was certain her mother was going to toss the water in her face. Slowly she brought the glass to her lips and took a demure swallow before her slightly shaking hand returned the glass to the table. "Is that why you're here, to find more ways to humiliate me?"

"You! This isn't about you. I've been lied to my entire life, made to feel as if my very existence was a burden, and I never knew why." She held onto the arms of the chair to keep from hurtling across the short space and strangling Lou Ellen Maitland right where she sat.

"Don't you dare raise your voice to me," she tossed back, unbent, unyielding.

"It's long past time for whispering, Mother, or should I say, *Grandmother*."

Lou Ellen audibly gasped. She pressed her hand to her chest.

"You know exactly what I'm saying, Grandmother. My alleged brother was my father. Kyle." Her voice wobbled. "He had a child—me—with Rose Bennett, the daughter of our housekeeper, Ms. Claudia. Now I know why she loved me the way she did. I was her daughter's child—her grandchild."

Lou Ellen's lips tightened into a thin unmovable line.

"I know. Everything—almost everything. You can't lie to me anymore. How could you have done something like that? Do you have any idea what you've done to me, to my children, to my marriage, to Rose?"

Lou Ellen slowly turned her head toward Kimberly. A frightening expression of defiance was cast on her face like a plaster mask. "Don't you mention her name in my house," she practically hissed. "You have no idea about anything. Every privilege that you've enjoyed since you entered this world; from the best schools, the finest clothes, world travel, is because of what I did! You've met dignitaries and hosted them in our own home. You married well. Practiced law. Your life was so rich and orchestrated that you even made a run for higher office. Do you think any of that, any of it, would have been possible without the Maitland name and all that it represents? Do you? That *girl* could have ruined it all!" Her blue eyes flashed. The soft fabric of her clothing fluttered from the trembling of her limbs.

Kimberly pushed to her feet. "The Maitland name," she said, her voice flat and distant. "The legacy of the Maitlands." She tossed her head back and expelled something very short of laughter. "Our legacy! Our legacy is one of bondage and dehumanization, built on the backs, sorrows and misfortunes of others. That's who we are."

Lou Ellen lifted her chin. "Who we are?" She sneered. "You don't know what it is to come from *nothing*." She spat the word. "Nothing but dirt, and hunger, and hand-me-downs and soup lines and bug bites and sleeping on floors and turning your still childlike body into something useful so the family could eat." Disdain and the echo of the Appalachian life she'd escaped laced her voice. "What do you think you know, chile?"

The woman in front of her was not a woman that she knew. Gone was the soft spoken, genteel Southern matriarch that she'd grown up with. This woman embodied all the hurts she'd inflicted, from the cold stare of her eyes to the hard edge of her sudden, deep twang.

"So that justifies the things that you've done?" Incredulity lifted Kimberly's voice.

Lou Ellen's steely expression faltered but only for an instant. "Yes. And I'd do it again."

Whatever was left of Kimberly's soft insides were carved out and tossed with her mother's words of finality. She was emptied. Hollowed out. She stared at her mother and no longer saw her. She pushed unsteadily to her feet. Nothing looked familiar. A wave of nausea assaulted her. She stumbled off the veranda and ran through the house, and didn't stop until she'd reached her car. She dropped her key several times before her shaky fingers were able to stick it in the ignition.

She drove and drove. The maelstrom of her thoughts and emotions swirled mercilessly, leaving her disoriented and physically weak. Blaring horns and remnants of a driver's instinct were the only things that kept her from some head-on disaster. Maybe that would be best. Simply end it all. What did she have anyway? Her family, her marriage, her livelihood, her reputation, her sense of self—gone, destroyed. Why go on, for what? For who?

She drove until she found herself near the Quarter. The sun had begun its descent, casting orange and gold bands along the Mississippi River. The flow of wide-eyed tourists, resident party-goers and hawkers of every ilk moved in synchronized waves down the wide avenue. Zydeco, blues, and R&B blared from the open passageways of the bars along the strip. Aromas of shrimp po' boys, crawfish étouffée, jambalaya, and gumbo spiced the air. Kinetic energy vibrated through the concrete and cobblestones sending vibrations of joy up through the limbs of night owls making them dance and skip from one doorway to the next.

Kimberly parked on a side block and walked over to Bourbon Street. Mardi Gras had come and gone but the party that was the French Quarter needed no holiday to vibrate with vitality, something she'd discovered when she and her one friend ditched classes, and missed curfew for tall glasses of Hurricanes and pralines and two handsome, much older boys that promised to show them around. They stumbled in and out of bars and shops and hotel lobbies, and laughed and kissed and touched in narrow alleyways until the sun set as it did now. She'd never before or since felt so free.

She pulled open the heavy wood and chrome door of Jacques Lounge and was dragged into the heat of bodies, the thrum of music pounding from the speakers and the cacophony of voices raised in jubilation. Here in the dimness she could simply be one of many, forget who and what she was. She ordered her first Hurricane.

———◦◦◦———

Oblivion was what she sought and it was what she found when she opened bleary eyes and found herself naked in bed with a man she did not know. Prim, proper, well-raised Kimberly Maitland would be appalled beyond words. This naked woman—that still felt the pulse of sex and sticky afterglow between her legs—didn't care.

She squinted against the pale daylight that peeked beneath the half-drawn shade. Her head pounded. She tossed the sheet aside. The nameless man groaned and turned onto his side but didn't wake. She studied the ripple of muscle in his broad back. She'd never been with a black man before and wished that she could remember what it was like.

She put her feet on the floor and slowly stood. The room swayed then settled. She looked around. It wasn't a hotel room. She wasn't sure if that was a good thing or not. Gingerly she walked through the railroad flat until she found the tiny but neat bathroom. After relieving herself and tossing water on her face, she went in search of her clothes.

His wallet was on top of the badly scarred dresser. She flipped it open. His driver's license read: John Warren. 8701 Matchaponix Lane. New Orleans. 9/1/78. At least he was legal and she was still in the state. She located her purse under John's discarded blue jeans and found everything intact. She picked through the debris of their tossed clothing until she'd retrieved all of hers and got dressed. She wrote 'thank you John' on a fifty-dollar bill, left it on the dresser and quietly shut the door behind her.

It took her more than an hour to locate her car but once inside she had no idea what to do or where to go. Oblivion devolved into reality and everything that she'd tried to forget roared back in full Technicolor. She let out a keen, raw and ragged, lowered her head to the steering wheel and wept.

———————————

The following day Zoie was still rattled by her encounter with Lena. The idea that it may have been her sitting outside of their home hitched itself to her imagination. She'd seen one too many *Lifetime* movies featuring the mostly normal woman go pure psycho over a man. It was certainly possible that Lena could get pushed over the edge. Who could blame her if she did? She was carrying the child of the man she'd loved who was now with another woman. A woman he had a long history with.

She turned into the parking lot of the mall. Jackson wanted to take her to a fancy dinner and fancy attire was not in her MO. What she really needed was Miranda's eagle designer eye. She connected her blue tooth to her phone and dialed Miranda's number. If she couldn't be there in the flesh to help her shop, at least she could help virtually.

Instead she found a back booth of a dimly lit franchise restaurant, ordered up a margarita in the largest goblet she'd ever seen, and began laying out her suspicions with Miranda who was always up and ready for a good bestie convo.

"Now you know your aunt Hy doesn't always have all the groceries in the cart," Miranda was saying.

She chuckled at the analogy. "Of course. I felt the same way until I saw the car and then I saw Lena."

"Girl, how many white cars are zooming around 'Nawlins'?"

"I know. I know. Coincidence. I don't believe in coincidences."

"Until you know otherwise, that's all it is. Let it go before you make yourself crazier than you already are."

"Very funny."

"On another note, what you should be concerned about is this clause in the will. Why didn't the lawyer say anything a year ago?"

"Apparently, this part of the will was not to be disclosed until my year was up."

"Nana Claudia was one tricky sister. What are you going to do? Basically you're free and clear of any more obligations to run the business. The house and the land go to your mom and your aunties and you can move on, build your life with Jackson. Get back to writing."

"Hmm." She loudly sipped her drink.

"What are you drinking?"

"Girl you have no idea how big this damn glass is. Lucky thing the drink is weak or they'd have to carry me out."

They laughed.

"Damn, I miss us hanging out, setting this town on fire," Miranda lamented.

"Yeah, me too."

"You have the opportunity to come back to New York if you wanted. I know Mark Livingston would give you your old job back at the paper," she said, her words like a bee to honey to Zoie, who'd toyed with the idea of going back to the thrill and challenges of New York, but still struggled with all that she'd accomplished in New Orleans.

"That's just it. As tempting as it is to return to my life in New York, I don't know if it's what I want. Most of my life I spent wanting to have a relationship with my mother. I finally do—well at least we're heading in that direction. My entire career I've worked for someone else, doing what they needed when they needed it. Running my grandmother's business showed me that I can be more than a byline. And of course there's Jackson."

"I think it's pretty telling that you mention Jackson last."

"Meaning?"

"Meaning that the old Zoie would have had Jackson at the top of the list and the last person would have been your mom."

Zoie sipped. "I hadn't even . . . I didn't think of it that way."

"Exactly. Nana Claudia knew what she was doing when she

wrote the will. This first year changed you—for the good. If this was a year ago you would be ranting about how you couldn't wait to leave. Now you can't see how you would."

Zoie stared into the bottomless depths of her glass. She and Miranda had been friends for so long that they knew each other inside and out. One thing they'd always promised was they'd be honest with each other no matter what. Miranda was right, she had changed. Her priorities were different. She was a gentler version of herself but she was a work in progress like one of her pieces for the paper. Before going to press her story was researched, planned, drafted, tossed, drafted again, edited and proofed. She was still in the early draft mode—putting the pieces of her life together, and she still was not sure what the final product would look like.

"I'll figure it out," Zoie finally said.

"I know, you always do. Now put down that supersized drink and let's find you something to wear."

When Zoie pulled on to her street the first thing she did was check to see if the white car was around, but there was no sign of it. She parked in the driveway and just as she was getting out, the front door opened. Arm-in-arm, Sage and Hyacinth gingerly walked down the steps to the landing.

"Out for your evening stroll, Aunties?"

"Would do you some good to walk instead of riding around everywhere," Sage admonished. "Makes your behind big. All that sitting."

Zoie tucked in her lips to keep from laughing. "Yes, ma'am."

"Men like big behinds," Hyacinth said with a snicker. She winked at Zoie.

"Come on crazy woman, putting foolishness in that child's head." Sage ushered her sister down the lane to the street.

Zoie watched them go and shook her head in amusement. Any

other time she would have taken offense to her aunt's comments but she'd slowly begun to understand that Sage's caustic tongue wasn't one of malice. It was her own odd way of showing she cared.

——◦—

"Hey, Mama."

Rose was sitting in the family room reading. If Rose wasn't cooking or cleaning, she could be found curled up with a book. Zoie was sure that she'd inherited her love for reading from her mother, or really both her parents. Rose, unlike her older sisters, went to the best schools in New York, got a college education, and for several years she worked in management. When she'd returned to New Orleans, she went to work as a school teacher until she retired.

The house she'd grown up in with her parents was filled with books and laughter. She remembered sitting on her dad's lap while he read the newspaper to her in a variety of cartoon voices that made her convulse in delighted laughter. At bedtime, her mom would hold her close and read wondrous stories of kings and queens and pyramids and jungles in faraway places. She and her mother had no other choice than to return to Rose's childhood home to live with her sisters. She needed her family to help her raise her daughter. Hank Crawford's name was never uttered out loud, only shared with silent knowing looks of recrimination. Hank Crawford became the invisible elephant in the Bennett sisters' household. Zoie asked and begged and cried for a reason why her daddy was gone, until she'd finally tucked away her questions and pain where it sat and festered shaping her into the relentless seeker of truth—at any cost.

"Hey, sweetheart." Rose put down the novel she was reading and took off her glasses. "Find a dress?"

Zoie dropped her shopping bag next to the armchair and plopped down on it. "Yes, I had a virtual shopping trip with Miranda."

"What?"

She explained that she had Miranda on the phone with her while she shopped.

"Technology," Rose mused.

"What are you reading?"

"*Sugar* by Bernice McFadden. Reminds me of folks I know."

"Oh. I heard her read from it a couple of years ago at a Barnes and Noble. Pretty good."

"Didn't realize it wasn't new." She smiled. "But it's new to me."

Zoie crossed her legs and leaned back. "Remember when Dad used to read the newspaper in cartoon voices?"

Rose gazed off. "I remember." She pressed her hand to her chest.

"You used to laugh, too. We all did when Dad was around. He took your laughter. Took a part of you. Maybe a part of me too."

Rose's long lashes lowered. "Your father was larger than life. He took up all the oxygen in the room."

"You never got over him, did you?"

Rose picked up the novel she'd set aside. "It's the past Zoie. I've moved on."

Zoie leaned forward, pinned her mother with a steady gaze. "Have you, Mom? I mean really?" She watched the light dim in her mother's eyes, the sweet smile sour, the open expression close. This was the mother she remembered best, distant, emotionless. "I haven't."

Rose shot Zoie a look. Her breathing escalated.

"I haven't," she repeated.

Rose's nostrils flared. Her lips tightened into a lemon sucking pinch. She looked away, pushed to her feet. "Then it's time that you did."

"Why did he leave? Just tell me why?"

"What does it matter!"

"It matters to me, Mama!" She poked at her chest then jumped up and paced. "It's colored everything in my life, you, Auntie

Sage and Hy, even Nana Claudia. How I live my life, my obsession with digging for the truth, my inability to trust—anyone." She stopped, swung toward her mother. "It matters!"

Rose dragged in a long breath, raised her chin, turned, and walked away. "Let it go. Please," she said softly, before leaving the room.

Zoie stood at her bedroom window, palms braced on the white sill. The conversation with her mother—or lack thereof—sat like a stone in the center of her chest. All the progress they'd made toward reconciliation over the past year crumbled like a stale cracker. Why was it so wrong to finally know what happened to her father?

There was one year that every Sunday morning she combed through the obituaries in the newspapers. She visited the morgue and hospital emergency rooms. All she'd known about her father's background was that he was from New York. It was where her parents met. Was that what drew her to that city, of all the places she could have run to? She went through the Yellow Pages and found countless Hank Crawfords, none of whom were her father, or so they all claimed. All her journalism training, all her searching had yet to provide her with the answers she sought.

She turned away. Jackson would be there in an hour.

CHAPTER 6

Zoie leaned over the gears and gave Jackson a light kiss. "Hey," she said against his lips.

"Hey yourself. Looking good woman," he said, taking a long drink of water look at her.

"Why thank you, kind sir," she said in an exaggerated drawl. "You're not too bad yourself." She tweaked his tie.

Jackson winked. "Ready?"

"Yep."

"I should have come in and said hello to everyone." He put the gear in drive.

"They're all settled in for the night."

He pulled to the intersection. "Seven? Early even for them. Your mom is not up reading?" he asked off hand.

"Didn't see her when I walked out." She folded her hands on top of her purse.

Jackson snatched a quick look at Zoie. "Something wrong?"

"No. Why would you say that?"

"Because I know you and I know that tone."

She pressed her lips together. "Maybe we can talk about it later." She looked at him. "After dinner. Don't really want to get into it now." She turned her face toward the window.

Jackson's jaw clenched. He was not going to let it be one of those nights. He knew from the tightness around her eyes, the flat edge to her voice that something was simmering beneath the surface ready to overflow and scorch them both. When Zoie sunk into that place where she would retreat, she'd gather her weapons of words and research and attack the adversary. Sometimes the victim of her tenacity was truly worth investigating, much as she'd done when writing the series on the 9/11 attacks that uncovered the vulnerabilities of the buildings, and the money that was made by hedge funds. But he'd seen that same tunnel-vision determination unleashed on her own family. She didn't speak on it much but he knew she continued to struggle with what she'd done to Kimberly. She'd been relentless, turning over every rock, peeking between every crevice, hurt feelings and reputations be damned. Now she had to live with it, and make amends, yet here was that look again and he wasn't sure if he wanted to know why.

He reached toward the dash and turned on the radio.

"You didn't say where we were going, just someplace fancy," Zoie finally said, breaking the ice with a teasing tone.

"Can't surprise you," he tossed back and winked. "Emeril's. We haven't been there since you've been back, and I know how much you love the food."

She squeezed his thigh. "Now that's a pleasant surprise."

He cleared his throat. "I should have said something sooner."

"About Emeril's?" She scrunched her face and waved her hand in dismissal. "Please. Don't even think about it."

"Not Emeril's."

Her right brow flicked upward. "Oh. You're losing me."

"Two of my business connections that want to invest in the development will be joining us—for after dinner drinks. Other than that, the evening will be just me and you. Promise."

"Oh. Okay. I mean I would have loved that it was just us—*all* evening—but dinner at Emeril's takes the sting out." She smiled.

He released a breath of relief. "I was hoping you'd say that. Miles Cyrus and Victor Branch are from one of only two black financial investment firms in all of Louisiana. Can you believe it, in this day and age?" He huffed in frustration, made the turn onto Tchoupitoulas Street, pulled in front of Emeril's and was met by the Valet. He handed over his keys, helped Zoie out of the car and gave her another hungry look before walking into the famed flagship establishment.

Emeril Lagasse launched Emeril's New Orleans in 1990 in a renovated pharmacy warehouse that was transformed into one of the most famous restaurants in the country. Beyond it being a tourist attraction, due to the exquisite cuisine and stellar service, not to mention the larger-than-life personality of its owner and founder, getting a reservation was akin to striking gold.

A hostess greeted them at the door. "Good evening. Welcome to Emeril's."

"Good evening. Reservation for Fuller."

She scanned the register, located his name then tapped some keys on the computer. She looked up and smiled. "Yes. Your table is ready." She signaled for a waitress. Another young woman approached. "Rachel will show you to your table. Enjoy your evening."

"Thank you. There are two others that are meeting us."

"When they arrive, we'll escort them to your table," the hostess assured.

"Thanks," Jackson said.

The restaurant's circular tables were covered in white linen, topped with candle centerpieces in glass bowls and gleaming silver flatware. Yet even for its understated elegance there was a down-home feel to the space that said it was okay to laugh loud and long, have more than a glass of wine and ask for seconds, and if it was a lucky night Emeril himself may drop in.

Jackson held the chair for Zoie as she sat. The waitress placed a menu in front of each of them.

"Can I start you with a drink?"

Jackson deferred to Zoie.

She scanned the drink list. "Hmm, I'll have the Moonshine Margarita."

"And for you sir?"

"Bulleit Buzz."

"Great choices. I'll be back with your drinks shortly."

Jackson linked his long fingers together. "Did I tell you how fabulous you look?"

Zoie's cheeks got hot. "Yep. But you can tell me again."

"You look fabulous."

They laughed.

"So, you never got a chance to tell me what happened with the attorney," he said as a way of leading up to their little exchange in the car.

"Apparently there was a clause to the will . . ."

Zoie explained to him what she had learned from her meeting with the lawyer.

"Wow." He sipped his drink then put down the glass. "I don't understand why you weren't told this at the reading."

"Same thing I wanted to know. Those were my Nana's instructions."

Jackson gave a slight shrug. "Well, it may be annoying that you didn't know, but it still works out. You were planning to stay anyway."

The waitress arrived with the dinner they'd ordered while they'd talked.

Zoie turned her full focus on her grilled Gulf swordfish and pasta. "This looks delicious." She cut into the fish.

Jackson took a mouthful of andouille hash while thoughtfully watching Zoie. Another one of Zoie's 'tell' signs was that when she was ducking a subject she either changed the topic or totally avoided looking you in the eye.

"How is it?" Jackson asked, testing his theory.

"Hmm, amazing," she said without looking up. "You?"

"Great. Have you thought about hiring more help?"

She reached for her drink. Her lashes shielded her eyes. "Not at the moment. The two assistants I have now are fine."

"Is something else going on, Z?"

Finally she looked at him. "What do you mean?"

"You're doing that thing you do when you don't want to talk about something."

She put down her fork, wiped her mouth with the linen napkin then placed it next to her plate. "That *thing* I do?"

"Yeah. You either avoid the question or avoid looking at me."

"Seriously, Jax. You're going to do this here?"

He wagged a finger at her. "And that. You go on the attack."

She pushed back from her chair and stood. "Need to use the restroom."

He watched her walk away and shook his head in frustration. He'd been down this road with her over and again; the hot, cold, off, on, accuse, defend scenarios. Zoie was amazing in so many ways that all too often he was blind to her faults, those things that drove him crazy. Most of her behaviors stemmed from the broken relationship with her family. He knew that, and so he made excuses for her to appease himself so he could justify staying. He loved her, always had, but she was making it so hard. It didn't have to be this hard.

The waitress was walking toward the table with Jackson's two business associates.

Jackson stood, extended his hand. "Miles, Victor. Thanks for coming."

They exchanged greetings and settled in their seats.

"Can I get you gentlemen a drink?" the waitress asked.

"Bourbon straight up," Miles said.

"Make that two," Victor added.

"I thought Ms. Crawford would be joining us," Victor said.

"She just stepped away."

"We made a quick site visit again today. Real progress being made," Miles said.

"I'm very pleased. We're pretty much on target and on budget." He glanced up. Zoie walked toward the table. "Here she is now." He put on a smile. The three men stood. "Zoie Crawford. This is Miles Cyrus and Victor Branch. The two men I told you about."

"Nice to meet you both." She sat. "What did I miss?"

"Not a thing, just ordering drinks," Jackson said. He checked her demeanor. Her body language was fluid, but her facial expression was unreadable.

"I understand from Jackson that you would be the one overseeing the community garden and the market," Miles said.

Jackson's gaze slid toward Zoie hoping that she would take the conversation in stride. True, they'd talked about it, but she had not fully committed and her no response to his earlier statement about her staying in NOLA gave him real pause.

"Actually, after Jackson talked you up and what you were able to accomplish in just a year, that was the dangling carrot that got us on board," Victor said.

Jackson saw the brief line that pulled her brows close and the forced smile that followed.

"Jackson is the great negotiator," she said throwing a look in his direction.

"We'd love to hear how you envision the two projects," Miles said.

Zoie cleared her throat. "I really was not expecting an impromptu presentation."

Jackson reached across the table and covered her hand. She balled her fingers into a fist. "No presentation. I thought it would be good for Miles and Victor to meet you since I pretty much sold them on the idea because you were going to be a part of it."

She slid her hand away, turned a warm smile on the duo. "What would you like to know?"

"I—we were really impressed with the fantastic growth of your business. It's only been a year, correct?"

"Yes."

"What's your secret? Because to be honest, the concept for the community garden and the market is a great one, but it is self-contained within the complex. How would it grow?"

"If you are getting into this to see phenomenal growth and franchises all over NOLA then this is not the project for you." She linked her fingers together, looked at Miles then Victor. "This is about doing right by a community that has seen nothing but dismissal. It's about providing a life and a lifestyle that they deserve. I'm sure you are aware of the history of disparity in the Ninth Ward. The goal of the community garden and market is a way of trying to level the playing field. If you're looking for this concept to grow," she looked at Jackson, "then you should consider partnering with Jackson to develop more affordable housing projects with the Healthy Choice Initiative."

Victor smiled. "Healthy Choice Initiative? Hmm." He turned to Miles. "We're just hearing the slogan, but I like it."

Jackson smothered his surprise. It was the first time he was hearing it as well, and it was damned good. For someone that didn't want to make a presentation, not only did Zoie knock it out of the park, she articulated a concept that was just what he'd need to get more financing to replicate the concept. With the right branding, the Healthy Choice Initiative would become a national movement. Damn, she was amazing; poised, controlled, clear. She exhibited a feeling of reassurance that rolled off her as easy as breathing. When she was in her element, her ability to pretty much seduce listeners into believing what she said was a skill that should be packaged.

"I told you Ms. Crawford was special." He slid a glance at Zoie and smiled. She lifted her glass to her lips.

Miles finished off his drink. "I like what I've heard."

"Absolutely," Victor added. "I can see the concept taking off, and whatever we can do to make that happen, I'm in."

Jackson nodded in appreciation of their support. He'd been

confident that Miles and Victor would be on board. They were already impressed with the work that Jackson had been doing in the 9th Ward and across Louisiana's depressed areas. Bringing Zoie into the mix, and now with her Healthy Choice Initiative tag, the deal was solid.

"We'll let you two get back to your dinner." Victor stood, extended his hand to Jackson, then turned to Zoie. "It was a pleasure to meet you." He held her hand for a moment longer that Jackson would have liked. "Hope to see you again."

Zoie offered a tight-lipped smile.

"We'll be in touch," Miles said to Jackson, gave Zoie a nod of acknowledgment and headed off.

"Enjoy the rest of your evening," Victor said.

"You were brilliant, babe. Was the Healthy Choice Initiative something you'd been thinking about?"

"Not consciously." She frowned, bemused, as if just realizing what she'd done. "It just came out."

"Well it was genius. It says everything about what we're trying to do. That's why you're so important to this whole thing."

She focused on the remnants of her drink. "Look, I'm not committing to anything and to be honest, no matter how brilliant the idea may have been, you shouldn't have sprung that on me." A simmering swirl of agitation that she'd tamped down began to gain in strength. "I felt like my back was up against the wall. I want to support you. I think your project is amazing, but I don't want to be blindsided like that. It's not cool." She reached for her glass, saw that it was empty and that annoyed her even more.

"You're right. I was out of pocket to toss you in the mix like that without talking to you first. I'm sorry. I really am. It won't happen again." Jackson heaved a breath, anticipated her response, but got nothing but a distant look.

"Tired of people telling me what they feel like telling me when they get ready," she muttered loud enough for Jackson to hear.

"What is it? What is wrong? It's not all about this meeting. Talk to me."

She clicked her fork mindlessly against her plate. She wiped her mouth with the napkin, pushed out a breath. "Tonight only added onto the crappy day I had." Her lips pinched. "Got into it with my mom this afternoon."

His brows lifted. "Oh. I thought things were better between you two."

"They were."

"So, what happened?" Before she even explained it, his gut told him that the reason for the latest blow up was due to something Zoie did or said. There was a part of her that he never fully understood: her relentlessness that often pushed people beyond their breaking point when she wanted something. She would become blinded by her own need to know. A great attribute to have as a journalist, but in day-to-day living it was definitely a flaw.

Zoie sucked in her cheeks. "I'm sure you think it was my fault."

"I didn't say that."

"You don't have to. It's all over your face, in your tone."

"Z. Don't do this. I'm asking because I want to know, because I want to understand what's bothering you so that maybe I can help. But you make it so fucking hard, Z."

Her nostrils flared. Her bottom lip trembled.

"Talk to me," he urged, his tone softening.

Her lashes fluttered. "It was about my dad."

That gave him pause. The name Hank Crawford was *persona non grata* in the Bennett household. It was never quite clear to him what happened all those years ago and no one would talk about it. He could understand Zoie's desire to find out why her dad walked out the door one day and never came back. In her shoes, he'd want to know the same thing. What was generally a problem was not that Zoie wanted answers, but the way she went about trying to get them.

"What happened?"

In alternating levels of anger, sadness, and frustration she relayed what had transpired between her and her mother. She knuckled aside a wayward tear, sniffed hard.

"I'm sorry, baby." He covered her hand with his. "I know it's hard for you to understand why your mother won't talk about your dad. But think about how hard it was and probably still is for her," he gently said. "It's a time in her life that changed her and everyone around her. The hurt of it is probably more than she wants to deal with."

Zoie leaned in. "What about me?" she asked through clenched teeth. "Don't I have a right to know?" A tear dripped from her left eye.

He squeezed her hand. "Z, sometimes, just sometimes, knowing isn't everything. Sometimes we have to let things go and move on. Sometimes we have to put aside our personal wants for the benefit of others."

She pursed her lips, took a shuddering breath. Her voice wobbled. "It's not right." She lowered her head. Her shoulders shook.

Jackson slid over into the seat closest to her and pulled her into his arms. She buried her face in his chest.

"If . . . if I knew," she cried, "maybe I would be different. Not so angry and vindictive . . . unlovable."

Jackson stroked her back. "You may be all those other things, but you are definitely loveable. Haven't I shown you that?"

She lifted her head from his chest and looked into his eyes that held the light of mirth in them.

"Did you just say that I was angry and vindictive?"

He gave her his best puppy dog look. "But I did say you were loveable."

She swatted his arm and sat upright then took the napkin and dabbed at her eyes. He kissed her forehead.

"I've really been working on being . . . better," she said.

He smiled, lifted a wiry tendril of hair away from her face. "I know, Z. You are a work in progress."

She smothered a laugh. "That is definitely true." She tugged in a settling breath and quickly scanned the room. She cupped his chin in her palm and moved in to kiss him.

"Let's go home," she murmured against his mouth.

"Ahhh, dessert," he teased.

"You catch on quick, handsome."

"One of my hidden talents."

———————

"I'm sorry ma'am, the card was declined."

"That can't be right. Please try it again," Kimberly said to the hotel clerk.

The woman swiped the card again. "Sorry." She handed the card back. "Maybe you can try another card?"

Her heart pounded so violently she began to sweat. Her hand shook as she went through her wallet. She pulled out her Visa. "Try this one."

The woman forced a smile and swiped the card. Kimberly held her breath. He wouldn't do that. He wouldn't. Her thoughts raced in every direction.

"I'm sorry Ms. Maitland." She handed back the card.

Kimberly's cheeks were on fire. She felt sick. "Is there an ATM or a bank nearby?"

"There's an ATM right down the corridor near the business office."

"Thank you." She shoved her wallet back in her purse. With as much dignity as she could summon, she walked away and out. She wouldn't bear the humiliation of this woman seeing her card declined in the ATM as well.

Once outside she reached out and grabbed the pillar to keep from collapsing. She ran her hands through her hair, looked

wildly around. Rowan had always made her feel safe and protected, provided for. That cloak of protection had been torn away.
She may as well be naked. He was the finance person. He paid the
bills, managed their investments while she built her law business.
She couldn't think. There had to be some reason, beyond the one
that was playing with her head, as to why her credit cards were
declined.

"Welcome to the Hilton, Ms. Maitland." The clerk beamed.

Kimberly blinked. Her heart pounded. When she focused, she
was looking into the face of the young woman who moments ago
had turned her away—or so she'd imagined. But it was all in her
head, the horrible ordeal of what could have been. She slid her
card back in her wallet.

"How many keys would you like?"

Kimberly tucked her hair behind her ears. "Just one. Thank
you," she said softly.

The clerk processed the room key and handed it to Kimberly.
"1601. Do you have luggage?"

"Just one bag."

She signaled the bellhop. "Ms. Maitland is in 1601."

The young, red-jacketed man picked up Kimberly's bag and
put it on a rolling cart. "Right this way." He started off toward the
elevators.

"Enjoy your stay, Ms. Maitland," the clerk said.

Still shaken by the scenario that whirred in her head, she
merely nodded and followed the bellhop.

She registered the click of the door closing behind the bellhop.
She should have given him a tip or something. He seemed nice.
Maybe he wasn't really. Maybe he hadn't closed the door behind
him and he would come back and attack her in her sleep. She hurried from the bedroom to the front door. She slapped the security
lock in place, spun around and rested her back against the door,
breathing hard. She pressed the heel of her palm against her forehead.

What was wrong with her? Thinking crazy. Imagining things. She pushed away from the door and shuffled over to the sitting room, slid open the doors to the terrace and stepped out in the humid night air. She dragged in a long deep breath in the hopes of clearing her head.

Downtown New Orleans spread out below, dotted with multi-colored lights and waves of people flowing along the avenues. Trails of laughter and the strains of music floated up to her, drawing her into the city's seductive embrace. There was a magic to Nawlins, a mystery that she never quite experienced in all her years in New York. The vitality of the city was palpable. Whole neighborhoods, the above ground cemetery crypts, the cobblestone streets, all paid homage to a bygone era that continued to thrive like no other city, bubbling over like a pot of spicy gumbo. A city that pulsed with drama, romance, and of course Mardi Gras. It was in her blood—this place, from the heat that floated in waves from the street and curled your hair into ringlets, to the aromas of jambalaya and red beans and rice that traveled along the Mississippi River breeze.

She'd shed this skin when she'd moved to New York to build a life away from the influences of her parents. She'd transformed herself into a slick Big Apple attorney, smothered the heaviness of her Nawlins twang, lived in a penthouse with a wealthy husband, and associated with a gaggle of so-called friends whose greatest ambition was to spend the summer in Fiji. That is who she became, but never who she was. Now she was in a kind of limbo, a purgatory of otherness, not belonging in either world. She gripped the rail of the balcony. A tear dripped onto her lip. She licked away the salty taste. Who was she now?

She looked down the sixteen floors. What would they put on her stone? How would she be remembered—*the woman who never was.*

Zoie stared up at the ceiling while she listened to Jackson's soft breathing. Funny, he didn't snore, but he swore she did which she heartedly denied—not that she would know. He'd always threatened to record her just to prove his point. He never did.

She turned onto her side, away from him. She was at a crossroads—torn. Her blind drive—that character flaw—had wreaked havoc with Kimberly's life and her mother's. And now her persistence had frayed the already tenuous thread that held her and Rose together.

Her commitment to her grandmother was complete, but her stubborn pride urged her to stay and keep control over what she'd built. She wished she could say the sole reason she would stay was for love. She sniffed. But it was like Miranda said, Jackson was number three on her list. Was that even enough to build a life with someone? Not to mention that he was having a child with another woman—the woman who may be stalking her and her family. And now she was entwined in his development project, whether she wanted to be or not. At the very least she owed it to him to stay and get the project off the ground. But what about what she wanted? She curled her knees toward her chest. There was a time she knew what she wanted. Truth. Justice. Look how that turned out. Now she was no longer sure.

Jackson moaned softly, turned and draped an arm across her middle, spooned his body with hers. "Why are you awake?" he asked, his voice raspy with sleep.

"How do you know I'm awake?"

"One, because you answered me, and two because I know you. You always curl up like that when you're thinking, troubled, can't sleep." He pulled in a breath, urged her onto her back. "Talk to me. What's keeping you awake?" He propped his head up on his palm.

"I don't know. A bunch of stuff and nothing." She sputtered a laugh. "My mom, Kimberly, the will, you and Lena, partnering with you on the development . . ." She hesitated to tell him of her suspicions about Lena.

Jackson stroked her hip, placed a light kiss on her shoulder. "You can't tackle it all on your own," he said softly. "I can take some of the pressure off. If you have doubts or issues about overseeing the garden and market, I get it. I put that on you and then dragged you in almost like a bargaining chip with Miles and Victor. I shouldn't have done that. I'm sorry. I can't apologize enough for putting you in that position."

"Jax, you didn't do anything wrong. Really," she said with a light chuckle. "We talked about it . . . maybe not as fully as we should have, but—we did toss the idea around."

"You're being generous." He traced the outline of her ear. She wiggled against him. "As for me and Lena. It's a big ask. Hell, it's more than any woman should have to deal with. I know we've been down this road. I tried to be as plain as I could about where I stand and what the agreement is between me and Lena. On that score, I don't know what else I can do."

"I know," she whispered.

He kissed the lobe of her ear. "You and your mom . . ." He blew out a breath. "At some point, you're going to have to let some stuff go, Z. I know it's hard as hell for you not to dig a tunnel to China every time you don't get the answers you want, but it may be more than your mom can handle to have to resurrect what happened between her and your dad."

"After my father left, my entire family changed. There was always a weird tension between my mom and my aunts. Now I know why of course. My mother had her reasons for clinging onto me, demanding so much. I get it." She turned her head so that she faced him. "It doesn't change the fact that I want to know why my dad left and why no one will tell me the reason." She looked upward and watched the shadows change shape across the ceiling. "There's something else. I wasn't going to say anything because it sounds crazy and it's probably nothing."

"What's probably nothing?"

She clasped his hand and told him about her aunt Hyacinth's insistence that she saw someone in a car outside the house, her own spotting of the car and then running into Lena.

"Wait." He sat up. "Are you trying to say that you think Lena is sitting outside of your house?" His voice kicked up in pitch. "Are you serious?"

She sat up, pulled the sheet up to her chin. "I know it sounds crazy but yeah, that's what I'm saying."

Jackson tossed the sheets aside and swung his feet to the floor. He rested his elbows on his thighs, placed his head on his palms. "Zoie, I've tried. I really have. I've pushed things aside that maybe I shouldn't have, but I did it because all I was concerned about was keeping you happy, making things easier for you. But this," he glanced over his shoulder. "I can't get with this Zoie. Lena wouldn't do something like that. And for what?"

"I don't know for what," she snapped. "Forget it. Just forget it. I knew I shouldn't have said anything."

"Yeah maybe you shouldn't have." He got to his feet. "I'm going to the kitchen." He stalked out.

Why should she have expected any other kind of reaction? It did sound crazy. But a part of her expected Jackson to accept the craziness that ran through her head, because to not accept it was to not accept her. What stung was that this was the very first time that he hadn't, and it was because of Lena.

Jackson slammed a cabinet door shut. She flinched. Bang. Another one. Her body tensed. After her father left them, Rose slammed cabinet doors, room doors, closet doors, anything that she could shove to generate the sound of impact. Zoie saw herself crouched in the corner of her bed, with her knees pressed to her chest and her hands covering her ears, like she was now. Slamming doors equaled unhappiness, and men that you loved left.

Jackson returned to the bedroom. He sat on the side of the bed. "Made some tea," he said, his voice flat. "Want some?"

"No. Thanks." She unfolded her body and sat up. She placed her hand on his back. "Jax. I'm sorry."

"Nothing to be sorry about. It's what you think and how you feel. I just don't happen to agree."

She dropped her hand to the bed. "So we can agree to disagree?"

"Seems that way." He pushed to his feet. "I'm going to take a shower and get dressed. Have a full day."

"I can take a taxi home."

"If that's what you want to do." He walked away without a backward glance. "I'll call you."

—————

Zoie turned the key in the lock of the front door. The murmur of voices coming from the kitchen greeted her, that and the tempting aroma of fresh-baked biscuits that teased the air. The scent of baking bread with a hint of cinnamon evoked a sense of comfort, warmth, home. Yet, she felt none of those things at the moment, even as her mouth watered. She turned toward the stairs and started up.

"That you, Zoie?" her aunt Sage called out.

"Yes, Auntie."

"Gon' come in all times of the mornin' and not speak?" She appeared in the doorway, wiping her hands on a dish towel. Her near waist-length, almost all gray hair was plaited in two long braids and pinned on top of her head.

"I'm sorry, Auntie." She stepped back down, walked over and pecked Sage's cheek.

"Breakfast is almost ready," she said while looking Zoie up and down. "For someone that spent the night in a man's bed you look pretty weak around the eyes."

Zoie felt her cheeks heat. She bit on her bottom lip, feeling like the teen she'd once been under this roof rather than the grown woman she'd become.

"You go on in there and speak to your mother," Sage advised, shooting Zoie a no nonsense, all-knowing look.

She started to protest but knew it was useless. She hoisted the straps of her purse higher up on her shoulder and walked into the kitchen.

Rose was pouring a cup of tea for Hyacinth. She glanced up when Zoie walked in.

"Good morning," Zoie murmured. She walked over, leaned down and kissed Hyacinth's cheek. "How are you this morning, Auntie?"

Hyacinth angled her long neck to look Zoie in the eye. "I'm doing just fine," she said in a voice that hinted at a secret. "Been with that cute fella Jackson?" she said with a wink and a chuckle.

Zoie patted Hyacinth's shoulder, rounded the table and approached her mother. "Good morning, Mom."

Rose sat down and dragged the spindle-back chair along the tile floor bringing it closer to the table. "'Mornin'" she said without looking at Zoie. "Coffee is ready if you want some." She lifted her mug to her lips.

Zoie took a step back. "Maybe later."

Sage brought the basket of fresh biscuits to the table and placed it next to the platter of scrambled eggs and sliced ham. "You should eat something," Sage said before lowering her wide hips onto the chair.

Zoie's stomach reached for the spread on the table even as her hips warned her to step away. She'd put on at least ten pounds since she'd been back and it was all due to not being able to push away from the table of temptation.

"Not really hungry. Thanks." She walked over to the sink and took an apple from the bowl. "Enjoy, ladies. I'm going to get ready to work."

"Saw that car out there again," Hyacinth mumbled.

Zoie stopped short. She turned toward her aunt. "What did you say, Auntie?"

"Car was out there all night."

"How would you know, Hy?" Sage taunted. "You were fast asleep."

Hyacinth stabbed a piece of ham with her fork. "That's what you think." She hee-hee'd and brought the ham to her lips.

Sage waved her hand in dismissal. "Talkin' crazy."

Zoie wanted to believe that it was all in her aunt's head, but she was beginning to think that was no longer true.

CHAPTER 7

Kimberly pulled herself out of bed and went to answer the knock on her hotel room door.

"Good morning, Ms. Maitland Your order." The room service staffer wheeled a food cart into the suite. Light bounced off the silver covered plates. "Where would you like me to put this?"

"Over by the terrace please." She looked around, frowning at the disarray. Her clothes were tossed everywhere, her shoes were slouched under the table, and her purse was opened on the couch, its contents littering the surface.

"Of course." He pushed the cart near the terrace doors, opened the leaves on either side of the cart, transforming it into a small linen covered table. He locked the wheels and turned to Kimberly with a practiced smile. "I hope everything is to your liking." He produced her receipt in a black leather billfold, which she signed and added a sizeable tip.

He gave a short bow of his head. "Thank you. Enjoy your meal, Ms. Graham."

She walked behind him to the door and locked it. Returning to the table the first thing she did was pour a cup of coffee. Her head still pounded. She wasn't sure if it was lack of sleep, stress, or the two empty bottles of wine that lay on the floor next to her bed. Probably a combination of everything. She'd requested a bottle of aspirin along with her breakfast. She struggled with the child-proof top which she always thought was ironic since she consistently had trouble opening medicine caps. She shook three tablets into her palm then downed them with large swallows of coffee. She picked up the bottle. 'Extra strength.' Yes, that's exactly what she needed, extra strength to do what she must.

She opened the doors to the terrace. The drapes fluttered against the warm, late morning breeze. Disjointed images suddenly flashed in front of her. It was dark. Loud. Music. A tree-lined street. She was in the pink dress that was now on the floor. Her pulse quickened. The pictures felt so real. She didn't know why. She swung away nearly colliding with the cart. What happened last night?

Her long fingers stroked her throat. Where had she been—another night with a random stranger? Bar hopping? Or had she stayed in all night and simply drunk herself into a stupor? Her heart tumbled. She didn't know and that was more frightening than anything else.

She flopped down on the chair closest to the cart and lifted the silver cover that revealed the fruit platter with two slices of toast, and an egg white omelet. Her stomach rolled, bile rushed to her throat and burned. She gripped the edge of the table and squeezed her eyes closed as she drew in long, deep breaths.

Slowly her lids fluttered open as her stomach wobbled then settled. Her hand shook when she reached for the glass of orange juice. She took a sip then a long swallow. Juice dribbled onto her chin. Absently, she wiped it away with the back of her hand.

What the hell happened last night? Her gray-green eyes scanned the mess she'd apparently created. She tried to bring the images that bounced around in her head into some kind of focus and couldn't.

Her eyes clouded with tears. Everything was spiraling out of control. She desperately missed her daughters and the life that had been snatched from her. What Rowan was doing was beyond cruel. How could he be so utterly different from the man she'd met and fallen in love with?

When they'd met over fifteen years earlier, Rowan Graham was an up-and-coming tech guru with designs on launching his own firm and snatching up all the corporate contracts that he could handle. He was larger than life and made her believe that together they could walk on water.

She was captivated by Rowan's energy, but mostly for the way he made her feel. With his sandy brown hair, chiseled physique, and piercing blue eyes, he was a matinee idol come to life. Everywhere they went together women had no problem giving him an extra look, a subtle smile even if she was standing right next to him. And he would slide his arm around her waist, pull her close and whisper in her ear how good she looked and that he couldn't wait to get her home. His words of love and encouragement always shoved her insecurities aside and cooled the 'come ons' from the countless female admirers. He was always her biggest cheerleader and moral supporter.

So how could all that turn into *this*? How could he simply stop loving her? She was the same person she'd always been. Did her lineage change her worthiness?

She nibbled on a strawberry, still plagued by not remembering what happened the night before. Whatever it was, her only hope was that it was nothing that would come back to haunt her.

———◦———

Feeling a bit more human after a long shower and a longer washing of her hair, she sat on the side of the bed wrapped in the hotel robe, her hair turbaned in a towel and reached for her phone. She'd been out of the office for more than two weeks. She hadn't spoken to Gail in almost as long. She'd missed or ignored several calls from Gail and had not returned the messages left on her voice mail. She owed it to her long-time employee to at least check and see how she was doing and if she was able to secure counsel for her clients.

Kimberly scrolled to Gail's number, tapped the phone icon and waited. She started to hang up, end it all before it began. What could she possibly say?

"Ms. Graham?"

Gail's incredulous voice broke through Kimberly's fog.

"Gail. Hello. How are you?"

"How am I? How are you? Where are you? I've been so worried."

Kimberly closed her eyes. Emotion swelled in her chest. The idea that someone cared was almost more than she could take.

"Ms. Graham?"

Kimberly took a breath, cleared her throat. "I'm sorry, Gail, about everything and the position I put you in."

"I'll be fine. My concern is you. Maybe I can help. At least I can listen. This is so unlike you. Talk to me," she gently urged.

"I . . . wouldn't even know where to begin."

"Why don't you start by telling me where you are."

"In a hotel, The Hilton . . . in New Orleans."

"Okay. Isn't that where your family is from? Did something happen with your family?"

Kimberly sputtered a withering laugh. "Family! I don't have a family."

"Of course you do. You have a husband and two beautiful daughters."

Tears slid down her cheeks. "No I don't. He . . . took everything . . . my children." She wept openly. The sobs shook her body as she rocked back and forth.

"What do you mean? He who? Your husband?"

Kimberly stared at the white wall. "Yes. Rowan. He changed the locks. He took my girls. He won't answer my calls."

Gail was quiet for a moment. "What about your parents?"

She laughed. "My parents! They're at the root of all of this. All of it," she cried out. "I'm sorry. This isn't why I called." She swiped at her eyes and sniffed. "Were you able to get services for our clients?"

"Yes. Everyone is taken care of. I've been doing some temp work, but I've been thinking about taking some time off myself. Maybe . . . take a trip to New Orleans. I've always wanted to see the city."

A knot formed in Kimberly's throat. "Really?" Her voice wobbled.

"Which Hilton are you in?"

"On St. Charles."

"Do you think you can hang in there for a couple more days until I get there?"

Her lashes fanned her eyes. "Yes."

"Good. Please take care of yourself until I get there. Please."

Kimberly sucked in air. "I will. Thank you, Gail."

"I'll call you once I make arrangements."

"Okay."

Kimberly rested the phone on her lap. She pressed her fist to her lips. Someone cared. Her brow tightened. She lifted the phone and called Rowan.

As she'd expected the call went to voicemail.

"What you're doing is wrong Rowan. You know this. Those are my children, too. I have a right to see my children! You're punishing me for something that was out of my control. I'm the same woman that you claimed to love all these years. The same woman! Are you really the kind of human being that bases their feelings about someone on race? As long as I was white, I was good enough be your wife and the mother of your children. But now . . ." The automated message advised her that the time for recording was up. She called back, then again. Paced. Each time becoming more enraged, more frantic, swinging from fury to pity, to utter despair and back again.

By the time she threw the phone across the room she was spent. Her throat was raw. Her eyes burned. Her right temple thumped. She heaved in air until her heart slowed to a reasonable rhythm and the sting had lessened enough that she could see.

She tugged off her robe, tossed it to the floor and went to look for something to put on. She pulled off the towel from around her head, dropped it on the floor and shook out her strawberry blond hair. She scanned the chaos of the suite while she picked up and put down items of clothing, kicked shoes out of the way. Thank goodness for housekeeping service.

Zoie went up to the attic that she'd converted into her office. Once upon a time the attic was no more than storage for all the things that couldn't find a home. It was where she'd discovered her grandmother Claudia's trunk that had the journals and photographs that set her on the path to discover what really happened between her family and the Maitlands.

She rolled the chair away from the antique roll top desk and sat down. So much had changed since she'd first sat at this desk. She'd been so angry with her grandmother for tying her to this place, forcing her to stay among women that she believed would rather see her any place other than here. What did she know about running a fruit and vegetable business—any business for that matter? She'd been so fucking pissed that she couldn't see clearly, total tunnel vision. She went on a scorched earth agenda and didn't care who got burned in her process.

She rested her head back against the chair and rolled her gaze up to the raftered ceiling. What was she going to do? Tensions were renewed between her and her mother. Jackson was pissed at her, and the business was doing well. She sucked on her bottom lip. There was nothing holding her here anymore. Maybe she could do like Miranda suggested and get her old job back at *The Recorder*. She did miss it. She missed the pace, the hunt for clues, putting the pieces together, and she desperately wanted to find her father. But digging up the past regarding her father was a no-win situation if she stayed here. She'd made enough of a mess.

She reached for the business ledger to review the scheduling of deliveries to the local market and private customers and cross-checked the information on the computer. She ran her hand along the bumpy green leather and the red trim binding. The gold foil lettering had long ago worn away leaving behind flecks of the letter 'R.' Her grandmother was all pen and paper, meticulously noting every bag of seed purchased and every dollar and cent on her investment. When she'd taken over, she'd initially thought the process antiquated, but there was a certain kind of comfort in penning the information, watching the numbers add up over time, page after page. And if there was one thing she'd learned as a journalist, computers crashed but notebooks didn't. The ledger was her go-to. The computer was only backup. She flipped to the next page, looked up and stared out the tiny attic window. At some point, she was going to have to tell her mother and her aunts what the lawyer told her about the will. Based on their response she would make her final decision.

She reached across the desk and turned on the little portable radio. Jackson had rigged it some kind of way that allowed her to get reception, but only on one local station. After a bit of static, and jiggling the dial like Jackson showed her, the station came through loud and clear. The host was giving a news run-down. Apparently, Michael Jackson had caused an international stir when he dangled his infant son Prince Michael II over a balcony. *Who does that?* She hit the keys, copying the entries from the ledger. What made her sit up and pay attention was when the host segued to national news. President Bush announced a change in Middle East policy stating that the U.S. would not recognize an independent Palestine until Yasir Arafat was replaced. And the U.S. was in the process of creating a new division called Homeland Security in the wake of the World Trade Center attacks.

Those were the kinds of stories she wanted to sink her teeth into. Some of her best work was her series on the World Trade Center disaster. She shut the ledger and sighed, pushed away from the desk and stood. She arched her stiff back and rotated her neck.

While she'd been working, it had grown dark and begun to rain. Fat pellets popped against the window and bounced off. Dammit. She needed to check the tarp on the garden. She walked over to the window. In just a matter of moments it was difficult to see out to the street. She started to turn away but stopped. She pressed her face closer to the window, trying to make out the forms beyond the swirling mist. Her heart thumped. The car. The white car.

She spun around and ran down the stairs, along the hallway. She grabbed a coat from the rack, draped it over her head, flung open the front door and darted out onto the porch. The car was pulling away. She couldn't make out the driver or the plate. The rain came down in sheets, so hard and fast that she might have imagined that she saw a car at all.

"Chile why are you standing there with the door wide open in this weather? Gon have the whole front hall full o' water," Sage fussed. "Close that door, girl."

Zoie backed up into the house and shut the door. Robot-like she took the coat off her head and hung it back up. Slowly, she looked across at her aunt.

"What in the world is wrong with you? Eyes don't look right."

Zoie had to catch her breath, think about what she was going to say because she knew if it came out wrong, she would sound just as crazy as her aunt Hyacinth who may not be as disconnected as everyone thought.

Zoie swallowed the truth. "Sorry Auntie. I started to go out to see about the garden and it was raining too hard."

Sage frowned and held her rooted to the spot with a 'don't try it with me stare.' "I look stupid to you? Since when you go to the vegetable garden out the front door?"

Zoie forced a wobbly smile. "That's just it Auntie, I wasn't thinking. I was upstairs working on the books and saw the rain." She wiped some water from her forehead. "I just ran out." She sputtered a laugh. "But I do need to go check on the garden and make sure the tarps are secure."

"Did that already," she said, slowing Zoie's escape. She planted her fists on her hips. "Listened to the weather this morning. Knew a storm was coming."

"Oh." Zoie blinked rapidly. "Thanks, Auntie."

"Hmm, umm," she hummed in her throat while she watched Zoie go back up the stairs.

Zoie went to her room and shut the door. Had the car really been out there? Was it even a white car? It was so hard to tell between the fog brought on by the heat and the downpour. Maybe it was gray or light blue. She didn't know anymore.

She sat on the window seat and tried to make out the shapes in the distance. She was starting to feel that she was in some kind of Hitchcock thriller, complete with a mysterious car and a dark and stormy night. She gave a little shiver and went over to her bed. Maybe it was all a crazy coincidence. Like Jackson said, why would Lena do something like that. It didn't make sense.

—————

Over the pulse of pounding music, voices raised in conversation and laughter, Kimberly signaled the bartender for her fourth refill. She was finally becoming numb, and wasn't that the reason why she'd fled the confines of her hotel room to find solace in the warm brown liquid surrounded by strangers? As much as she wanted to sink into a solitary pit of oblivion, the part of her soul that still pulsed with any kind of humanity needed the pressing of flesh, the sound of something other than her own twisting thoughts.

Periodically she'd check her phone. Maybe Rowan called and she missed the ring because of all the noise. He hadn't called.

"Think you should slow down a bit, take it easy, ma'am," the bartender said when he put her drink in front of her.

She cupped her hands around the tumbler and slid it toward her. "I'll take it under advisement," she said, her words flowing in slow motion from her brain to her mouth. She lifted the glass to her lips and took a swallow. The usual kick and burn of that first gulp had lessened and she wasn't sure if that was good or bad; either she was growing immune or he was watering down the drinks.

Through a gaze clouded by tumblers of whiskey, she studied the crowded space; the bodies leaning in, on and around each other. Polished mouths and swinging hips, bulging biceps and bellies over belts, decked up and down in rainbows of colors.

Everybody had somebody, even if only for one night. Yet, in a room overflowing with people she was still alone. The way she'd been most of her life. She'd become so accustomed to being her own best friend that she was ill-equipped to navigate the waterways of friendship. That quality of being able to stand alone, on the outside looking in, made her an excellent attorney. The only one who'd been able to open her up was Rowan, and then her daughters. She was broken now—vulnerable. Loving and being loved was a cruel trick of emotion that had stripped her of the bits and pieces of existence that she'd spent her life putting together.

A plate of hot wings with celery sticks and blue cheese dressing appeared in front of her.

Her eyes lifted. He had a nice smile.

"Eat something. On the house."

She bit down on her lip to keep from crying. "Thank you," she managed.

He eased her glass of whiskey away and replaced it with a glass of ginger ale.

She blinked back tears. "Why?" she asked.

"That's a pretty big question. Eat first, and maybe then we can talk about the age-old question why." He grinned and walked down to the other end of the bar.

She picked up a sticky wing, brought it to her lips and bit off a piece dripping in sauce. Her belly sang in delight. When was the last time she'd eaten anything? She didn't remember, but before she knew it the plate was a pile of bones swimming in sauce and blue cheese.

Her head was beginning to clear. At least enough to determine that this wasn't Kansas.

"Can I get you anything else, ma'am?"

He was maybe thirty, thirty-five. Hard to tell in the dim light. The black t-shirt outlined a firm but slim body. He had nice eyes, kind eyes.

"Umm, do you have French fries?"

He chuckled. "Sure do. Coming right up."

Dipping each fry in a mini pool of ketchup, she chewed slowly, actually appreciating something as simple as a good French fry.

The bartender returned. "How are they?"

"Good."

"Need anything else?"

"You're very kind. Whoever you are I have always depended on the kindness of strangers." The famous line spouted by the ill-fated Blanche DuBois in *A Streetcar Named Desire* popped into her head. How apropos. Would she too be doomed to be carted off to an institution—abused by everyone she allowed herself to care for?

He leaned in just a bit, close enough that she could smell the mint on his breath. "You are no Blanche DuBois." He refilled her glass of ginger ale from the tap.

"You were going to tell me 'why.'"

He half-smiled. "You seemed like you needed something, not another drink. And you remind me of someone."

"Oh. Not sure if that's good or bad." She shifted her bottom on the barstool.

"It's mixed," he said with a sad smile.

"Who do I remind you of?"

"My sister. Twin."

"Twin sister. That must have been fun. I don't have siblings. I do—not really." Her features tensed. She threaded her fingers through her hair, picked up a fry then put it back down. She pushed the plate aside.

"Yeah, it was pretty cool. Couldn't play pranks 'cause obviously folks could tell us apart," he said with a chuckle. He took a damp, white cloth from beneath the counter and wiped off the bar top. "Besides looks, we were night and day in personality." His gaze drifted away for a moment then returned to settle on Kimberly. "She didn't know where she belonged either."

Kimberly stiffened.

"Our family comes from a long line of octoroons. Most could pass easy as the sun rises. Some crossed ovah to the other side, some only when it was convenient. Me, I decided to take my chances on the 'dark side.' Nila, that was her name, she couldn't ever figure out what side of the fence she wanted to be on."

"Can we get some service down here?" someone at the other end of the bar yelled.

"Be right back."

Her chest heaved. What would make him say those things to her? More importantly, what made him feel like he could? Her years of being paid deference in any situation kicked in, overrode the fact that she was a woman alone in a bar who needed a bartender to slow down her drinks to keep her from falling over or worse.

Her back straightened with indignation, anyway. He was being too familiar, as her mother would say. Speaking to her as if they were equals.

Octoroon. The word bounced back in her head. She blinked, rapidly peeling back the years to her days on the playground when Ella Delange was called out and humiliated by Susan Langford and Mary Ellen Tully. They'd called her half-breed and said her mother slept with a monkey. 'If we throw water on you, I bet your hair will nap right up. Just like a nigger,' Susan taunted. A crowd had gathered and circled Ella. Tears streamed from her hazel eyes, but more than that, Kimberly saw real fear in her eyes. At the same time, she wasn't sure if the fear was because of the crowd or something else. Ella tried to run, but each time she attempted to break free of the circle that surrounded her, she was shoved back to the center as the crowd grew more frenzied and vicious. They pulled and tore at her hair freeing the once-neat twin braids. They tugged at her bright white blouse until the tiny buttons danced and popped across the concrete. Ella tried to cover herself but it was too late. The crowd fueled by teenage hormones and century-old ingrained prejudice descended on Ella like vultures. Her tears and her pleas fell on blind eyes and deaf ears. If anything, the crowd became more incensed.

Somebody, she couldn't remember who, held a small white bra up in the air, waved it over his head. "If she got brown nipples she a nigger for sure." She could still hear Ella's screams that finally brought the teachers. Everyone scattered. What was left was what used to be Ella Delange. In her place was a wild-haired, wild-eyed fourteen-year-old, half-naked girl trying to cover her ripe breasts with trembling hands. When she went home that day and told her mother what happened to Ella, Lou Ellen Maitland simply said, 'that's what happens when them coloreds try to pass.'

"Are you okay?"

Kimberly glanced up. Her vision was cloudy and her cheeks were wet.

He put a paper napkin in her hand.

She sniffed hard, took the napkin and mumbled her thanks.

"Food can't be that bad," he teased.

"I should go." She dug in her purse for her wallet.

He placed a hand on hers. "On the house, remember?"

She dragged in a breath, dabbed at her eyes. "You never finished telling me why?" She needed to know now more than ever.

He rested his forearms on the counter. She watched the muscles harden.

"Because I couldn't save my sister."

She frowned. "Save her from what?"

"Herself. Society." He pursed his lips as if contemplating his next words. "Nila wanted to be what she could never be—white. She wanted the acceptance and the privilege that went with looking how we appeared. But to do that she had to shut the door on everyone who loved her."

"I'm sorry," she stammered, not sure what else to say. What she needed to do was leave, get away from him. He was picking away at what was left of her protective covering, seeming to be in search of an opening.

"I don't know your story, but I can guess that you're carrying something heavy."

"You don't know anything about me," she fired back.

"You're right. I don't. But when you've been behind this bar as long as I have you get to know people. Some people come in just for a good time with friends. Others come to find someone. Then there are those that want to lose themselves, wash away what ails them." He angled his head to the side. "I place you in that group."

Kimberly glanced away, fidgeted with her empty glass of pop.

He took the glass, refilled it from the tap, then placed it back in front of her.

Her gaze lifted. She clasped the glass with both hands. "You're right, you know," she quietly admitted. "I do want to get lost." She blinked rapidly. "But the truth is I've been lost all along and never knew it. I don't know who I am and you can't lose what you never had."

He studied her for a moment. "I'm pretty sure you don't mean that literally. I don't get that I'm talking to Jane Doe."

She felt the halo of a smile tug at her lips for the first time in weeks. "No, you're not. My name is Kimberly," she said on a hesitant breath.

"Nick," he returned with a nod of his head.

The tightness in her chest lessened. "Nice to meet you."

He lightly tapped the counter with his palm. "Now that we have formalities out of the way I'm gonna check on my other customers. You sit there as long as you need to."

From the corner of her eye she watched Nick charm and cajole his customers, while periodically throwing a glance in her direction. Did he want to make sure she was still there or was it simply habit to check his work space? She preferred to think the former. And as the effects of the whiskey continued to recede she realized that she had in fact accepted the kindness of strangers, but she would not become Blanche.

———— ·•· ————

Bit by bit the clientele continued to morph from the high-energy crowd of earlier to a more subdued group who'd settled in for the long haul. It was coming up on one in the morning. She couldn't sit there forever or expect Nick to ignore his customers to keep her company. But she didn't want to go back to her hotel room alone either.

Nick sauntered over to her, leaned on the counter. "You good?"

She pressed her lips tightly together and nodded.

He seemed to study her for a moment. "I get off in like twenty minutes."

The words hung in the air between them.

What did he want her to say? "Oh. I probably should get going myself."

"If . . . you don't mind waiting." He gave a slight shrug. "I can walk you to your car . . . make sure you get there safely."

She swallowed down any hesitation. "Sure. I'll wait," she said before she changed her mind.

"Good."

Why was she leading him on? What did she hope to gain? Did she plan to fall in bed with him like she did with a perfect stranger—John? Before that escapade—that she still could not fully piece together—she'd never been with another man other than her husband. Her gaze slid down the length of the table to settle on Nick. At least—if things got interesting—she was alert enough to know what she was doing. Whatever that might be.

CHAPTER 8

Kimberly stood outside of the bar waiting for Nick to come. She wished she smoked—at least if she did, she could do something other than stand there as if she wanted to be picked up. Some remnants of propriety still lingered when she considered what it might look like to others, with her walking out with the bartender. Now she considered what she must look like standing outside of a bar at two a.m.

The glass and chrome door pushed open. Her heart jumped with anticipation. It wasn't Nick. She tamped down her anxiety and refused to begin pacing. But the longer she stood there, the more exposed she felt.

"Sorry to keep you waiting. Last minute stuff," Nick said, coming up behind her.

Her stomach tumbled. She licked her suddenly dry lips. "No problem. Nice out."

Nick gazed skyward. "Rain tomorrow."

"You sound pretty certain," she said, thankful for a topic as mundane as the weather.

They began to walk with no specific destination in mind.

He chuckled. "Grew up on a farm."

Her brows shot up. "Really?"

"Yep. Learned early how to search the clouds, the movement

of the wind, and the rise and fall of temperatures so we'd know when to plant and when to pick."

"What did your family farm?"

"My grandparents, actually. Sugar cane was the money maker. We also had peach trees . . . and a cotton field."

She snatched a look at his profile. "Cotton," she said, the historical implications well understood between them.

"The irony of farming cotton for my family was that it was being done by a black family and employing black labor. From the outside, we looked like a white privileged family exploiting our position. When me and Nila would visit for the summer, Nila embraced it, flaunted all the prestige that came with having a wealthy family. Me on the other hand . . ." He gave a slight shrug. "I had a hard time wrapping my mind around it—at least when I was old enough to see the bigger picture." He looked in her direction. "What about you?"

Her body tightened. "What about me?"

"Your 'Nawlins drawl comes and goes. How long you been away from home?"

Her nostrils flared as she sucked in air. Her stomach clenched. "I'd rather not talk about that."

"No problem." He slowed. "Where are you parked?" he said over a slight chuckle. "We're just kinda walkin'."

"I'm staying at the Hilton. I didn't drive." She threaded her fingers through her strawberry blond tresses, moving the thick mane away from her face.

"Then we should head this way," he said, lifting his chin in the direction they should follow.

"You never said what happened to your sister."

"One day she said she was leaving. She'd met someone. She wasn't coming back and we shouldn't look for her."

"Wow. Just like that?"

Nick dragged in a breath. "Naw. She'd been building toward that moment most of her life."

"How long has she been gone?"

"Fifteen years now," he said in a wistful voice.

She caught the shadow of sadness pass across his face. "You haven't seen or spoken to her?" she asked, trying to imagine her twin girls living without each other. She couldn't.

He shook his head. "No."

She found her hand on his arm. "I'm sorry."

He glanced down at her hand in his as if this was the way they always were with each other. "You learn to live with things. Even the unpleasant things."

"How?" Her brows drew tight.

"One day at a time." He gently squeezed her hand that still rested on his arm. "Find happiness where you can, mostly."

She was no longer sure if that was a possibility for her. Not without her girls.

They made another turn and continued down the narrow streets in companionable silence, occasionally bumping elbows or thighs.

Did she know as much about her own husband as she did about this man that she'd just met—the why and the how of the man Rowan grew to become? It never occurred to her to look beneath the surface—his pedigree spoke for him. His father was a broker and his mother the director of a real estate investment firm. The Grahams were new money. New York money. He'd attended Yale for his undergrad and graduate degrees. He was a phenom, having built his tech company—InnerVision—from a two-man operation to two-hundred plus with offices in New York, Tokyo and London. But none of what was obvious about Rowan would lead her to believe that underneath all his golden glitter was aluminum foil.

"How long do you plan to stay in town?" he asked, interrupting her thoughts.

"Not sure."

"No plans at all?"

She snapped her head in his direction. He was looking at her with such grave sincerity that the terse response that laced her tongue burned on its way down her throat. She was no different from Nila, whether consciously or not. She'd deployed her privilege with precision each time she was extended the extra courtesy or was not required to justify her existence, when men desired her, lifted her onto a pedestal simply because of how she looked. She filled an ideal—she was Nila. And like Nila, she was only a representative, a stand-in, not the real thing. Had she known of her true heritage would she have chosen the red pill or the blue— Nila or Nick?

"I didn't know who I really was until recently," she said with her head lowered, her words hitting the concrete and bouncing back. "My parents . . . aren't who I thought they were. My husband left me—or forced me to leave him. I guess." She swallowed the dry knot in her throat hoping to stem the burn in her eyes. "My girls." Her voice broke into pieces.

Nick stopped walking, turned her toward him and pulled her gently against his chest. Without a word or any cooing and soothing sounds, he held her while her sobs shook her body.

The sea of strollers, party-goers, and city explorers parted around them. How long they stood there, Kimberly had no idea, until her tears were spent and she found herself sitting molded against Nick on a loveseat in the hotel lobby of the Hilton.

"I am so sorry." She sniffed and wiped her eyes with a handkerchief that Nick had miraculously produced. He didn't seem like the handkerchief type, she mused in a moment of lucidity.

"Nothing to be sorry about. We all got laundry that tumbles out of the closet every now and then." He offered her a smile of understanding.

She sniffed. "Thank you."

He waved off her thanks. "No need." He took his arm from around her shoulder and pushed to his feet. "You gonna be okay." It was more of a statement than a question.

She nodded.

"Okay Kimberly. It was good talking with you."

Panic exploded in her belly and she reached for his hand, grabbed it. "Please. Don't leave. I . . . really can't be alone tonight. I'm not asking for or expecting anything," she implored, her eyes wide and wet. "I just don't want to be alone."

Nick looked down into her eyes, studied the pained expression on her face. He ran his tongue across his lips, shifted his body weight from left to right. "Only until you fall asleep, then I'll leave. Deal?"

She nodded in agreement and stood, gazed down at her feet, suddenly shy. "Thank you."

Kimberly slid her card key into the slot on the door to her room. The light flashed green and the locks clicked open. She pulled in a shaky breath before stepping inside. She flipped on the light and was immediately thankful that housekeeping had taken care of the mess she'd left earlier.

Nick closed the door behind him, slid his hands into the pockets of his jeans and followed her into the main living space.

"Can I get you anything?" She offered a wan smile. "My turn to play host."

"I'm good. Thanks." He wandered over to the couch and sat.

Kimberly toed out of her shoes, took them into the bedroom and returned barefoot. She sat on the club chair opposite him, tucked one foot beneath her. She rested her arms on her thighs. "Thanks for being here."

Nick nodded. He leaned back against the couch headrest. "Stayed in a hotel room like this once." He glanced around from his reclined position.

"Really? Where?"

"Aruba."

She smiled. "Never been. What was the occasion? Vacation? Business?"

He rocked his jaw. "Honeymoon."

Her eyes darted to his hand. His ring finger was bare. "Oh."

"Doomed to fail. I was surprised we lasted the two years. No kids, luckily."

"What went wrong?"

"Pretty much everything." He choked a laugh. "She was in it for the family money, or at least what she thought she could get. When she found out that my inheritance was beyond air tight, she filed for divorce."

"I'm sorry."

"I was too, but I got over it. Never fall for a pretty face," he warned, but only half in jest. He draped his arm along the back of the couch.

"If you don't mind me asking—"

He held up a hand. "So why am I working in a bar?" He grinned, then put his index finger across his lips. "I own it," he whispered. "A string of them actually. Two in NOLA and two in Baton Rouge."

She tossed her head back and laughed, a deep belly laugh. "Guess we both got the last thing we expected."

"Why did your husband want you gone?"

Her cheeks flushed. She blinked rapidly. "It's a long, ugly story."

He shrugged. "I thought that was the real reason you wanted me to stay, so you could finally tell someone."

The tips of her fingers pressed into her thighs. She turned her face away then looked right at him. "Until a few months ago I believed that my real father, my biological father, was my brother."

His brows shot up for an instant.

Bit by bit, she turned the pages to the sordid story of her life. "Kyle, my father, had an affair with our housekeeper's daughter, Rose . . . I always wondered why it was so hard for my mother and father to actually love me." She pressed her fist to her mouth. "I lived the life I thought I was supposed to live. I married Rowan, had beautiful twin girls, built my law practice, ran for office." Her nostrils flared. "And then Zoie Crawford tore it all apart, cracked the glass of the fantasy that was my life and everything fell apart." She got up, walked to the terrace window. "When I dropped out of the race, Rowan was livid. He couldn't understand. I had to finally tell him the truth."

"And he felt betrayed, couldn't accept that he'd married a black woman."

She turned around slowly. "No. He couldn't. I thought our love would be enough to get us through it." She blinked away the burn of tears. "I'm still me."

"Not to him."

Her insides twisted even tighter. "It's her fault!"

"Who?"

"Zoie Crawford and her fucking snooping, investigating. If it wasn't for her I would probably be a congresswoman, still with my husband and my children. I'd still have my life!"

Nick got up and came to her side. "You can have whatever life you want. I don't get the feeling that you're the kind of woman that simply backs down from a fight. You fight for your clients, don't you? Why aren't you fighting for yourself?"

She whirled away, stomped off to the other side of the room, away from him and the challenge of his words. "You don't know Rowan."

"But you do."

She looked at him over her shoulder. Why did she tell him anything? He was a bar owner. What did he know of her life to cast judgment? She walked over to the mini fridge, tugged it open and took out the travel-sized bottle of Hennessey and quickly poured it into a glass.

"That's not going to change anything," he said pointing to the bottle and the glass.

"For a little while it will."

"And then what?"

She brought the glass to her lips and stopped. "I only need a little while at a time to get from one little while to the next."

He stood in front of her, pinched the glass from her fingers and put it on the counter.

He was so much taller than her now that she was in her bare feet. Her pulse quickened. This was what she wanted, wasn't it? To succumb. To be used. To pay for her crime of false existence.

"Nila felt the same way after a while."

She looked at the glass then at him. "You said she's been gone for years. You haven't seen her. How do you know?" she asked, pinning him with her stare, accusing him with her question.

"She thought she'd found someone who loved her, too, that she could live the life she believed she was entitled to, until it all fell apart." He shoved his hands in his pockets and walked away from her. "She called me . . . she was wasted out of her mind. I never knew who he was, only what he wasn't. He wasn't the man she thought he was. She didn't tell me how he'd found out about her, only that her life was over. I begged her to come home. She said she couldn't. She told me to tell our mother that she was sorry. The last thing I heard was the shot."

Kimberly gasped. "My god. I . . . I'm so sorry." She came over to him and placed her hand on his back. His muscles flexed beneath her fingertips. "That's what you meant when you said you couldn't save her."

He nodded.

She walked over to the couch and sat. She linked her fingers together on her lap. "And you think the same thing could happen to me."

"Could it?"

Her lips tightened. A tear slid down her cheek. "At times . . ." Her voice cracked, "I think so." Her shoulders shook. "I believed that I was what he wanted, that he loved me. But that was as long as I fit into the frame of his expectations. The minute I didn't fulfill his image, he withheld love, support, understanding. That is the man I actually married, not the person he projects to the world. I guess we're both frauds. But how could he take my children? They're my life," she sobbed.

Nick sat beside her and pulled her tightly against him. "Then you get yourself together, clear your head, and fight for what's yours."

The first beams of morning light slid between the terrace drapes. Kimberly moaned softly. Her lids lifted then closed. Her thoughts were a jumble. She opened her eyes. She was lying on Nick's lap. He was fast asleep, head lolled to the side.

Gingerly she eased up, groaned as her stiff joints rebelled. She tiptoed away into the bathroom and quietly shut the door. In less than a month she'd spent the night with two men that weren't her husband. What did that say about her? She stared at her reflection in the mirror. At least she hadn't slept with Nick.

She turned on the faucets, grabbed a cloth, and scrubbed the makeup and the night from her face. She brushed her teeth, rinsed and turned off the water. She opened the bathroom door and peeked out to the living room. Nick stirred but didn't wake. She'd told him things that she'd never told anyone, not even Rowan. Her fears, her loneliness, her doubts of self-worth. He'd listened. He didn't judge or offer useless advice. He'd shared the guilt that lived with him about his sister Nila and what drew him to her—because of what he saw in her.

She returned to the living room. "Hey," she said softly. She gently shook his shoulder.

His eyes cinched tight then opened. A slow smile lifted his lips. "'Mornin.'" He rotated his neck. "Did we pass out on the couch?" He covered his mouth and yawned.

Kimberly laughed lightly. "Yep. That we did. I'm going to order breakfast."

Nick stretched his arms over his head and slowly got up. "I need a shower." He ran his hands across his jaw. "And a shave."

"Bathroom is all yours. Clean towels, robe."

"Thanks. I'll take the full monty on breakfast. Starved."

She grinned. "Got it."

The bathroom door closed and shortly after she heard the rush of water. She envisioned him stripping out of his clothes and wondered what his body looked like wet and soapy. She shook her head, scattering the image, but as quickly as the pieces dispersed they fused back together. Her heart beat faster and a warmth spread through her body as she found herself walking toward the bathroom. Her hand shook as it hovered above the knob. She took a deep breath and slowly turned the knob, pushed the door partly open.

The clear glass enclosure put Nick on full display. He turned, froze for an instant at the sight of her standing in the doorway. Water sluiced over the hard contours of his body. Her eyes followed the water's path as it cascaded downward then curved into an arch when it reached his cock, which even in a flaccid state was a thrill to behold.

"Come in and close the door. You're letting in a draft."

She blinked. Her lips partially parted. She stepped in and closed the door behind her. Nick half smiled and continued lathering his body.

Kimberly's heart was pounding so hard and fast she started to feel light-headed.

"Coming in?" he asked off-handedly.

She swallowed. The steam had begun to obscure him, only his outline and the sound of his voice remained. She unfastened the sash at the side of her dress that held it in place. She let the dress fall to the floor. Her bra and panties followed. Her stomach did a complete three-sixty as she reached for the handle of the shower door and pulled it open.

Nick's hickory-brown eyes glided over her. He took a step back to give her room to get in. "I'll do your back if you do mine," he said, his tone casual and matter of fact. He handed her the mini bottle of shower gel and the cloth then turned his back to her.

His back was as delicious as his front. She squeezed some gel onto the cloth then in slow circular motions cleansed his back. She took her time, moving from the base of his neck down to his ankles, cleansing, massaging and exploring, letting the soap and water slip and slide between the ripple of sinew and muscle. His skin was smooth, blemish-less, and reminded her of that perfect color brown that was never in the crayon box, but only in your imagination.

Her eyes fluttered closed as she inhaled the freshly washed scent of him. She opened her eyes and found herself facing him. He looked down into what she knew must be an expression of unadulterated lust and smiled, almost shyly.

"Your turn." He held out his hand for the cloth.

Her gaze drifted downward and her breath caught in her throat. He was fully erect, at least she hoped it was as erect as he could get. She wanted to touch him, to see if her fingers wrapped around him, and feel him pulse in her grasp. Her eyes jumped back up to his. She put the cloth in his hand and turned around.

How many showers had she taken with Rowan over the years? Too many to count, but maybe none at all. She was no longer sure, because even if they did indulge in the sharing of water, it was nothing like this. This was a performance in the art of seduction.

One hand moved down the center of her spine with the soapy cloth followed by the other—only fingertips that rose and settled the fine hairs on her body. A soft sigh slipped from her lips. Her knees weakened as the soapy cloth, guided by his sure hand slid between her thighs and down the inside of her legs. She pressed her palms against the white tiled walls to keep herself upright and bit down on her lip to keep from crying out.

His arm looped around her, lathering her belly, the swell of her breasts until her nipples hardened to perfect peaks. His free hand slipped between the apex of her thighs. His finger slid along the slick folds of skin until she trembled and whimpered.

Nick lifted a thick handful of hair away from her neck and placed a hot kiss there. She felt the waves of desire course through her from the soles of her feet to the top of her head.

"Are you sure this is what you want?" he whispered into her ear.

She looked at him over her right shoulder. "Yes."

Nick cupped her chin, lowered his head and kissed her slow and deep, tasting her with his tongue.

Kimberly turned into his arms, his stiff erection jutted against her belly.

Water and steam wrapped around them. Nick opened the shower door, took Kimberly by the hand and led her across to the adjoining bedroom.

"Are you sure?" he asked again before nibbling her neck.

She sat on the side of the bed and pulled him down next to her. "Yes."

Nick threaded his fingers through her hair, drew her to his mouth.

Their damp bodies fused, limbs entwined, and hands and mouths explored. He took his time with her as if every inch of her body was a rare find. He was gentle and insistent at the same time.

For a moment, when she lay beneath him, she hesitated. This thing with Nick was more than a fling—more than something to do. She felt something, a connection, and that realization scared her.

He stroked her hair away from her face, looked into her eyes. He leaned down and tenderly kissed her parted lips. The moment of hesitation dissipated. She wrapped her arms around him, arched her hips and enveloped him in her body.

Sighs mixed with deep groans. Kimberly held tight, needing to disappear beneath his skin, to cast the world and her troubles aside and relish being cared for body and soul, even if at the hands of a basic stranger.

"You're incredible," Nick whispered into her ear, still a bit breathless.

She drew in a shuddering breath. The warmth still pulsed in her veins. It could be so easy to fall for a guy like Nick—if she were someone else. She curled closer to him. The closeness somehow eased the guilt of what she'd done—broken her vows. For as much as Rowan seemed so willing to discard everything they meant to each other, even with all that had happened, she didn't want out of her marriage. She wasn't ready to toss it all away. There was a part of her that needed to believe that Rowan would come around and realize that their love was more important than DNA and melanin.

She squeezed Nick's hand that rested on her stomach. "So are you."

He kissed the back of her neck. "We don't have to talk if you don't want to."

"Thank you," she whispered. Her lids slid closed. "I never did get around to ordering breakfast, and now I'm really starved."

"You and me both. Want to stay in or do you feel like going out to eat?"

She shifted her body and turned around to face him. "Let's stay in." She frowned. "Do you have to work tonight?"

"I go in at eight. Why?"

She looked into his eyes. "My assistant from my office in New York is coming in this afternoon. Would you mind driving me to the airport to pick her up? I have a rental, but I really don't want to drive."

"Not a problem." His expression softened as his gaze drifted slowly across her face. "I'm not quite ready to be away from you either." He leaned close and kissed her.

Kimberly smiled. The simple words warmed her like a hot toddy on a winter night. She stretched out her arm, pulled the phone toward her and pressed the button for room service.

<hr />

Zoie sat on the ledge of her bedroom window. The sky was overcast, pretty much a reflection of how she felt inside. Ash gray clouds hovered along the horizon. Why would she think that Jackson would believe her suspicions, especially anything having to do with Lena? She should have kept her mouth shut until she was sure. Now, she'd created a brand-new rift between her and Jackson.

She sighed heavily. Maybe they weren't meant to be. For the duration of their relationship they'd been butting heads on one thing or the other. It seemed as if they were always standing on opposite sides of whatever the issue was, no matter how big or small. Passion drew them back together, but was passion really enough?

Whether she was ready to admit it to anyone or not, she now had options that she didn't have this time a year ago. She had her out according to her lawyer. She could walk away and let her aunts and her mother deal with the business. She'd gotten it on solid ground, all they needed to do was maintain it. Jackson would be a father in a matter of months. She wouldn't stand in the way of that. She'd shared her idea for the garden initiative. Jackson could run with it on his own. All the pieces were in place. Life would go on without her in the pot, stirring up conflict.

She sniffed, rested her chin on her knees. *Go on without her.* The gray clouds grew closer. Why did she always feel like the overcast gray cloud that always brought on the storm, the puzzle piece that didn't quite fit? The only place that she felt whole and needed was when she was digging for information for a story. It made her feel alive, vibrant and relevant. A drumbeat of thunder rolled in the distance, punctuating her mental point. It was who she was, the only person she knew how to be.

She swung her bare feet to the floor and stood. What choice did she have? She'd tried for most of her life to fill the void that her father left behind; anger at her mother, distance from her aunts, sabotaging every relationship she'd been in as if needing to abandon them before they abandoned her. If she ever wanted to find out who and why she really was she needed to find out who Hank Crawford really was and why he left her.

She pulled her cell phone from her pocket, scrolled through her contacts and pressed the New York number for Brian Forde, her one-time love interest and major competitor at *The Recorder*. Although she and Brian were always going toe-to-toe for a byline, Brian was one of the best investigative journalists she'd ever known—other than her of course. But now that she was no longer on the desk at *The Recorder,* she didn't have the same access and resources that she once did.

She pressed his name on the screen and the phone began to ring on the other end. Her romantic history with Brian was hot and intense. But he'd always believed that he was the fall back guy, the placeholder for Jackson. Maybe he was. She was never really sure. The bottom line was she didn't know how to be in a relationship, no matter who it was. And she didn't think she ever would be, until she wrestled the demons away.

"Forde."

Brian's familiar baritone drew her back. "Hey, Brian, it's Zoie."

"Zoie. Wow. How are you? Still in NOLA?"

"Yes. I am. Doing pretty good. You?"

"Can't complain. You know in the city that never sleeps, the stories never stop."

"I know."

"You're missed around here."

Her heart thumped. "Really?"

He snuffed a laugh. "Yeah, really."

"Guess that's a good thing."

There was an awkward silence.

Brian cleared his throat. "So, what's up?"

"Well, I probably told you at some point or another about my father."

"You mentioned him once or twice. No real details."

She swallowed. "My dad just up and left one day and never came back. No goodbye. No calls. No explanation. Nothing. I was ten. My mother refused to tell me anything. To. This. Day. My aunts . . . same thing. He is *persona non grata* in the Bennett household."

"Did anyone—"

"Nothing," she said, cutting him off. "By the time I was really old enough to do anything, he'd been gone for so many years . . . Everyone keeps telling me to leave it alone." Her voice trailed off. "I'm no psychologist, but I clearly have daddy issues. I know that's why I dig so deep and so hard." She pushed out a breath. "I want to try to find him. I need to. For all these years, my father has hovered in the back of my mind. Like a shadow. Images. Some things I wasn't sure were real or imagined. What I do remember like it was yesterday was the last time I saw my father." Her voice hitched. "It was a Saturday afternoon, a week after my tenth birthday. Usually on Saturdays my dad would take me into town and we would window shop, and Dad would tell me to pick out one thing I wanted more than anything else in the window and why."

"Seems kinda tough on a kid," Brian said.

Zoie huffed a laugh. "Yeah, I thought so too. Thought I'd have to always come up with the right answer ya know. It wasn't until years later that I realized what he was trying to teach me. '*You can't just want the thing that catches your eye. What is that 'thing' going to bring to your life?*' he'd always say. '*And if you really want it bad enough you gotta work to get it.*' Humph. Well, that Saturday I got up early like I always did, ya know. All prepared to convince my dad that the bike we saw the week earlier was not only something that I wanted, but with a new bike I could sell more papers on my route and it was safer than the one I had." She smiled at the memory. "But when I got up and went to look for him he wasn't anywhere in the house. My mom was in the backyard, just standing there, staring," she said, her voice drifting to that morning when no one would tell her where her dad was, when he was coming back, why did he leave without taking her with him. "No one would tell me." Her voice cracked. "Ever. Ever. I guess the only way I was able to handle the hurt was to bury it, because when I thought about him just leaving me . . ." She swallowed. "I tried intermittently to look for him over the years, but there was so little to go on and so much time had passed. I patched up the hole he'd left in my life and moved on. At least I thought I did."

"Do you really think finding your father is going to change who you are?"

She pushed out a heavy sigh. "I don't know. Maybe. At least it would give me some answers."

"It might not. Finding him may not be what you want it to be. There could be very good reasons why your family wants the past to stay in the past."

"The whole legacy of my family is built on lies and deceit and secrets."

"And you're the one to right all the wrongs."

"Is that a question?"

"No. Simple statement of fact. Remember, I know you Zoie. You're always on a one-woman crusade."

"Someone has to."

"Be careful what you wish for, Z."

How well she knew that axiom. She'd been down this road before. This same fire in her belly, the dog-with-a-bone tenacity fueled her when she went after Kimberly. Yes, the truth was ugly and painful and it upended lives and opened old wounds, but it had to be done. Even if she felt like crap about it in the end.

"I'm pretty sure you didn't call to get my blessing. So . . . how can I help?"

She smiled. "I was hoping you'd say that."

Zoie relayed all that she remembered about her father, that he grew up in Brooklyn from what she could remember, and that he'd met her mother while she was living in New York.

"Not much to go on Zoie. Do you remember ever hearing about where he went to school or who *his* family was?"

"No. Not really." She frowned. "I don't think so." She paced the cool wood floors then went to stand in front of the window. Rain splattered against the pane.

"You remember what he did for a living?"

A streak of lightning lit up the sky. Zoie peered through the gloom. The car.

"It's out there again."

"What?"

"The car. It's out in front of the house again."

"What are you talking about? What car?"

"I'll call you back." She ended the call and raced downstairs. But by the time she got outside, the car was gone. Again. She was really beginning to believe that she was imagining the whole thing. That didn't account for her aunt Hyacinth. She shut the door and returned inside.

Sage stood in front of her. "You have that look on your face again. What is it?"

"I thought I saw that car again."

"I saw it too, the other day," Sage admitted.

Zoie's eyes widened. "You did? Why didn't you say anything?"

Sage pursed her lips. "I'm fixing some gumbo. Should be ready in about an hour." She turned and headed back to the kitchen.

"Aunt Sage!"

Sage waved her off and continued on.

Zoie released a breath of frustration. What was it with this family and secrets? She returned to her room. She needed to call Brian back. This time she got his voicemail. She apologized for cutting their call short and asked that he call her back.

She tossed her cell on the bed and her body right behind it. Prone, she stared up at the ceiling. It didn't make sense for Lena to keep coming around, especially being pregnant and all. But, she'd always heard that hormones during pregnancy could make a woman a little crazy. *Still*.

Her phone chimed. She picked it up. "Hey Brian. Sorry about that."

"Yeah. No problem. You said something about a car."

"Hmm, yes. No big deal. You'll think it's crazy."

"No crazier than any of your other ideas and hunches. Try me."

Every time she said the words out loud she realized how ridiculous it all sounded. She tried as best she could to sound matter-of-fact as she told Brian about the car, Lena, her aunt Sage. "Crazy, right?" she asked.

Brian was quiet for a moment. "Maybe, maybe not."

"Seriously?"

"If there's one thing I know about you, Zoie, it's that you have great instincts and you might put a little extra sauce on things, but I've never known you to be wrong about your hunches. Clearly from what you're telling me, someone, maybe Lena, maybe not, is watching your house." He paused. "I know we're . . . not that couple anymore but . . . how in the world did you get yourself into a relationship with a man who's having a child with another woman? I get that you and Jackson have history." He snorted a laugh. "He always was the third person in our relationship."

"Thanks for the reminder."

"Hey. I'm sorry. That wasn't necessary." He blew out a breath. "I'll see what I can find out on this end about your father. If you come across anything on your end let me know."

"Thank you, Brian. Really."

"I'll be in touch. Take care."

The call disconnected.

Zoie squeezed her eyes shut. Brian really was a decent, stand-up guy. They may have been rivals at work, but Brian put his entire self into their relationship. But she'd never given him the chance that he deserved. He was right. Jackson had been the third person in their relationship. And for the first time she fully understood how Brian must have felt.

"What time does your friend's flight get in?" Nick asked, finishing off his western omelet with a long swallow of coffee.

"Her flight lands at three."

"We have plenty of time."

"I, uh wanted to show you something first."

He angled his gaze toward her. "Show me what?"

She lifted her chin. "Where it all began."

"The house is around this bend and then up the road. We'll be able to see it from the street."

"You still haven't—"

"Right there." She pointed to the wrought iron gates that guarded the drive to the house.

Nick slowed the car then stopped.

Kimberly gripped the handle, opened the door and slowly got out. She walked to the front of the gate. Nick followed.

"This is where I grew up."

"Damn. This looks like one of the plantations."

"It was a plantation. You can't quite see it from here but over to the far left behind the main house is a row of shacks. They once were used for the slaves. I had no idea at the time. All I ever knew them to be were horse stables, storage, and places to hide."

"When did you find out?" he asked, his voice turning distant.

The fingers of her right hand wrapped around one of the pillars of the gate. "I was about thirteen. My parents . . . were hosting one of their annual fundraising dinners. There was this couple." She shook her head slowly as if trying to clear the images. "They were looking at one of the portraits on the wall. I heard the woman say that the history of the Maitlands goes back more than one hundred and fifty years. They were one of the early land-owners and were able to buy slaves. Most of their fortune came from slave labor." She turned away from the house. "I remember feeling . . . unsettled inside, trying to wrestle with what that all meant. When I asked my parents about it, my mother was practi-cally indignant. She asked me how did I think the family was able to live the way they did and contribute to the community? I'd asked her wasn't she ashamed of what the family was, what they'd done? My father told me that the Maitlands had nothing to be ashamed of. It was a way of life and it provided everything we now enjoy. He'd laughed. 'It's not as if we still have slaves.'"

The first drops of rain began to fall. Typical Louisiana spring. They started back to the car in silence.

"That's what I have flowing through my veins," she practically whispered. She turned to look at him and saw her sorrow and shame reflected in his eyes.

"Every family has skeletons in the closet. Some closets are big-ger than others." He offered a half-hearted smile. "Can't change a past that you had nothing to do with."

She lowered her head. "I know. It's the ugly irony of it all. I'm sure that's why Kyle did community work and ran for office, and I wound up doing pretty much the same thing. I guess subcon-sciously it was a way to get the stench off." She sighed heavily. "This family has so many ugly secrets." Her features tightened. "It's no wonder they hid the truth about my birth, who my real parents were. It would have destroyed the image, tarnished the name. My parents were willing to do whatever it took to preserve the Maitland name. No matter the cost." She snapped her seat-belt into place.

Nick reached over and gently squeezed her clenched fists. "None of this is your doing."

"No. I'm just collateral damage." She stared straight ahead.

The rain fell steady now.

"One more thing I want to show you before we go to the airport."

They drove for about twenty minutes to the other side of town. Block by block, the landscape shape-shifted from sprawling mansions and massive weeping willows, to small gated communities, and one and two family homes some with a footprint of land, others with more.

"You can make a left. It's the only house on that side."

Nick made the turn onto Jessup.

She absently grabbed his thigh. "Right here," she said on a breath. She stared at the house.

Nick peered through the pelting rain and building fog.

"That's where my real mother lives." The frown line between her brows deepened. "And where Zoie lives."

Nick's brows rose. He turned halfway in his seat. "Have you seen her since you've been here?"

She slowly shook her head.

"Why are you doing this? Why are you here?" he asked, low and even.

She swallowed. "I'm not . . . sure. I think maybe I wanted someone—" she turned to him, "—you to see who I really was, what I came from."

Nick looked at her for a long moment. "At some point, you're gonna have to do more than sit out front of this house, *cher*. You're gonna have to cross the threshold and deal with all this shit or you'll always sit in your rage."

He turned the key in the ignition and headed for the airport.

"I still can't believe you came all this way," Kimberly said, her voice breaking with gratitude as Gail embraced her.

"You sounded like you needed more than someone on the

other end of a phone. Besides," she added, "this gave me the perfect reason to visit the Crescent City."

"Is that your only bag?"

"Yes. I travel light," she said smiling. "I'm only going to stay through the weekend." She looped her arm through Kim's as they navigated the terminal toward the parking lot. "How have you been?" she gently asked.

"Day by day. I . . . met someone." She snatched a quick look in Gail's direction. "He actually brought me to the airport to pick you up."

"He?" Her brow lifted in question.

"Yes. It's a story for another time. His name is Nick."

"I see."

They crossed through the lot, winding their way around the multitude of cars until they reached Nick's Acura. He hopped out.

"Let me get that." He reached for her suitcase.

"Nick, this is Gail Sorenson. Gail this is Nick." As she said the words she realized that she didn't even know his last name.

"Nick Bordeau," he said as if reading her mind. "Pleasure. Kim's been looking forward to your visit." He lifted the suitcase and placed it in the trunk.

"Nice to meet you." She turned to Kim and gave her a wink. Gail got in back. Kim sat next to Nick.

Conversation was light, mostly about the weather in New York and how this was Gail's first time to New Orleans.

"Safe and sound," Nick announced when he pulled to a stop in front of the hotel.

A red-vested valet came to the car. Nick popped the trunk and the valet loaded the suitcase onto a rolling cart.

The trio got out of the car.

Kimberly stood in front of Nick. She took his hand. "Thank

you. For everything," she whispered. "For last night, this morning, for listening and not judging."

He leaned down and lightly kissed her cheek. "You take care of yourself."

Her throat clenched. "Will I see you again?"

"Up to you. You know where to find me if that's what you want."

She bit down on her bottom lip and nodded.

Nick turned toward Gail. "Enjoy your stay."

Kimberly released his hand and he turned and got back in his car and drove off.

Gail came to stand beside Kimberly while she watched Nick's car until it was out of sight.

"He seems really nice," Gail said.

Kimberly pushed out a breath. "Yes, he is." She turned to Gail, pushed a smile onto her face. "Come, let's get you settled."

Kimberly went with Gail to her room.

"This is lovely, " Gail said. She left her bag in the short hall and walked fully inside.

It was a simple one bedroom unit with a separate seating area that had a small terrace. Kimberly had a full kitchen. Gail did not, but she did have a mini bar and fridge.

"Perfect. Thanks for setting this up."

"The least I could do with you coming all this way."

Gail faced Kim. "I came because I care. And I was worried about you." She drew in a breath. "I know we weren't besties back in New York. We did keep employee, employer lines clear." She gave a light shrug. "Now . . ."

"I can't tell you how much I appreciate this."

"Don't mention it. "

"I'll let you get settled. I'm in 1601."

"Give me about an hour. I want to get out of these things. Wash off the plane ride."

"Whenever you're ready. We can meet for drinks and dinner." She walked to the door.

"I'll meet you in the hotel restaurant in an hour?" Gail said.

"Perfect. See you then."

———————

Kimberly adjusted her chair beneath the table. Now that Gail was actually here, she'd begun to second-guess how much she wanted to reveal. She took a sip from her glass of water and absently glanced around at the stream of evening diners that had started to fill the restaurant. Her insides were still broken and her heart badly bruised but she didn't feel as incredibly vulnerable and defeated as she had when she and Gail last spoke.

In that moment, she had been at the lowest point in her life and found herself doing and being in situations she could have never imagined. She'd wanted to destroy what was left of herself and she nearly did and probably would have, if she hadn't met Nick. She would have wound up drunk out of her mind in the bed of another strange man who may not have been as relatively decent as John. She gave a little shiver just thinking about what could have happened to her.

She placed her small purse on top of the linen covered table and inched her chair closer.

"What can I get you to drink?"

Kimberly glanced up. Her heart slammed in her chest in that moment of recognition, pounding so fast she could barely breathe.

He smiled benignly. "Glass of wine?"

She swallowed and blinked rapidly to clear her vision.

"Are you all right miss?"

"Yes. Yes." She forced a smile. "Sorry." She waved her hand. Her laugh trembled along the edges. "A million things on my mind. I'm actually waiting on someone. She's in the rest room, but a glass of wine in the meantime would be perfect."

"Red or white?"

"White. Thank you."

"Be right back."

What she should do is leave before he returned and recognized her—made a scene. But maybe it wasn't John at all, and just her imagination and guilty conscience working overtime. He didn't act as if he recognized her.

She fidgeted with the clasp of her purse and suddenly wished that she smoked.

"There's always a wait in the ladies' room," Gail announced upon her return. She pulled out her chair and sat. "Even in the best of places." She reached for her glass of water and stopped. She leaned in. "Are you okay? You're actually pale." She tucked a lock of sandy blond hair behind her ear.

Kimberly blinked Gail into focus.

"Sorry. Daydreaming. I just ordered some wine. I hope you like white."

"Sure." She released a breath and took a slow look around. "Very nice place. And these are great seats. Get to see all the comings and goings." She linked her fingers on top of the table. "You've been gone from here for what, almost twenty years, right?"

Kimberly slowly nodded. "Twenty-two to be exact. Wow." She sputtered a laugh. "Hard to believe it's been that long."

"Ever miss it?"

"Hmm." She pursed her lips. "Not really. I mean not in the way most people miss home." Her gaze wandered away. "I didn't have any real friends. I was never close to my parents. No . . . siblings. I guess what I missed was . . ." Her eyes danced around the dimly lit room. "The culture, the mood."

The waiter returned with a bottle of wine. He turned over the wine glasses, opened the bottle and poured. "I'll be back shortly to take your orders."

Kimberly reached for the glass.

"You're shaking. What's wrong?"

Kimberly brought the glass to her lips and took a long swallow before returning the glass to the table. "I . . . know him. At least I think I do."

Gail frowned. "Someone from when you lived here? Why are you so upset?"

"From the other night."

"He's someone you met the other night?"

Kimberly bobbed her head. Her eyes darted around her immediate space.

Gail reached across the table and covered Kimberly's hand. "Do you want to leave? We can leave."

Kimberly dragged in a shaky breath, ran her tongue across her bottom lip. "Pretending it didn't happen isn't going to make it go away."

"Make what go away? What happened?" she implored, her voice low and insistent.

Kimberly closed her eyes for a moment. "I was such a mess," she said, slowly opening her eyes. "I'd been drinking for hours . . . I think." Her brow tightened. "When I woke up I was in bed with . . . the waiter." Her stomach twisted. She dared to look at Gail, expecting censure, but only saw empathy in her eyes. She swallowed. "I found his wallet on the dresser. His name is John. I put fifty dollars next to his wallet, got dressed and left. I . . . didn't think I'd ever see him again. Or maybe I just hoped that I wouldn't."

"Are you ladies ready to order?"

Their heads snapped up.

Kimberly's breath hitched in her chest. She shifted in her seat.

He looked from one to the other. "Should I come back?"

"Um." Gail took a quick look at Kimberly who gave her tight-lipped nod of approval. "No. We're ready to order," Gail said. "I'll have the lump crab cakes, seasoned fries and salad."

"And you, ma'am?"

Kimberly's lashes fluttered. She swallowed over the knot in her throat. "Make that two," she managed.

He took the two menus and tucked them under his arm. "Good choice. Should be about twenty minutes." He turned and walked away.

Gail leaned in. Her fingertips pressed into the table. "Are you sure? He doesn't seem to recognize you."

Kimberly tucked in her lips, slowly shook her head. "I would swear it was, but maybe it's just my conscience."

"You did say you'd had a lot to drink. You don't even know how you got to his apartment. You're probably wrong." She offered a hopeful smile.

"You're right. I'm making myself crazy." She finished off her glass of wine.

"I'm not going to ask you more than you're willing to share, but whatever happened with 'John,' did it happen with anyone else?"

Kimberly vigorously shook her head.

Gail exhaled. "Then let it go." She refilled their wine glasses. "Shove that skeleton in the closet and lock the door."

Kimberly sputtered a laugh. She lifted her glass. Gail did as well.

"Thank you for being here," she once again reiterated.

Gail touched her glass to Kimberly's. "Now do you want to tell me what happened?"

Kimberly drew in a breath, took a sip of wine. "My parents aren't my parents . . ."

She poured out the sordid story of the Maitland legacy, what they had done, the people they'd hurt, the secrets kept and how Zoie Crawford, who'd initially been sent by her paper to do an in depth piece on 'the candidate' began turning over sticks, stones and boulders and uncovered her family's sordid history. She'd planned to print everything that she'd discovered." She swallowed, gazed away.

Their food arrived, served by a waiter other than 'John.'

"I couldn't risk having my family's dirty laundry hung out for all the world to see. That's why I dropped out of the race, and Rowan . . . he lost it. I didn't know how to tell him and he couldn't understand why after all we'd been through that I would drop out without explanation."

"I can't imagine how hard that must have been for you. The weight of it."

Kimberly speared a forkful of salad. She chewed slowly. "When I told him the truth . . . about me, who and what I really am . . . he put me out and took my girls." Her voice cracked as her eyes filled with tears. She reached for a napkin and dabbed at her eyes.

Gail put down her fork and wiped her mouth. She leaned forward. "Listen to me. I'm not here to judge. I got plenty of shit in my own life. Next to dysfunctional family is a picture of mine. Alcoholic, abusive father, my mother had so many 'uncles' and 'prospective daddies" running though our lives it would make your head spin. My sister got pregnant at fifteen, ran away. My brother was locked up for petty theft and robberies more times than I can count. I was the youngest." She swallowed, looked off into the distance. "I come from a long line of ignorant people, racists, rednecks. The ones you see riding in pickup trucks, shooting off rifles and chugging down jugs of moonshine. That shit is real." She laughed derisively. "All I dreamed about was getting out of that backward ass Arkansas town and making something of myself. I did and I don't regret a fucking thing I did to get here." She licked her peach-tinted lips. "The way I see it, you're a victim in all this. But don't you reduce yourself to acting like one. You're an amazing attorney. Use what you have. You can't let him get away with taking your children without a fight." She pursed her lips. "It may not be what you want, but the truth is going to have to come out if you want your girls. If your husband wants to play dirty, then you play dirty, too. He wants to use your heritage against you," she paused, "you beat him to it and use it against him."

Kimberly rested her slender fingers on the table. "What do you mean?"

"Obviously, your husband doesn't want the world—or at least his circle—to know that he married a black woman, or half black, whatever." She waved her hand. "You have nothing to lose now. This is not the 1950s. Being bi-racial is exotic, acceptable. Own it. You champion everyone else's cause, champion your own."

CHAPTER 9

Zoie began her morning in the office attic reviewing the books and following up with deliveries. The two young men that she'd hired to do the harvesting were already at work, picking and packing the tomatoes, cucumbers and greens. She watched their progress from the attic window.

She was still torn about what she should do about the business and about Jackson. Although she was beginning to believe that the relationship between her and Jackson had hit a major crossroads, there was still a corner of her heart that wasn't quite ready to let go. In the past, it had been her and her relentlessness that led to the downfall of their relationship. Was she using her need to find out about her father regardless of the cost to others merely as a smokescreen for her inability to truly commit? And then there was Lena.

When he'd first come to her and told her of Lena's pregnancy her initial reaction was shock, but she gave herself enough room to understand that it would have never happened if she'd never left. Jackson made it clear that his heart was with her, not Lena, and he wanted to make it work, but he would be a father to his child. Lena insisted to him that she would continue to work her job at Xavier College, her sister would help with the baby, and that she did not want a relationship and he'd agreed. He'd pressed that point. She believed him. She convinced herself they could make it work. Yet, again, as soon as things seemed to be on solid ground, she sabotaged it. Why? Why? What was it in her DNA that refused to allow her to be satisfied and happy?

She turned away from the window, walked to her desk and put away the ledgers then went to look for her mother.

※

Zoie found Rose sweeping the back porch, humming to herself. She paused at the door, taking the moment to enjoy the lilt of her mother's voice. When she was little, the earthshaking thunderstorms that raged across NOLA would send her racing to her mother's bed. She'd burrow under her mother's arm while Rose cooed and soothed her, stroking her hair and planting calming kisses on her cheeks. But it was only her mother's angelic voice that ultimately quieted the tremors and slowed her racing heart. Even now, all these years later, her mother's voice still settled the restlessness inside of her.

But since she'd confronted her mother about wanting to know what happened with her father, conversation between them had been reduced to basic pleasantries. It had taken literally tearing her family apart with her digging into the past and finding out the truth about Kimberly and the Maitland family before she and her mother ventured on the road to rebuilding a mother-daughter relationship. They were getting to a good place until she blew everything up again with her need to know. She silently wished that the only thing she needed right now was her mother's singing to make things right.

"Mornin' Ma."

The note hung in the air. Rose stopped sweeping and slowly turned toward her daughter. "Mornin'. You didn't come down for breakfast. Left you a plate in the oven." She went back to sweeping.

"Thank you." She let the screen door close behind her. She

shoved her hands into the back pockets of her jean shorts and drew closer to her mother. "I need to talk to you."

Rose's gray-green eyes slid toward Zoie then returned to her task at hand. "If it's about your father, I done told you . . ." She shook her head as if she could scatter the words away on the morning breeze.

"It's not about my father."

Rose propped the broom up against the wood railing and stared at her daughter. "What is it then?"

"It's about Nana's vegetable business. I went to see the attorney about the clause, since my year is up . . . actually passed."

Rose's doe-brown face darkened. She walked over to the padded rocker and sat. She folded her hands in her lap. "Ready to cut and run," she quietly accused.

Zoie would not allow herself to be baited. It's what they did with each other, but not today. She walked over and sat in the chair next to her mother.

"Nana's will stipulated that I had to remain here for one year and run the business or the house would be lost." She cleared her throat. "There was a clause that I was not privy to until the year had elapsed. It states that at the end of the year if the business is successful I would turn everything over to you and the aunties and go back to New York." She pulled in a breath. "Or I can retain full control of everything."

Rose leveled her gaze on her daughter. "And? I'm sure you've come to a decision or we wouldn't be sitting here."

Zoie rested her forearms on her thighs. "When I first came back for Nana's funeral, the only thing I wanted to do was honor my grandma and get back to New York on the first thing smoking." She snorted a laugh. "Nana had other plans."

Rose almost smiled. "Mama always did things her way."

"But she knew what she was doing. She knew I needed to stay, and forcing my hand was the only way to make that happen. She wanted it for *us*." She looked her mother in the eye. Rose pressed her lips tightly together. "For a while it worked, at least I thought it did, until I screwed up again pressing you about my father." Rose's nostrils flared. Zoie reached over and clasped her mother's fingers. "And I'm sorry. I'm sorry for upsetting you, I'm sorry for cracking the fragile glass we were walking on. But Mama, I'm not sorry for who I am. I won't apologize for wanting to know all about the pieces that made me who I am." She paused. "And that includes my father."

Rose turned her face away, gazed off into the distance. "But look at what you needing to know and digging has already done."

Zoie tugged in a breath. "No, the outcome wasn't perfect. But you finally found out what happened to your daughter and all the reasons why she was taken away. We all did."

Rose turned a hard look on her daughter. "And to what end, Zoie? What good did it do any of us? And I'm sure that's the reason behind Kimberly dropping out of the race and who knows how it affected her family." She sighed heavily. "And I still have no daughter. I don't know if it's worse believing for years that she was dead at birth or to find out years later that she's alive and doesn't want to have nothing to do with me—cause I'm the wrong color." She snorted a laugh and looked away. "That's what all your diggin' brought us." She rested her elbow on the wooden arm of the chair and propped her chin on her fist. "Now you wanna go digging up Hank Crawford. How much more do you want to hurt me, Zoie?" she said, her voice barely above a whisper.

The vice of her guilt tightened around her throat. Her eyes stung. "Mama, I—"

Rose flicked her hand in dismissal and turned her face away.

Zoie straightened then got to her feet. She wanted to share with her mother her fears and reservations, her doubts about Jackson and what she should do. She wanted her mother to simply stroke her hair and tell her that everything would be fine, that she was a wonderful daughter in every way, and that she was loved. She sniffed. That's all she needed.

She opened the back screen door and went inside. She'd never gotten around to talking to her mother about everything the lawyer said or ask what she should do. She checked her pockets for her keys and cell phone.

What difference did it make anyway? There was no point in hoping to get counseling from her mom. They had not had that kind of relationship since she was a teen.

She took off at a slow jog down the lane from the house that led to the street. Running helped to clear her head and burn off the fire that constantly simmered in her belly. When she ran, her mind focused on her body; the beat of her sneakered feet against the pavement, the speed of her heart, the racing of her pulse, the beads of sweat that trickled down her spine, the flex of her muscles. The humid air coated her skin, turned her hair into sparkling ringlets. How many miles had she run away from what plagued her thoughts? Not far enough. It seemed that no matter how fast or far she ran, the euphoria of being disconnected from her fears and troubles was temporary, just like the buzz from the rush of adrenaline. Once she wound down from the high, her reality came racing back. But at least for now she could put a mile or two between her and what ailed her.

She turned the corner intent on cresting the rise before completing two laps around the track at the park. Her Blackberry chirped. She reached into her back pocket and pulled out her phone. There was a news alert on the screen; an explosion had gone off on the campus of Xavier College, several casualties, dozens injured.

Zoie frowned while she read. Her pace slowed. Journalistic instincts kicked into gear. She turned and raced back to the house, thankful that she'd kept her company account with *The Recorder* that maintained its subscriptions to all the major news outlets. Even though she wasn't doing the hard news she'd been accustomed to in New York, she still kept her hand in and her skills sharpened by periodically writing articles for *The New Orleans*

Clarion, and her monthly small business column was beginning to get some notice.

Breathless, she hurried straight to the family room. She turned on the television. The screen filled with first responders, fire trucks, police vehicles and smoke. In the corner of the screen was an insert showing the panicked surge of bodies being herded to safety by the police.

The entire country was still in recovery from the devastation of 9/11. The images and the losses were still fresh. Every fire, loud boom and low flying plane fed the trauma. Mammoth holes and mountains of debris in lower Manhattan were physical reminders that would take years to rebuild. Now this.

According to the broadcaster, it was unclear if it was an act of terrorism or something else. The explosion was confined to the academic affairs building. The names of the deceased and the injured were being withheld pending the notification of family.

Sage and Hyacinth meandered into the room.

"What's going on?" Sage asked, coming to stand next to Zoie.

Hyacinth plopped down on the couch. "Looks bad."

"Explosion or something at Xavier University," Zoie replied, with her eyes glued to the screen.

"That's where that nice girl works. Jackson's friend," Hyacinth said.

"What?" Zoie said.

"Use to bring her 'round." Hyacinth frowned. "Ain't seen her in a while. Not since you been back." She smiled at Zoie. "Lisa, Laura . . ." Hyacinth struggled to recall.

"Lena," Rose said, joining the gathering around the television.

Zoie's cell vibrated in her hand. She turned the phone over. Her old boss's name appeared on the screen.

"Mark. Hey. Yes, I'm watching right now. Really? Not a problem. I'll get right over there. Yes. I still have my press pass. Sure. I'll get back to you as soon as I have something."

"Who was that?" Rose asked.

"My managing editor from New York. He wants me to go over to the college and cover the story." She hoped she didn't sound as excited, almost giddy as she felt. But the mere idea of running down a story, for her, was like giving a kid a bag of sugar. "I need to get ready." She started to leave.

"I hope that girl is okay," Sage said and shot Zoie a hard look.

Her aunt Sage had a sweet spot for Jackson, even though she'd put him through the wringer when he and Zoie were together years earlier. And although she was happy that Jackson was "back in the family," she barely disguised her displeasure of how Jackson and Zoie were reunited. 'No good ever comes from the heartbreak of others,' she'd warned Zoie.

"I'm sure she's fine." She hurried away and went to her room.

The first order of business was her press pass which she found in the top drawer of her dresser. Hopefully it would give her all the access she needed to ask questions and take some pictures.

She checked the battery life on her phone. Dammit. It needed charging. She'd do that in the car. The drive was about thirty minutes. That was plenty of time. More than likely the streets surrounding the college would be blocked off. There was no telling how far away she'd have to park. Comfortable shoes were definitely in order.

She took off her tank top and shorts and changed into a T-shirt, jeans and sneakers. She hung her press pass around her neck, the grabbed her backpack and filled it with her notebook, pens, her tape recorder and charger. That was everything.

Ticking off the list of things she needed kept her from zeroing in on what hovered in the back of her mind. *Lena*.

She stopped at the entrance of the living room on her way out. The family was still gathered in front of the television.

Aunt Sage glanced up. "Six confirmed dead."

Zoie's stomach tumbled. "I'll be back as soon as I can."

"Be careful, Zoie," her mother said with the first note of care in her voice since they'd argued about her father.

Zoie offered a tight-lipped smile. "I will. Thank you," she added.

As she backed the car out of the driveway, from her rearview mirror she spotted the white car parked across the street from the house. By the time she reached the curb, the car sped off and turned the corner. Her desire to know battled with her commitment to the story that lured her like a seducer. Torn, she succumbed to the lure of the journalistic beast and drove off in the opposite direction.

She turned on the radio to catch any updates. One building had almost been leveled, there were now fifteen confirmed dead, dozens missing. Covering disasters was nothing short of life altering; the devastation, the lives upended, the aftermath. As much as journalists were trained to be objective and impartial, it was impossible not to be impacted by the pain and loss of others. When she'd first witnessed the destruction of 9/11, photographed the ruins of the iconic markers of New York City and talked to first responders and survivors, she understood, perhaps for the first time in her career, the importance of getting it right. She didn't dig into stories for sensationalism or personal glory, but to reveal the truth for the world, no matter how ugly. Because, for her, knowing the truth was what set you free and put you on a path not to make the mistakes of the past. The events of 9/11 had begun to change the world. It changed the rules, it changed how large groups of people were viewed and treated. It changed laws, chipped away at personal freedoms. What was once considered impossible—no liquids on planes, no shoes during check-in, cameras on every corner, invoking war, orange alerts, and an entire branch of government formed to oversee and root out terror—was now becoming normal. She believed in her bones it was her responsibility to tell that story, not from the view of the government, but the voice of the people who would never be the same. Her series on 9/11 had won her numerous accolades and there'd been talk of a Pulitzer until she was reassigned to cover Kimberly Maitland-Graham. *Look how that turned out.*

The cry of sirens signaled that she was closer. The muffled commands from bullhorns grew louder as she neared. The air turned gray the closer she got. The smell of burnt wood, metal and something unnamed assaulted her. Flashes of the huge holes in the ground, the smoke that still rose from the ground days and weeks later, the eerie silence around ground zero, loomed in front of her, as vivid as the day it happened.

Barricades set up two blocks away from the campus stopped her from going any further. Police, donned in tactical gear and long guns, manned the corners. Red and blue lights from police and fire department vehicles swirled in the gray cloud that hovered above the entire area.

A local cop, dressed in his uniform and an iridescent orange vest, waved her away.

She rolled down her window and was hit with cloying fumes. "I'm with the press." She held up her pass.

The officer leaned closer. "You can't bring your car in there. You'll have to walk. You need to back out and park on a side street."

"Thank you. How bad is it?"

His expression darkened. "Pretty bad."

She rolled up her window and went in search of a parking space.

———◆———

"I thought about everything you said last night at dinner," Kimberly said to Gail as they walked through the quarter, stopping every now and then to peek into some of the shops.

Gail peered into the window of a handmade jewelry and candle shop. "Oooh, I love that necklace. Let's go in here." She pushed open the door. Kimberly trailed behind.

"So what are you going to do about what I said?" Gail asked while she lifted the chain onto her palm. It was jade-colored stones, embedded on an oval-shaped base that hung from a thin gold chain. There was a wide band bracelet to match.

"Before my life totally blew up in my face, my half-sister Zoie had planned to write an entire expose about me. The true story."

"I met her—briefly—didn't I?" she asked with a frown of concentration knitting her brows together.

"Yes! That's right you did. She came to the office once."

"Hmm." She flipped the base of the chain over to check for the price. "What? Two hundred and fifty bucks! Are they serious? Definitely not handmade prices." She shook her head. "So, go ahead."

"I was thinking it's time I contacted her. Contacted . . . my family." She swallowed. "I want her to write the story. Get it published. Call out my family, and Rowan. He won't be able to simply get away with what he's doing. The one thing he hates is bad publicity."

Gail stopped examining jewelry and looked right at Kimberly. "Are you sure that's the route you want to take? It could get messy."

"It can't be any messier or any uglier than it's been."

"Hmm, that's true." She placed her hand on Kimberly's arm. "You need to be prepared for the fallout."

She nodded. "I know. But if it'll peel back the ugly curtain of who my family is and get my children back, it will be worth it."

"Are you ready to meet your real mother?" she asked softly.

Kimberly's nostrils flared. "I think so."

"Good. However I can help, I will."

"Thank you." On impulse, she pulled Gail in for a hug and it felt good to realize that she had a real friend. She stepped back, a bit flustered by her uncharacteristic behavior—but she'd done a lot of things out of character lately. She smiled. "I'm in the mood for a beignet. You haven't lived until you've had a for real Louisiana beignet."

Gail laughed. "I'm along for the ride."

They walked out.

———•◆•———

"So what's the story with Nick?" Gail asked as they sat at an outdoor cafe. She lifted the delicate pastry filled with fruit to her lips and took a bite, and the sweet confection tossed in powdered sugar was like manna from heaven. Her lids fluttered closed in euphoria. "Oh, my goodness. This. This is delicious."

Kimberly laughed. "Told you. It is one of my absolute favorite decadent treats." She lifted her cup of latte. "I was having another 'bad day' and wound up in a bar on Bourbon Street. Very apropos," she said wryly. "Anyway, I'm on my third, maybe fourth drink and he stops me. Makes me eat. Starts talking to me. I mean actually talking to me and for whatever reason, I didn't take it as a come on or a 'this is what bartenders do' kind of thing. He seemed to actually care. We talked off and on all night until he got off. I . . . brought him to my hotel room." She held up her hand when Gail's eyes widened. "Nothing happened. We talked until we fell asleep."

"Seriously?"

She nodded yes. "The next day was a different story." She felt her cheeks heat.

"Umm, umm."

"Silly, but afterward, as wonderful as it was, I felt guilty."

"Guilty. Why?"

"I mean that thing with John . . . that was . . . crazy."

"And dangerous."

"I know. But Nick . . . it was different. My head was clear and I knew exactly what I was doing. He asked me three or four times if I was sure. So I went into it with my eyes wide open."

"And?"

"It was the first time that I'd knowingly cheated on my husband. Until this week, I'd never been with another man besides Rowan."

"I totally get it. But," she leaned in, "you have nothing to feel bad about. It's not as if you set out to hurt him or deceive him. You were looking for something that you needed and you found it in Nick. For whatever it's worth."

Kimberly sniffed. "I suppose," she said.

She stretched her hand across the table. "Don't be so hard on yourself. You've been through hell. If anyone deserves to be taken care of, it's you. Just continue to keep your eyes open. When we're hurt it's easy to confuse lust with deep like."

Kimberly snickered. "I'll keep that in mind."

"So, what are you going to do about Rowan and your family?"

She pushed out a breath. "I need to speak with Zoie and I want to meet Rose, my real mother. I'm going over there. Today. Now. Before I change my mind." There, she'd said it, over the pounding of her heart.

Gail slowly nodded. "I'll go with you."

When they left the cafe and wandered back into the flow of human traffic it was clear that something had happened. There were pockets of people gathered around cell phones. Anxious faces replaced relaxed ones. That old flutter of anxiety rippled through Kim's stomach. That feeling of absolute terror for her children and her husband swept through her like a raging storm. She knew those looks. She'd lived it the day the towers fell.

"Something's going on," Gail said, as they passed a group huddled near the corner.

"Yes." She pulled out her Blackberry from her tote. It took a while to get a signal before she could search for the big news outlets. There were several notifications from the news services that *The Recorder* subscribed to. CNN, *The Washington Post, The*

New York Times, all blared the headlines of a possible bombing at Xavier University. There were multiple casualties.

"Oh my god," Kimberly muttered and shared the screen with Gail.

"Oh no. Is it an attack?"

"It doesn't say. Still investigating."

"How far is that from here?"

"From what I remember maybe about fifteen, twenty minutes from here." She looked around and every face that her eyes landed on had that same stunned expression, the same expression that had gripped the nation little more than a year ago. "I need to get my car."

"We're not going over there are we?"

"No." She dragged in a breath. "We're going to see Zoie and my mother Rose."

Zoie wound her way back along the streets crowded with double and triple parked cars, emergency vehicles, knots of on-lookers, and first responders wheeling the injured into ambulances. The air was thick with acrid smoke that hung velvet drape heavy. It stung her eyes and burned her nostrils. She squeezed past bodies, flashing her pass when required until she got as far as the police would allow.

Controlled chaos. Rubble. Smoke. The ominous black zip-up plastic bags that lined the street.

She finally spotted the command vehicle and cornered one of the officers. After identifying herself, the captain shared what details he could and informed her that there would be a press briefing in about a half hour.

While she waited, she moved through the crowd and lucked out on finding a young woman, Madeline Fuller, who had been inside the building but managed to get out moments before the explosion. The shock still registered on her face and her voice shook as she spoke. She shivered beneath the blanket that EMS had put around her. The noise she kept saying over and over. "Screams. Glass everywhere. The blast threw me to the ground. I didn't know what happened at first. My friends . . ." She began to cry.

"Do you know if they got out?" Zoie gently asked.

She shook her head no. "I don't know. I don't know." Her shoulders shook with her sobs.

An EMS worker came to her to let her know that transportation was ready to take her to the hospital.

"Where are they taking the injured?" Zoie shouted to the worker over the continued wail of sirens.

"The most serious are going to University Medical Center, the rest to LSU Medical Center." He helped Madeline into the ambulance.

Zoie turned in a slow circle. It was déjà vu. Trauma revisited. But she couldn't let her own feelings of helplessness overwhelm her. She was there to cover a story, to get the word out to the world about what had happened here so that maybe, just maybe, it wouldn't happen again.

She was able to get a few words from an exhausted rescue worker before inching her way over to where the makeshift podium had been set up for the press conference. The minute it was over she was going to drive to University Medical, talk with the staff and maybe some family members of the victims.

She took her tape recorder from her bag and turned it on when the mayor stepped to the microphone. She aimed her recorder in the direction of the mayor. She didn't want to miss a word.

Mayor Hatchett adjusted the microphone and looked soberly out onto the gathering. He cleared his throat and straightened some sheets of paper on the podium.

"This morning at approximately 11:45 am, there was an explosion in the Academic Center Building. The blast leveled the second floor, which collapsed onto the first. Once the structure was compromised the building fully collapsed at twelve thirty." He took a handkerchief from the breast pocket of his blue suit jacket and dabbed at his forehead. "At the present time, we have twenty confirmed fatalities, multiple injured. The injured were taken to local hospitals. We will not release the names of the victims until all families have been notified. Rescue crews are continuing to search the debris for survivors. According to the most current information we have, there are forty employees unaccounted for." He lifted his chin. "We have no idea how many students may have been in the building at the time of the explosion. We will keep you all updated as more news becomes available. I will take a few questions."

Everyone shouted out questions at once hoping to get called on.

"Do you know if it was a bomb? And are there any suspects?" a reporter from the local news channel yelled.

"ATF has determined that it was a bomb. But I don't have more details than that. And no, we have no suspects and no one has admitted to the crime."

"Had the college received threats? Could it have been a student or disgruntled employee?"

"We are investigating every possibility." He held up his hand to tamp down any more questions. "That will be all for now. There will be another briefing later this evening when hopefully we have more information." A trickle of sweat slid across his forehead. "In the meantime, please pray for the families of the lost, the survivors and our university. Thank you." He turned away from a barrage of more questions that went unanswered.

Zoie turned off her recorder and stuck it back in her bag. She needed to get to the hospital.

"That's the house," Kimberly said when they pulled the car to a stop in front. For several moments she simply sat there.

Gail touched her hand. "You don't have to do this if you're not ready."

"I have to do this." She unfastened her seatbelt, opened her door, and got out.

Together they walked to the front door.

Gail stroked Kimberly's back. "I'm right here," she said softly.

Kimberly gave a tight-lipped nod and then rang the bell.

It was several moments before the door was opened.

Aunt Sage answered. "Yes? Can I help you?"

"I'm Kimberly Maitland."

Sage blinked. "What?"

"I'm Rose's other daughter. This is my friend, Gail."

Sage gripped the doorknob. "Kimberly? Is that really you?"

"Yes. It's me."

Sage stood there, frozen, staring in disbelief. Finally, she gathered her wits and her manners. "Come in. Come in." She held the door open and stepped aside.

"We prayed and prayed that you would come one day," Sage said while she closed the door behind them. She stared into Kimberly's face. She reached out and caressed her cheek. "You have our eyes."

Kimberly's throat clenched.

Sage took Kimberly by the hand and led her to the sitting room. "Please sit. I'll get you some refreshment and . . . Stay right there." She ambled out of the room as fast as her weight and feet could take her.

"You okay?" Gail asked as Kimberly folded down onto the couch.

"I think so. I don't know. Wasn't sure what to expect."

"Who was that? One of your aunts?"

"I believe she's my aunt Sage, from the pictures that Zoie showed me." Kimberly looked around in wonder, taking in the homey atmosphere from the overstuffed but well-worn couches and chairs, the mantel lined with family photos and souvenirs. Sheer, off-white curtains gently fanned in and out of the bay windows. There was an old record player in a place of honor on a gleaming wood table, and a piano that looked to have had better days. A far cry from the mansion she grew up in or her lifestyle in Manhattan, yet there was a warmth here that was missing in her high-end abodes.

She turned at the sound of a gasp. A woman with skin the color of warm honey and waves of thick black hair that fell around her shoulders, stood frozen in the doorway. Her hand flew to her mouth. Another woman, not Sage, stood next to her. Those same eyes but a bit unfocused. All three women were versions of each other.

"Kimberly," came a timid whisper, a combination of a question and a prayer. Rose tentatively took a step into the room.

"Who's those white ladies?" Hyacinth asked, peering at Kimberly and Gail from the doorway.

"Hush," Sage cautioned. "That's Rose's girl, Kimberly, and her friend."

"Well now. Ain't that something," Hyacinth said and clapped her hands.

"Kimberly," Rose whispered again. She walked closer.

Kimberly licked her lips. "Yes, it's me."

"Oh god, oh my god." Rose's eyes filled with tears. She walked up to Kimberly and cupped her cheeks in her hand. "I didn't know if I would ever see you." Her voice cracked into tiny pieces. "I . . . they told me you were dead. That you'd died during birth." Tears flowed freely down her cheeks. "Zoie found you." She blinked rapidly, wiped her eyes. "She found you." She wrapped her arms around Kimberly and hugged her stiff body against her own. "She found you," she repeated. Slowly she let go and took a step back. She wiped her eyes, focused on the patch of floor between them. "I'm sorry. I shouldn't have done that."

"No," she shook her head. "It's fine. Really." She glanced around nervously.

"This is your aunt Sage." Rose extended her hand toward Sage. "And that's your aunt Hyacinth." She wrung her fingers together. "Let's sit down."

"Why don't I take your friend out to the kitchen for some refreshment," Sage said.

Gail jumped up from her seat. "Thank you. I'd like that."

Sage grabbed Hyacinth by the arm. Gail followed them out.

Rose walked over to the velveteen love seat and sat. Kimberly sat opposite her on a matching side chair.

"How much do you know about what happened?" Rose tentatively asked.

Kimberly's face tightened. "Only what Zoie told me . . . and my . . . mother didn't offer much."

"You talked to her about everything?" Rose asked, incredulity lifting her voice.

"Lou Ellen Maitland is not someone you actually have a conversation with. It's generally an exchange of sound bites, directives, declarations, and observations." She glanced away, lowered her head.

"All these years I didn't know," Rose said softly. She linked her fingers together on her lap. "I was so young. But I was in love." A wistful smile teased her lips. "Kyle," she quickly looked at Kimberly, "your father was an incredible man. So smart, and caring and handsome." Her gaze drifted away. "It was all a fantasy. I know that now. Back then a wealthy, well connected white man, marrying the barely of age black daughter of the housekeeper was unthinkable." She drew in a long breath. "My mother sent me to New York. Well, I found out much later that it was the Maitlands that took care of everything, including faking your death certificate, paying my mother to never speak a word of it by taking care of all my college and living expenses. My sisters resented me for years because of that. They knew why girls got 'sent away' and felt like I was being rewarded for being a slut." She snorted a laugh. "I was so broken after believing I'd lost you, I didn't care. I didn't want to come back. And Kyle was dead. I had nothing to come back to."

Rose looked at her daughter who'd risen from her seat.

Kimberly walked toward the window with her arms folded tightly around her slim body. "Secrets are an ugly thing," she said in a faraway voice. "I don't know who I am. I've lost everything because of secrets and lies."

Rose came up behind her and placed a tender hand on her back. Kimberly shrugged her away. "As much as I despise what my mother did, I benefited from it. I had a good life, loveless, but good. I had a career and aspirations. I married well. I have two beautiful daughters. All of that is gone now. I have nothing. Zoie did that. If she had only left things alone." She slammed her hand against the wall.

Rose lowered her head. "I never stopped thinking about you," she said softly. "What you could have been. What you would look like. When I lost you, I lost a part of myself that was never really filled." She frowned in thought. "I think at times I even blamed Zoie."

Kimberly turned around. "Why?"

"I wanted to make her into what I thought you would be and that wasn't fair to her. I held on." She fisted her fingers. "So tight. I wanted to bind her to me because I was so afraid of losing her. I couldn't lose another child." She crossed the room and sat back down. "But I lost her anyway." She sniffed, wiped away the tears from her eyes and looked up at Kimberly. "The two of you favor each other."

"Where is she? Zoie?"

"She's at the University. The explosion. Did you hear about it?"

"Yes." She paused. "I suppose she's covering the story."

"Yes."

"Humph. It's what she does isn't it. Uncover things."

"Would you have rather not known the truth? Would you have rather gone on for the rest of your life not knowing your family? Me? Your aunts and yes, your sister."

A tear spilled from her eye. "Yes! I want my life back! She ruined it all with her digging and probing." Her body shook.

Rose tried to touch her.

Kimberly held up her hand. "Don't." She snatched up her purse from the couch. "You can let her know she finally got what she wanted," she said, a coating of defeat weighing down her voice. She strode to the door. "Gail!" she called out.

"Kimberly don't leave like this, please," Rose begged. "Stay, let's talk."

"What else is there to say? Nothing. Nothing. Nothing!"

Gail emerged from the kitchen with Sage and Hyacinth close behind.

"Let's go."

"Thank you for the cake and tea," Gail said and rushed behind Kimberly to the door.

The three sisters stood in the doorway, watching Kimberly and Gail get into the car and drive off.

Sage put her arm around Rose's shoulder. "You okay?"

Rose hung her head and shook it slowly. "No," she whispered.

<hr />

All the major news outlets had the same idea that she did. When she arrived at University Hospital the street and the parking lot were littered with news vans and satellite dishes. Zoie found a place to park a block away and walked back to the hospital as two ambulances raced by.

The ambulance bay took in vehicles as quickly as they pulled out. Swirling red and blue lights spun through the sky. The pungent scent of fear, chaos and confusion burned her nostrils, setting off a physical reaction.

The scent hurled her spiraling backward. Images of destruction from that fateful New York morning flashed like strobe lights in front of her making her momentarily lightheaded, blurring her vision. She leaned against the side of a police van and dragged in gulps of air. She was never sure when the visceral reaction to scent would hit her. Since the day she'd stood frozen in terror staring upward as flames shot from the windows of the towers and bodies leaped to their deaths she'd had moments of flashback, usually triggered by smell. In the beginning, it was extremely difficult for her to work on her Trade Center series, but she'd pushed through. The doctors said it would take time, but eventually the symptoms would disappear. The episodes had lessened, but when they hit she was rocked.

She wiped the sheen of sweat from her forehead, adjusted her backpack and walked toward the hospital entrance where a cluster of reporters had gathered. She recognized several of the local anchors broadcasting for their networks. What she needed was access to either the doctors or emergency personnel.

She hipped and elbowed her way closer to the front. A reporter from WVUE Fox 8, WDSU, and WWL Channel 2 were doing their live broadcast. She took several photos of the entrance to the hospital to get her establishment shot. Her phone vibrated in her hand.

"Jackson?" She put a finger in one ear so she could hear him over the noise.

"Zoie I know you heard about the explosion at the university."

"Yes. I'm at University Hospital now," she shouted.

"So am I, but they won't let me in. I'm trying to find Lena. She's not answering her phone. She's not at home."

Her stomach knotted listening to the panic in his voice. "How can I help?"

"Would they let you in? Maybe you could find out something."

"I'm in the front of the hospital. Where are you?"

"Around the corner at the emergency entrance."

"Stay there. I'll come to you," she said. She disconnected the call, stuck the phone in her pocket and made her way over cables, around trucks and through the crush of media.

Jackson was pacing in front of the emergency entrance. "Z," he breathed in a moment of relief upon seeing her come around the corner. He walked up to her and grabbed her in a short embrace. "Thanks."

She nodded, tight-lipped. "I'm not sure how much I can do, but I'll try. So far, they aren't letting anyone in beyond the waiting areas, except victims and immediate family."

He heaved a breath, ran his hand across his face and turned in a slow circle. "This is making me crazy."

Zoie placed a hand on his shoulder. "I'm sure she's okay. Just out of touch for now. Maybe it's as simple as she can't get to a phone in all the chaos. I'm sure the lines are all down at the college. Let's not look for the boogeyman. Okay?" She squeezed his shoulder.

Jackson looked into her eyes. "I know this is awkward for you. I don't want to put you in a—"

"Stop. I'm here because I want to be, because you're important to me and you asked for my help."

"I appreciate that."

"Okay. So let me see if I can find out anything from the emergency folks. Sweet talk someone." She pushed through the revolving doors of the emergency entrance. The entire area was littered with stretchers, medical carts, bandaged and bleeding patients and harried staff trying to manage it all, mixed in with reporters and anxious family members. The blare of emergency calls over the loud speakers only intensified the scene of unreality.

"Wait right here," she said to Jackson. "I see someone I know from my grandmother's church." She wound around the obstacles and up alongside one of the nurses. "Miss Janet. It's me Zoie. Claudia's granddaughter."

Janet Felix frowned before her expression registered recognition. "Zoie. What are you doing here? Is someone hurt?"

"Actually, that's what I'm trying to find out. We think Lena Banks may be here. She works at Xavier and we've been unable to reach her since the blast."

"Zoie, I can't give out information on patients if it's not family."

"I know. I understand. All we want to know is if she's here." She swallowed and lowered her voice. "She's pregnant." She looked over her shoulder. "That's the dad over there in the denim jacket. He's going crazy with worry."

Janet craned her neck to see around the moving bodies and spotted Jackson. She pressed her chart to her chest then focused on Zoie. "I'll see what I can find out and only because Claudia Bennett would have cussed me out if I didn't. Give me a minute."

Zoie clasped Janet's arm. "Thank you, thank you. Whatever you can do." She walked over to where Jackson had begun pacing. "That's a woman from Nana's church. She's going to check and see if Lena is here. Okay? And if she's not here, maybe she's at LSU. Only the really critical were brought here. So, if she's not that may be a good thing."

He nodded, but Zoie wasn't sure if he'd actually heard her.

"Does Lena have family here, someone you can call?"

He shook his head, no. "Father passed. Her mom is in North Carolina. No siblings. I wouldn't know how to reach her mother."

"Friends?"

"Don't have numbers. Just the name of her one friend, Diane," he said as if realizing just how fragile relationships are. "They work together."

She linked her fingers with his. "We'll find her."

They found a corner of a space in the tightly packed area to wait for some word from Nurse Felix.

"Did you go to the college?" Jackson asked.

"Yes. I went there first." She stole a look at his stricken expression.

"I was in the car on my way to the housing complex when I heard the news on the radio." His features tightened into ridges and valleys. "I thought I was mistaken. I changed the station and they were saying the same thing." He shook his head.

An EMT worker rushed in pushing a stretcher. Jackson jumped forward trying to get a glimpse of the person being wheeled in.

Zoie grabbed his arm. "It's not her. It's not her."

His shoulders slumped, deflated as if jabbed with a pin. He leaned up against the wall and momentarily squeezed his eyes shut.

As much as she knew this entire surreal time was overwhelming and traumatic for everyone, it was still hard to watch Jackson's angst over another woman—albeit the mother of his child. She got it, of course. If he was indifferent or not overly concerned that would be worrisome. So why did she feel a way about his anxiety over Lena? He should. But was it simply concern for someone that he knew and cared about, or was it really more than that? Shit. What kind of person was she to even think along those lines? Always digging, always looking under rocks. She dragged in a breath.

"Hey, I'm gonna see if Nana's friend found out anything."

"Thanks."

CHAPTER 10

The ride back to the hotel was in relative silence, save for the voices of the newscasters relaying updates on the explosion at Xavier University and minimal comments from Kimberly and Gail.

As much as she tried to present a façade of indifference, Kimberly was deeply shaken by meeting her mother. She wasn't sure how she would react or feel seeing Rose for the first time, but to actually stand in front of her, hear her voice, and feel her touch was beyond anything that she could have ever imagined. Her emotions seesawed between fury and rage, longing, and confusion.

For her entire life, she'd lived with the belief that her grandparents were her parents. Yet, there was a secret part of her that always felt something was missing. Why didn't she feel loved instead of simply tolerated? She'd attributed it to Lou Ellen's standoffish persona and Franklin's tunnel vision about his empire, and that they were older than the parents of her classmates. It was never that.

"How could they do that to me?" she suddenly said.

Gail placed a comforting hand on Kimberly's shoulder. "There's no easy answer."

"Who am I really? The man I thought was my brother was my

father for Christ's sake! Do you have any idea what that feels like, how ugly and filthy I feel?"

"This isn't on you, Kim. It's not. You are the victim here. But you don't have to stay victimized. You're stronger than that."

Kimberly slid Gail a look. "Humph. I don't feel strong."

"I know you may not want to hear this right now, but you still have a family, and from what your aunt was telling me, a family that wants you to be a part of it, especially your mother. Think about what the lie has done to her. She's your mom," she gently added.

Kimberly sniffed back a fresh wave of impending tears and pulled into the driveway of the hotel, parked and got out. She handed over her keys to the valet then she and Gail walked inside.

"I need a drink," Kimberly announced and walked ahead to the bar.

"Martini," Kimberly said to the bartender. She placed her purse on the counter.

"Diet coke for me," Gail said. She angled her body toward Kimberly. "You have some decisions to make," she began. "Clearly the situation with your family can't stay the way it is. You're in limbo, and you're the only person that can change that."

"I . . ."She expelled a long breath fueled with sadness. "I don't know where to even start."

"I think you should start with your newfound family. If anyone can understand the trauma of losing a child it would be your mother. Talk to her about what has happened. Let them support you because you have to get your children back, no matter what happens with your mother . . . and grandparents."

The bartender returned with their drinks. Kimberly took a quick swallow of her martini then set the glass down. "Dealing with them would mean having to deal with Zoie." She spat the name as if it burned her tongue. "I'm still wrapping my head around what she did and what she was willing to do for a story. It still stings."

Gail wrapped her hands around her glass, stared down into the cool brown liquid. "She's your sister."

Kimberly's lips thinned into a solid line.

"No getting away from that. You may never have a loving sister relationship, but you'll always be bound by blood. She's the sister you never had. And she did some fucked up shit, but if she didn't, you would have never known the truth about who you are and your mother may have gone to her grave believing that the daughter she gave birth to was long dead. Truth always comes to light, Kim. No matter how hard people try to hide it."

Kimberly finished off her drink. "You make it sound so simple."

"Look, I've worked side by side with you for the past five years. I know what you're capable of and how far you're willing to go to bat for your clients. Now it's time to use that same tenacity for yourself. Your life, your family . . . this is the biggest case of your career, Kim. Are you willing to let the other side beat you?"

Kimberly turned to look at Gail and saw the challenge in her eyes.

"No. I'm not."

⇒•⇐

Zoie hurried over to Jackson, who leaped to attention when he spotted her.

She held up her hands to try to keep him calm while she explained what Nurse Felix told her.

"Lena's here," she said calmly. She pressed her hands to his chest. "She's in the trauma room."

"I have to see her." He tried to push past her.

Zoie gripped his upper arm and stood her ground, blocking him. "They're not going to let you go back there," she hissed through her teeth. "She's . . . unconscious, Jax. Some burns and a broken leg." She watched his expression shift from anticipated panic to outright fear. "They lost her once on the way over." She heard the sharp intake of breath. "They want her stable before they move her to ICU. They need to make sure that . . . there are no internal injuries. Once she's moved to ICU you will probably be able to see her."

He ran his hand over his face, turned his head up to the ceiling. "Fuck!" He slammed his fist into the wall.

"Jax . . ."

He walked to the exit. Zoie followed him outside. "They're doing everything they can. She'll come through this."

"What about the baby? Did she say anything about the baby?"

"No. I'm sorry. She didn't."

He pushed out a breath, nodded. He finally looked at Zoie. "Hey, thank you. Really."

"Of course. There's no thanks needed." She shifted the weight of her backpack. "It will be a while before you hear anything. The whole hospital is in chaos. There's no room to really wait. Where's your car?"

He looked around as if trying to remember. "Uh, about three blocks from here."

"Why don't I walk you to your car. At least you can sit down to wait. We know Lena is in good hands and there is absolutely nothing you can do right now."

He pushed his hands into his pockets. "You're probably right," he conceded.

"Which way?"

"Down Orchard."

She slid her arms through his. "Come on."

He glanced down at her and halfway smiled.

Her phone vibrated in her pocket. She pulled out her phone, saw the name and sent the call to voicemail. Mark would want an update and at the moment she didn't have one.

"You don't have to do this, Z. I know you're here working."

"As soon as I start complaining, you can send me on my way."

"Noted."

They stopped in front of his car. Jackson unlocked the doors and they got in.

"I'm going to try to find Diane's contact info. Maybe she knows how to reach Lena's mom."

"Doesn't Diane work at the college?"

"She does. But she's supposed to be on vacation this week."

"Oh." But then the brakes screeched in her head. How would he know that if he wasn't in contact with Lena on more than 'how are you and the baby feeling'? Her shoulders slumped under the weight of her realization, the burn of it flared in her stomach. She resisted her innate urge to ask how he knew that. The answer was obvious, but now was not the time.

She licked her lips. "I should get back over to the hospital and see if I can get some interviews for the article."

"Sure. Of course. Go." He leaned across the gears for an awkward on-the-cheek kiss. "Thanks again."

She opened her door. "I'll check in if I hear anything." She shut the door behind her without waiting for a response, suddenly hurt and angry, and guilty for being hurt and angry.

Halfway back to the hospital, she took out her phone to check the message from Mark. He wanted her to hook up with the local NBC affiliate news anchor on the scene, Anthony LeRoux. She shot Mark a quick text message to let him know she'd gotten the message and would look for LeRoux.

She picked up her pace, intent on leaving her shaky feelings behind.

When she returned to the vicinity of the hospital, the crowd and the controlled chaotic atmosphere had only intensified. The number of news vans seemed to have doubled, along with the on-air commentators that were broadcasting from every available spot in the area. News copters buzzed overhead. It would take a miracle to locate this LeRoux fellow. Maybe if she could get close to the WDSU van someone on the crew could point her in the direction of the anchor.

She squeezed between bodies, catching whiffs of stale sweat and coffee-tinged breaths to get to the other side of the restless crowd hoping to spot the WDSU van. She looked for the peacock-colored logo. As luck would have it, the van was at the far end of the street. "Scuse me, scuse me. Sorry. Excuse me . . ." she mumbled, moving through the gauntlet of bodies and equipment that was akin to traversing an obstacle course designed to make you fail.

"Hi," she greeted a cameraman sitting on the side lift of the van downing a can of soda. She held up her press pass. "I work with *The Recorder* in New York. I got a call from my editor to connect with Anthony LeRoux. Do you know where I can find him?"

He cupped his palm over his blue eyes, shading them from the setting sun and glanced up at her, took a cursory look at her pass. "He's in the truck." He hooked his finger over his shoulder.

"Thanks." She went around to the back of the truck. The door was partially opened. She stepped up on the lift and knocked.

Three heads that had been focused on transmission equipment and computer screens turned in her direction.

"Hi. I'm Zoie Crawford, with *The Recorder* in New York. My editor—"

"Hey," came a voice right out of central casting from the forth head at end of the row. He pushed his chair out into view and swiveled toward her. "I'm Anthony LeRoux. Mark told me to expect you. Come on in."

Holy ish. His smile should be patented. Anthony LeRoux was drop-your-panties gorgeous. Even in his seated position she could tell he was tall. His stark white shirt gleamed against skin that reminded her of long summer nights. She wanted to surf on the waves of his closely cut hair. Damn what time was he on the air? She needed to up her news watching game.

She stepped up into the van and inched her way to the back.

"Here, take my seat."

Anthony stood and just as she'd imagined he was tall. "Thank you."

He sat on the edge of the console and folded his arms. He focused on her like she was the only person in the room or the world.

"How can I help?"

"Mark wants me to team up with you, tag along for your coverage. I'll write up the events for print in New York. I guess he's thinking you may have more access, being local."

Anthony nodded. "Not a problem. This is the team Marvin Vance, Holly Spence, and Javier Ramos. And Allen Walters is outside."

They each nodded in acknowledgment.

"We have sodas, water and some sandwiches," Anthony offered. "You're more than welcome."

"Water would be great."

Javier handed her an ice-cold bottle of water from the ice chest.

"Thanks. Totally parched." She opened the bottle and took long, thirsty gulps nearly finishing off the bottle before putting it down. "Whew. I needed that."

Anthony checked his watch. "We go live in ten minutes. I'm going to get set up, find a good spot." He hunched his way down the narrow aisle to the exit of the truck. Zoie followed.

"I don't think I've seen you at any 'breaking news' events around here," Anthony said, once they were outside. "New to NOLA?"

"Actually, I grew up here, but I moved to New York about ten years ago. Did some stringer work for a while and then got a spot at *The Recorder*."

His brows knitted just a bit. "Wait," he pointed a slender finger at her, "you're the same Zoie Crawford that did the World

Trade Center piece," he said, his expression brightening with the realization.

She laughed. "Yep that's me."

"Damn good work." He stared at her. "Damn good work. So, what are you doing now? Connected to a paper here or what?"

"I guess you could say that." She nodded her head. "Long story. I recently started doing a monthly column and some articles here and there, to stay in the game, keep my skills sharp."

He adjusted his tie, just as Holly walked out of the van with the handheld microphone for Anthony and his earpiece. Marvin followed with the camera hoisted onto his shoulder.

"Gotta do my thing," Anthony said. "But we definitely need to talk." The corner of his mouth lifted. "I want to hear this long story of yours."

Zoie watched him take his place in front of the camera as his team prepped for his broadcast. With all that was swirling around her and them, the only thing she seemed to be able to focus on was Anthony LeRoux. There was something about him that dragged her to him. When she looked into his eyes, her heart actually raced. Maybe it was that charisma thing that a television personality had to have in spades in order to convince their audience of whatever it was they were selling.

She pulled in a long breath. Now however was not the time to muse over the merits of his appeal. She took out her camera and took pictures of the scenes in front of her just as Anthony was cued to start.

He was the consummate professional, totally focused on delivering the news to his audience, completely tuning out the tumult of activity behind and around him. Zoie found herself mesmerized by the movement of his mouth. Thankfully she'd turned on her recorder to memorialize what he'd said.

He suddenly pressed his finger to his earpiece then looked right into the camera. "We just received word that the police have a suspect in custody. He is alleged to be a student at Xavier, but the motive at the moment is unclear. Again, the police have a suspect in custody. We will continue to update this information as details become available."

Anthony got the cue that he was off air. He plucked the earpiece out and handed off the mic to Holly. He walked over to Zoie. "Wasn't expecting that," he admitted. "Quick work by NOPD."

"For real. What drives someone to intentionally hurt innocent people? What do they hope to gain? I still can't wrap my mind around it."

"A twisted sense of justice, misplaced feelings of being wronged by the world, or a government or a single person." He pushed out a breath. "Believe me, I don't get it either."

They stood in front of the vans taking in the activity that still swirled around them. And even with the scene's ugliness, standing next to Anthony, doing what they loved to do, felt like the most natural thing in the world.

"So how long will you be out here?" Anthony asked, cutting off musing.

Zoie blinked. Damn. Jackson. "Actually, I need to go and check on a friend. We're waiting on word of someone that was injured in the explosion."

"Wow. So sorry. I hope everything will be okay."

"Yeah," she said, "me, too."

"Listen, this might sound crass, but if the person you're checking on is okay and is willing, I'd really like to interview them. First-hand account."

Her brows rose. "Oh. Um. I'm not sure, but I can certainly find out."

Anthony nodded. "I have one more segment before I'm done." He held out his hand for her phone. "I'll put in my number."

She handed over the phone.

"Call me and we'll figure out how we'll work this explosion story; share notes, sources, access." He handed back the phone.

"Absolutely." She slipped the phone in the back pocket of her jeans and swore she felt the heat of his hand hugging her bum. "Okay," she said on a breath. "I'm gonna find my friend." She took the phone from her pocket, scrolled to his number and called him.

Anthony chuckled as the phone vibrated in his front pocket.

"Lock my number in. We'll talk soon." She turned and wove her way around the bodies and equipment, and wondered if Anthony was watching.

———————

Jackson hung up the call just as Zoie returned. He stepped out of the car.

"Hey, sorry it took so long. I had to meet up with a camera crew. Any luck reaching Lena's family.?"

"I actually found her friend, Diane."

"Great. How?"

"Blackplant.com. Can you believe it?"

"Good for something," she scoffed.

"Anyway, Diane said she'd seen the news reports and is headed right back. She's driving from Atlanta. She said she's about two more hours away."

Zoie nodded. "We should probably check and see if Lena's been put in a room."

"Yeah," he agreed. He locked the car. "Any updates on what happened?"

"Yes. While I was with the news crew he got an announcement that a suspect was in custody."

"Seriously?"

"That's what the police are saying."

"Do they know who it is?"

"No names, just that he's a student."

He muttered a curse under his breath. "All this death and destruction for what? Bad grades. Feeling unappreciated," he said, his words laced with contempt.

"Who knows. Whatever the reason, it will never be enough."

Jackson glimpsed her profile. "Did you say he? I thought you were with a crew."

She focused on the ground. "Oh, yeah. The anchor. Anthony LeRoux. He was the broadcaster. My editor back in New York wants me to work with the local television station here."

One thing he always admired about Zoie was that no matter how hard a conversation was, she never shied away from looking you in the eye—except when it came to her feelings. Those were the times that she found difficult—like now, and he wasn't sure why. But this wasn't the time to pursue it. Today had everyone on edge. Probably no more than that.

They arrived at the emergency entrance and entered through the sliding glass doors. The frenzy of hours earlier seemed to have subsided somewhat, though the staff still looked stressed and harried. The corridors had fewer patients lined up on stretchers which indicated that the triage process was under control or at least manageable.

Jackson and Zoie headed straight to the main desk. The nurse behind the desk barely looked up as she juggled the phone and recited information from the computer screen.

"Yes," she said on an exhausted breath. Her brown eyes looked swollen. "How can I help you?"

"Earlier today a woman, Lena Banks was brought in. She was in the explosion," Jackson said. "She was to be moved to ICU. They said I could see her once she was moved."

Zoie had her hand on his bicep and felt the tension ripple up and down the muscle.

The nurse typed some information. Her eyes roved quickly across and up and down the screen. She finally looked up. "Sixth floor in the next building over. The Pavilion."

"Thank you."

Zoie took his hand. "She's going to be fine," she assured, seeing the distress on his face. "Let's go this way." She led them quickly down the long corridor to the bank of elevators that would take them to the walkway that crossed to the next building.

They rode the elevator in silence, got off on the sixth floor and walked along the walkway to the Pavilion building. The telltale beep and hum of life monitoring machines and the disinfectant scent enveloped them.

"Over there," Jackson said, lifting his chin in the direction of the nursing station.

The horseshoe desk was lined with computer screens, with additional monitors hanging from above. As much as there was obvious activity on the ward there was an eerie kind of silence even as the staff spoke in modulated whispers.

"Excuse me," Jackson said. "I was told Lena Banks was admitted here."

The nurse looked up. "Banks?" she repeated.

"Yes. Lena."

"She's in B714 at the end of the hall on the right."

"Thank you." He hurried off without a backward glance at Zoie.

She followed him down the corridor. He stopped in front of a door and seemed to freeze. Zoie caught up to him.

Lena was not immediately recognizable. Her face was swollen and bruised, her head was bandaged and her left leg was in traction. Wires wound like snakes around and across her body. Bags of clear liquid dripped silently through the plastic tubing. The monitors beeped, slow and steady. There was a nurse at Lena's bedside checking the machines and the flow of fluids.

Jackson dragged in a breath, slid a quick look at Zoie, took one tentative step then another until he was fully in the room and at Lena's bedside.

"How is she?" he quietly asked.

The nurse entered some information on her chart. "Very lucky."

She offered a tight smile. "The doctor would have to give you details. You can only stay a few minutes. Okay. She needs plenty of rest."

Jackson nodded. "Thank you. Has . . . has she been awake?"

"Yes. She dozed off right before you came."

He hesitated to ask, but had to know. "The baby?"

The nurse pointed to the monitor. "The heartbeat is strong." She walked out, acknowledging Zoie in the doorway.

Jackson came up to the side of Lena's bed. He leaned over and tenderly kissed her forehead. He took her hand and brought it to his lips.

"Lena," he whispered. "It's me, baby. It's Jackson." He ran his thumb over the hand he held, comforted by its warmth. "You're going to be okay. Our baby is going to be okay. I'll be right here with you." His gaze ran over the roundness of her protruding belly. Their child. His eyes clouded. He blinked rapidly, turned behind him and pulled the chair next to the bed and sat. He gripped the cold metal railing on the side of the bed that kept him from crawling in next to her, holding her and their baby, promising them both that everything was going to be okay.

Seeing her like this, so still, so fragile was counter to everything that was Lena. Lena was vibrant, full of laughter and energy. When they were together, most weekends, they spent on the racket ball court, where she generally kicked his butt, or when they jogged along the banks of the Mississippi. Then there was their time away in the Bahamas when she'd dared him to parasail and bungee jump off a cliff. He smiled wistfully. He didn't consider himself soft, but Lena always made him step up his game. He dragged in a breath. That's the Lena he needed to come back to him.

He lowered his forehead to the side of the bed. He wasn't a religious man. Church on Sunday was not something he'd done as an adult. It had been longer since that he'd prayed, but he whispered words for mercy and healing. He clasped her fingers. "I was so scared when I heard, afraid of what could have happened to you." He kissed her fingers. "But you're here, and we're going to get through this."

Lena's fingers moved ever so slightly. His head jerked up. He jumped to his feet. "Lena?"

Her lashes fluttered.

"Lee, baby. Can you hear me?" He leaned over the bed.

She moaned. Her eyes opened then closed then slowly opened again.

"It's me, baby. Jackson."

"Jax," her voice was cracked and raw. "Jax." She struggled to swallow. "The baby. My baby." Her free hand went to cover her belly.

"Sssh . . . It's okay." His hand covered hers atop their child. "You both are going to be just fine." The fetal monitor beeped in apparent agreement.

A tear slid down her bruised cheek. She reached up and he pressed her hand against his lips. "It's going to be okay," he said, soft as a prayer. "I promise."

———◦◦◦———

Zoie had not moved from her spot in the doorway of Lena's room. She couldn't hear what Jackson said to Lena. She didn't need to. It was in the way he looked at her, touched her. And it had nothing to do with Lena's physical state or Jackson's fears. That was real love that flowed between them. She felt it from where she stood.

Something shifted inside her, an instant where she felt unmoored, that her world shook just a bit beneath her, and then in the next moment all was righted. She took in a deep reflective breath, turned and walked away.

———◦◦◦———

Zoie pulled into the driveway of her house, physically and emotionally exhausted. The devastation she'd witnessed today, compounded with her coming to terms that it was truly over between her and Jackson, left her in a space in which she was totally unfamiliar. She needed some time to process everything, and desperately wished that her best friend Miranda was down the street instead of halfway across the country. A long night of drinks and girl talk were in order.

The moment she walked into the house, her red-light senses went on alert. There was a vibe of tension in the air. She felt it, the way the hair on her arms tingled like when she was on the cusp of uncovering a major detail in a story. She shrugged out of the backpack and set it on the floor in the hall.

She walked down the short hallway and into the kitchen. The family was silently gathered around the table, a cup of tea in front of each of them. Her heart thumped. Who died was her first thought.

"What's going on?" she asked, stepping fully into the kitchen. She caught a glance at her mother. Her eyes were red and swollen. "Ma?"

"Two white ladies were here today," Hyacinth said with a giggle. She bobbed her head up and down. "Right in there." She pointed to the living room.

"What? What is Auntie talking about?"

Sit down, Zoie," her aunt Sage instructed.

Zoie's eyes darted around the table looking for some kind of clue. She pulled out the available seat next to her aunt Hyacinth and opposite her mother. Rose wouldn't look at her.

"Someone please tell me what's going on."

"Your . . . sister was here today," Sage stated and pinned Zoie with a hard stare.

Zoie blinked in her confusion. "What? Kimberly?" She looked from one to the other.

"She was here," Rose said, her voice thready and vacuous as if coming from some bottomless pit. She wrapped her fingers around her blue and white teacup. "She hates me. Hates you." She lifted her eyes to Zoie. "I tried to tell her what happened, how we'd all been used and tricked and lied to." Her throat worked up and down. She sniffed, reached for a napkin from the holder on the center of the table and dabbed at her eyes. She balled the napkin in her fist. "Worse now. Worse now. Wish I'd never known. Her too. She wishes she'd never known. Wants her life back but . . ." She pressed her fist to her lips.

"And you blame me," Zoie said.

Rose slowly lowered her hand, looked her daughter in the eye. "No. You're as much of a victim as I am, as she is."

Sage tapped Hyacinth's shoulder and helped her to her feet. "Ya'll two needs ta talk." She ushered Hyacinth out of the room.

Rose sat with hands still wrapped around her teacup.

"I'm so sorry, Mama."

"I know." She reached across the table and took Zoie's hand. "We talked," she began softly. "Not really a conversation. We just said things. I wanted her to understand how deep losing her affected me and how I treated you because of it. Don't think she was really hearing me." Her features tightened. "Her husband put her out. Kept her children."

Zoie flinched.

"She wants her life back, ya know, but it'll never be the same. I can't fix it. I want to help. I know what it's like," her voice splintered, "to lose your child," she focused on Zoie, "your children."

The burn of tears that Zoie struggled to contain slipped down her cheeks. "You haven't lost *me*, Mama." She dragged in air. "God, I'm so sorry. I let what I wanted overshadow everything at any cost." She swiped at her eyes. "I was so angry all the time. I didn't think about what it would do to you. Maybe I didn't care. What I wanted was more important than anything else. And now . . ." Her chest heaved.

"As much as it hurt and still hurts, I'm glad I know that my child is alive, that she had a privileged life. Can't change none of it. All I can do now is hope that she'll realize she isn't the only one hurt. I want her to know that she's loved," Her voice hitched, "that her children, my . . . grandchildren will be loved."

Zoie got up, came around to kneel in front of Rose. She rested her head on her mother's lap, wrapped her arms around her mother's thighs. Rose stroked her hair, quietly repeating that it would be all right.

She had to find a way to fix it; for her mother and her sister.

"I can't thank you enough for coming out here, Gail. It really meant a lot to me." Kimberly wiped her mouth with the linen napkin and reached for her martini.

"Please. I'm glad I could do it and it gave me an excuse to see New Orleans." Gail pushed her salad around on the plate with her fork. "Have you decided what you're going to do?"

"My list is long. Which 'to do'?"

"Touché. Your daughters for starters."

Kimberly sighed. "I'm not sure yet. But I'm not going to let Rowan get away with keeping them. That much I do know."

Gail's eyes caught the overhead light. "Now that's the Kimberly Maitland that I know. You'll figure it out and you know whatever you need, I'm here."

"Thanks," she said on a breath.

Gail paused. "What about your mom?"

Kimberly turned her face away, gazed off into the distance. "I wish I could," she shrugged slightly, twisted her wedding band on her finger as she searched for the right words, "just accept her and be her daughter, let her be my mother . . . but I don't know her. As much as I abhor what my . . . grandmother did, she was the only mother I've ever known."

"It's going to take time. I'm sure she's struggling, too. When you're ready you should give her a chance."

The waiter appeared at their table, the same handsome man that she'd thought was John from the other night, only to realize that he might resemble him, but his name was actually Corey. When he'd come to their table to take their order, he'd introduced himself as their server for the afternoon. Guilty consciences will do crazy things to the mind, she realized.

"Can I get you ladies anything else?" He looked from one to the other and Kimberly was once more amazed at the resemblance.

"No. Thank you. We'll take the check," Kimberly said.

"Of course. I'll be right back."

She turned her attention back to Gail. "Are you sure you don't want me to drive you to the airport?"

"No, no." She waved the offer away. "I'll take a cab."

Corey returned with the check. Kimberly handed over her credit card.

"Any plans with Nick?" Gail asked once the waiter was gone.

Kimberly smiled shyly. "Actually, we'll see each other later."

Gail winked. "Just what you need to take the sting out of the day." She turned her glass around on the table. "My only piece of advice . . . if you want it."

Kimberly tilted her head to the side, tucked a loose strand of strawberry blond hair behind her ear. The diamond studs sparkled in the light. "I'm listening."

"Nick seems like a really good guy, but don't lose yourself because you're hurt. Lust gets mistaken for something more all the time."

Kimberly's felt the heat rise up her neck to her cheeks. She pressed her hand to her throat. "I'll try to remember that."

Kimberly rested her head against Nick's chest. The steady beat of his heart was a comfort, reassuring her even as Gail's words of caution floated through her thoughts. There was certainly lots of lust between them, but it was more than that, and she didn't think it was entirely due to her emotional circumstances. Nick Bordeau offered her more than mind-altering sex, he actually heard her, shared himself with her—his own fears, and doubts, and hopes.

Her relationship experience was limited, she knew that. Rowan was her first and only love. Her youthful relationships were no more than hot kisses and quick feels in the backs of cars and college dorm stairwells. She'd always been too terrified that she'd somehow 'bring shame' to the Maitland name that she'd avoided going *too far*. Rowan became her knight in shining armor, rescuing her from the strictures of her well-appointed and organized life. He had a way about him, smooth and persuasive, without being overbearing. Rowan Graham could convince a broke man to spend his last dollar and they'd thank him for it. He brought a level of excitement to her life, and most of all a way out. Their life together was to be envied by most; he a highly successful tech giant, and she a respected attorney, although Rowan did express his distaste for her choice of clientele. "Why must you be the champion of the poor and downtrodden?" he'd asked one time too many. When she'd reply that it made her feel good to use her skills to help others less fortunate, he'd scoffed and told her that 'feel good' careers didn't pay the bills and it was a good thing that both of them didn't 'feel' the same way, or they'd be in the street. He'd kissed her then and told her he loved her and her bleeding heart. Did he really?

She supposed he showed his form of love in other ways. They lived extremely well, traveled among the New York elite, had a beautiful home, and two amazing daughters. But all of it was smoke and mirrors, an illusion. They both lived under a cloak of deceit. He was not the Eastern liberal he pretended to be, but a closet bigot. And she was not the fair southern belle he'd swept away, but the product of an affair with a wealthy white boy and the housekeeper's daughter.

Nick shifted, moaned softly. "What has you worried?" he murmured, his voice gravely with sleep.

"What makes you say that?" she whispered into the darkness.

"I can feel it in your breathing. Your body is tight. Talk to me." He brushed her hair away from her face. "It's about your mother—Rose."

"Yes."

"I know meeting her for the first time . . . had to be crazy. I'm not sure I would have reacted any different than you did. The thing now is what's next? What are you going to do?"

She splayed her fingers against his chest. "I'm not sure."

"You might not want to hear this, but I agree with Gail. You can't stay on the sidelines when it comes to your kids. You're a kick ass lawyer; force his hand the same way you would to an adversary in court. Plus, you now have a family that wants to embrace you—and your girls. If you let them. And you have me. You don't have to do this alone."

She lifted her chin to look at him. He kissed her forehead.

"I have been thinking of something."

"What?"

"Before my life blew up in my face, Zoie had written an exposé about me, a basic tell all. The only reason she didn't print it was because I dropped out of the race. At least I think that's why or maybe she had a sudden attack of conscience. I don't know. Anyway," she pushed up on her elbow. "Maybe now is the time for the story to come to light. The same way she planned to use it before, she can do it again. The last thing that Rowan wants is for it to 'get out' that he'd been duped. He'd never live it down."

She felt the rumble of his laughter.

"Nasty. But brilliant. And deserving."

Her own smile was short-lived. In order to do that, she'd have to speak to Zoie again.

———※·◇·※———

Zoie spent the morning working on her article for *The Recorder*. She had some pretty decent digital photos to accompany the article, but she couldn't focus. Her writing didn't have the punch and passion she knew it needed. She was distracted by her own real-life disasters.

She pushed back from the desk, spun her chair away from the laptop screen and got up. She walked over to the window of her bedroom. From where she stood, the sky was a cool blue, the trees were in full bloom, grass glistened on the lawns. The chirp and caw of birds filled the air. All appeared well with the world. But beyond her line of sight, life had been turned upside down. The remnants and stench of destruction were mere miles away. Her thoughts were flooded with issues much closer.

She crossed her arms and leaned against the frame of the window. For much of the prior evening, she and her mother sat side by side on the porch swing talking—really talking. After her return to NOLA following her grandmother's death, she and her mother had tried to bridge the gulf between them. On the surface, it seemed to have worked. But all it took was her own stubborn, tunnel vision to toss them both back into that dark place.

She didn't think she quite understood or accepted how devastated her mother had been by what had happened with the loss of her child, then a husband that walked out one day and never came back, and a daughter who seemed to want nothing more than to get away. Unlike her mother, she compartmentalized everything, placed gains and losses into boxes so that the totality of events didn't crush her. Or so she thought. What she had come to accept was that as much as she thought that was true, she was more like her mother than she'd realized. Everything that she'd done, the actions she'd taken, the decisions she'd made, and even the lives that she'd fucked up was a sum total of things that had happened to her. Yes, she put them in their own little boxes, tried to keep them separate and at bay, but she was not as good at it as she'd believed. The evidence was the debris that surrounded her: Brian in New York, her mom, her aunts, Kimberly, and her whole family and career . . . and Jackson.

She pushed out a long breath. She couldn't fix everything, but there were a few things she could do. At least she could try.

The buzzing of her cell phone on the desk drew her away from the window. She picked up the phone.

"Hello?"

"Hello Zoie. It's Kimberly. We need to talk. Can you come to my hotel," she said, all in one breath.

"Um, yes. Sure."

Kimberly gave her the hotel information.

"In about an hour?"

"Fine. I'll meet you in the lobby." She ended the call.

Zoie slowly put down the phone. Her pulse was racing. Kim wanted to talk—whatever that meant. But hopefully this meeting would give her the first step she needed to make things right with Kimberly—her sister.

———◆———

Zoie arrived at the Hilton. Of course, Kimberly would be housed in the most expensive hotel in the Quarter, she scoffed. *Jealous much.* If she was going to enter this conversation as a point of reconciliation, she would have to put her preconceived notions aside.

The valet opened the door and welcomed her. She pushed out a smile of thanks and walked into the sprawling lobby with its intimate seating, sparkling interior fountain, gleaming black marble floors, and wide-open space that led from one part of the hotel to the next.

They spotted each other simultaneously. Kimberly rose from the club chair as Zoie approached.

Zoie was again struck by their stark resemblance. It was like looking at a white version of her reflection. Although they had different fathers, the Bennett genes ran strong in them both.

"Hi Kimberly. Thank you for calling. I was actually going to call you," she babbled, suddenly nervous.

"We can talk in the restaurant," Kimberly said by way of a greeting, barely looking at Zoie.

"Sure." She walked alongside Kimberly into the hotel restaurant.

"Good afternoon ladies. Table for two?" the hostess asked.

"Thank you, yes," Kimberly responded.

The young woman took two menus from the holder. "Right this way." She showed them to a table in back. "A server will be with you shortly." She turned over the two goblets and filled them from a carafe of water. "Enjoy."

They sat opposite each other at a small banquette. Kimberly immediately reached for the glass of water and took a long swallow then settled her gaze on Zoie.

"I asked you here because I need your help."

Her cheeks flushed and her lips thinned as if saying the words were utterly distasteful.

Zoie linked her fingers together on top of the table. "Whatever you need."

Kimberly cleared her throat and straightened her spine. "It's about the article you planned to write about me . . ."

Over chicken Caesar salads and apple martinis, which they discovered was a favorite for them both, Kimberly spilled out all that had transpired since Zoie's mining of her life; her withdrawal from the campaign, the tension between her and Rowan as a result, her revelation to him, and his subsequent retaliation.

Zoie listened, and with every word, every crack in Kimberly's voice, every blink of her gray-green eyes to stem her tears, her soul ached. This was all her fault. Her blind sense of justice had ruined the lives of four people, maybe more. Would it have been so awful for Rose to go on believing that the child she'd given birth to in that New York hospital was dead, so that life, as it was, could continue? How much worse could it have been if she'd gone ahead and published the exposé? But it was that last call between her and Kimberly when Kimberly pleaded on behalf of her children. Zoie felt her pain, understood it in a way she hadn't before. Perhaps it was the tenuous bond she was building with her mother and finally coming to grips on how their fractured relationship had affected them both that softened that scabbed over pain in her soul. The call was the removal of her tunnel vision. It was in that moment that she knew she couldn't do it. All the steam, the misplaced animosity burned off like morning mist.

Kimberly lifted her glass and finished off her second martini. "So," she said on a breath, "I want you to send the story to him." She lifted her chin. "Let him know that you plan to release it unless he gives me my girls. And we can quietly get divorced." She pressed her lips tightly together.

"Of course. Whatever you need. Whatever I can do to make some kind of right out of this mess that I created."

Kimberly cut her eyes at Zoie, snorted a laugh. "You have no idea." She reached for her glass, realized it was empty and burst into tears.

Zoie quickly slid around on the leather seating and gathered Kimberly in her arms, held her tight, and the damn broke inside her as well. They'd never touched each other, held each other, confided in each other the way sisters do, the sensation of holding her sister broke down all the walls between them.

"I never told you how sorry I am," Zoie spoke into Kimberly's strawberry blonde tumble of hair. "I can never make up to you what I've done, how I've hurt you . . . and your children. I am so very sorry."

Kimberly's shoulders shook with quiet sobs. "I never thought I could actually hate anyone, but I hated you."

Zoie inwardly flinched, but she held her sister, knowing that she deserved her scorn.

"I hated that you'd ruined the fantasy. Maybe this would have all come out anyway, at some point. Who knows, but one thing I did learn in the midst of all this mess," she sniffed hard and eased out of Zoie's embrace, "Rowan is not who I thought he was, and whatever kind of love he had for me had nothing to do with who I am, only who he believed and expected me to be."

Zoie placed her hand atop Kimberly's. "We must definitely be related. I have come to a major realization about my relationship, too." She gave Kimberly an edited version of the ups and downs of her relationship with Jackson and the twist in the tale, aka Lena and the baby.

Kimberly's gray-green eyes widened. "Ouch."

"Hmm, exactly." She dared to look into Kimberly's eyes. "I know I may be a long way from being forgiven. Maybe never and I'll accept that. But . . . could you tell me a little bit about my nieces?"

A slow maternal smile of pure adoration lifted Kimberly's mouth. She opened her purse, took out her wallet, and proceeded to regale Zoie with anecdotes about her twin girls.

Their shared sorrow and their shared tears cleansed them, bound them and began to fill that space that had been missing.

Finally spent, their souls tender from the excavation, they looked into eyes that were identical and sputtered shaky laughter.

"If you're not busy," Zoie said, sniffed and wiped her eyes, "the Bennett women cook a mean Sunday dinner. We'd love to have you."

Kimberly's lashes fluttered. She bobbed her head. "I'd like that."

CHAPTER 11

Kimberly pulled her rented car in behind Zoie's on the driveway. She gripped the steering wheel when she was held in place by a series of possible scenarios that played out in front of her. In one version, she was surrounded by laughter as the family told stories about life in New Orleans, in others she was in a standoff with her mother, hurling words that she couldn't make out, and in yet another she sat alone, the outsider, the other sister, while the family ate from overflowing dishes.

She jumped at the sudden tapping on her window. She fumbled with the key and turned off the car, snatched her purse from the passenger seat and got out.

"Sorry," she murmured. She shut the door and began straightening her clothes and hair.

Zoie smiled, took Kimberly's hands to stop their nervous trek through her hair. She looked her in the eyes. "It's going to be fine," she assured softly. "The aunties are a handful, but they mean well." She turned toward the house with Kimberly's hand still in hers, and they began to walk to the front door. "Aunt Hyacinth is liable to say anything, so don't take offense. Aunt Sage is like an avocado." She grinned. "Tough outer skin and soft on the inside. And Mama," she angled her head toward Kimberly, "we're going to figure her out together."

They walked up the three steps to the front porch landing.

"Ready?" Zoie asked.

Kimberly took a breath. "As ready as I'll ever be."

Zoie opened the door and they were greeted by the aroma of bread baking.

"Mama is the baker in the house." She put her bag down on the table in the hall. "I'm sure they're in the kitchen."

Kimberly walked two steps behind Zoie and wondered if she could hear the pounding of her heart.

They reached the entrance to the kitchen. Aunt Sage glanced up from peeling potatoes. The knife slipped from her fingers and into the bowl.

Hyacinth glanced over her shoulder. "It's that white lady again," she announced.

Rose turned from the sink. Her mouth opened but no words came out.

"Hope it's okay to have a guest for dinner," Zoie said. She turned an encouraging smile on Kimberly.

Kimberly's eyes bounced from one shocked expression to the next. "Hello." She gripped her purse in her hand.

Rose wiped her wet hands on a dishtowel and tentatively came over to where Kimberly stood. She pressed her hand to her heart. Her eyes glistened. "Of course it's okay," she said, looking Kimberly in the eyes.

Kimberly's smile wobbled around the edges.

"Ya'll don't just stand there," Aunt Sage scoffed. "Wash the street off ya hands and come help with this dinner."

Zoie threw Kimberly an 'I told you so' grin, and tilted her head toward the sink.

Rose glided her hand lovingly down Kimberly's arm. "Go on. There's plenty to do."

Kimberly followed Zoie to the kitchen sink. Zoie snickered. "Told ya."

They washed their hands and Sage quickly got Zoie to finish peeling potatoes. "And you know how I like 'em done," she warned. She pushed to her feet. "I'm gonna sit on the porch for a few." She wagged a finger at Zoie. "They should be done when I get back. And don't cut 'em all too small. And dice up an onion when you're done. You can have her help you make the potato salad," she added, lifting her chin in Kimberly's direction.

"Yes, Auntie," Zoie said, taking the seat that Sage vacated.

"And you need to tie up all that yellow hair 'fore it get in my food. I know that much." She pulled a headscarf out of the pocket of her shift and handed it over to Kimberly. "Here, put that on."

Kimberly took the floral printed scarf. "Thank you, ma'am."

"I ain't no ma'am to you, I'm your auntie, girl."

Kimberly blinked rapidly, a proper response stuck in her throat. She awkwardly tied the scarf around her head, making sure her mid-back length hair was well out of the way.

"You know how to wash greens?" Rose asked Kimberly, giving her a reprieve from Sage's admonishing.

Kimberly's brow tightened. "Um, not really."

"Come on then. I'll show you."

Kimberly joined Rose at the sink.

Rose took a handful of greens in her hand and ran them under the water while she ran her fingers up and down and across the leaves and stems to rinse away any dirt and grit.

"These came right out of your grandmother's garden," Rose said.

"Really?" All her vegetables came with her weekly food delivery from the gourmet superstore D'Agostino's.

She passed Kimberly a handful of greens. "You try." Rose smiled wistfully. "Started off as a hobby, something for her to do as she got older." She washed some more greens. "Mama, your grandmother—loved gardening. It was just tomatoes at first, then the collards, cucumbers and spices. With all the land we have out back, there was room to grow. She turned it into a full-blown profitable business." She slowly shook her head in awe.

"That's amazing."

"We went from packing things up in the kitchen for our neighbors to hiring a driver and settling accounts with the local grocer. Got to be too much for us. Zoie mostly handles the business end of things now."

"I remember Ms. Claudia," she swallowed, looked at Rose, "my grandmother," Kimberly softly said, trying to get used to the idea. She gazed out through the kitchen window gathering the images of the past. "She was always so kind to me, took care of me and loved me in a way that my mother never did. Teased me and told me we were connected because we had the same eyes. Humph. Now I know why." She blinked away the past and turned to Rose. "I was here all the time," she said, her voice splintering.

Rose cupped Kimberly's cheek in her palm. "You're here now. Now," she insisted. "None of us can go back and fix the past, but we can work on the right now and on tomorrow. If you want to."

So much had happened in the past few months, few weeks. She stared down into the sink full of bright green collards, the running water swirling over them the way her mind and soul swirled in confusion. "I've done things . . . I never imagined I would do." Images of waking up in bed with a stranger exploded behind her lids, shortened her breath. "I've lost everything; my children, my marriage, my career, right down to my sense of self." She pressed her wet hand to her chest. "The pain—there are no words for the pain." Her eyes clouded. Tears slid down her cheeks. "I, I'm so lost." Her slender body shook with the force of her sobs. She gripped the edge of the sink for support.

Rose gathered her up in her arms, molding her to her body, pairing their breaths and heartbeats. "It's gonna be all right, sweetheart," she cooed. She stroked her back, squeezed her tighter.

"You gonna be all right. You have family. Right here. Family. My baby. My girl," she cried softly. "You have family. You have me."

Zoie quietly watched the exchange with a mixture of happiness and envy. She picked up the bowl of potatoes and the knife and tiptoed out of the kitchen. Maybe things would somehow work out for all of them. She pushed open the screen door and stepped out onto the back porch.

"Thought I should give them some alone time," Zoie explained in response to Sage's inquiring raised brow look.

"Hmm. All that schooling and fancy living in New York did you some good," Sage scoffed.

Zoie responded with mock sarcasm, "Thanks Auntie."

"And you just watch your tone, and stop cutting them potatoes so damned small."

Zoie bit back a laugh. "Yes, Auntie."

"You think that girl know how to make potato salad, 'cause you know she lived like white folks and white folks got a problem making potato salad," she said with a straight face.

Zoie burst into laughter. "I don't know Auntie, but I guess we're gonna find out."

"Humph. I guess we will."

⸻

Sitting down to dinner with the Bennett/Crawford women was an experience like no other. Kimberly was accustomed to light laughter and appropriate dinner conversation. This on the other hand was an event, from raucous laughter to ribald jokes, a parade of cuss words followed by 'help me Jesus,' and questionable commentary about every neighbor from here to the Mississippi. They teased each other, spilled secrets about who snored the loudest or who took the last of the jam and left the empty jar in the fridge. There was an ongoing montage of 'do you remember whens' that had them vacillating from tears of laughter to soft smiles of 'yes I sure do.' And never once in all the exchanges that flew back and forth across the table did she ever feel like an outsider. This was the part of her life that had always been missing, that she sensed in her soul but didn't know what it was. They included her in their tales of shenanigans, and even shared how they kept the creak in the steps so that they could hear Zoie when she'd sneak in after hours. They answered her questions about 'who was who' in their litany of stories and made sure that she sampled everything on the table at least twice.

Never in her life had she sat down to a dinner table loaded with so much food. From one end to the other it was lined with platters of collard greens laced with smoked turkey necks, peas and rice, sweet potatoes dripping in butter and syrup, macaroni and cheese that melted in your mouth, potato salad the likes of which she'd never tasted before but was proud to have a hand in, golden fried chicken, and succulent catfish. And the biscuits! They were bites out of heaven. She was actually relieved when Sage announced that they needed to start cleaning up the kitchen because if she took another mouthful of anything she was going to pass out.

It was nearly ten by the time the whole family walked Kimberly to her car. They stood around her like sentinels ready to guard and protect her from the known and unknown as they'd always done with each other, and she was one of them now and she felt the love and protection.

"Thank you so much for today." Her eyes danced from one to the other.

"Next time bring your own head scarf," Sage taunted as she eyed the scarf still tied around Kimberly's head.

"Next time I'll bring this one back," she rejoined.

Hyacinth burst into laughter. "I like her."

"You be careful out there on these roads," Sage warned, before turning back to the house and ushering Hyacinth along with her.

"When will you be coming back?" Rose tentatively asked.

"Very soon. I promise." She leaned in and kissed Rose's cheek.

"I'm going to hold you to that," she said, visibly relieved, then hugged her tightly before stepping back.

"I'll get to work on what we talked about," Zoie said. "First thing in the morning."

Kimberly nodded. "Thank you." She looked from one to the other. "Good night." She opened her car door, got in and slowly backed out of the driveway.

Zoie watched Kimberly pull off. If anyone had a reason to stalk her and her family it could easily have been Kimberly. But her car wasn't white.

Rose slid her arm around Zoie's waist, shorting out that line of thought, and they walked back to the house.

"What is it that you're working on for Kimberly?" Rose asked.

Zoie opened the front door. "I'll tell you all about it over a glass of sweet tea and a slice of your pound cake."

Rose laughed. "I'll get the plates."

———— ✦ ————

Zoie sat in the middle of her bed with all her notes and the original draft of the article she'd intended to write exposing the underbelly truth of Kimberly Maitland Graham and her *other* family's life of lies and duplicity spread out across the white down comforter.

She ran her fingers along the handwritten words, etched into the yellow legal pad and the transcribed typed pages. Before she could dangle the story in front of Rowan Graham she needed to make a few changes and updates.

As she reread the words she'd crafted months earlier, a stabbing pang of guilt jabbed and jabbed at her. The article was probably one of the most in depth exposés she'd ever done. It ripped off so many bandaged wounds that no one would have come out other than in a bloody mess. It was so good, so thorough, so scathing, so true, that it ended the launch of a rising political star, ruined a marriage, sabotaged a legal career, and estranged a mother from her children. That's how powerful her words were, how powerful words are.

She sat back against the headboard, tucked her legs beneath her. She had to make this right, whatever it took. She owed it to her sister. Her heart thumped in her chest. Her sister. Wow.

She reached for her phone and called Jackson. It was time she got to work on setting things straight on multiple levels.

He answered on the second ring. "Hey, babe, sorry I haven't been in touch."

"No worries. I totally understand. How is she?"

"Actually, I'm at the hospital." He sighed. "Haven't left. Anyway, the doctors say she's doing well. They want to monitor her and the baby for another day or two and then she'll be released."

Her spirit twinged just a little. "That's really good to hear, Jackson."

"Still working on the story?"

"Yes, actually since Lena is doing better I wonder if you could get away sometime tomorrow. And would you mind asking her when she's up to it if she would mind doing an interview with Anthony LeRoux for the television station."

"Uh, I'm pretty sure I can get away to meet you tomorrow. Lena's friend Diane arrived, so someone will be here with her. And I'll ask her about the interview."

Zoie squeezed her eyes shut for a moment, willing herself not to twist her emotions the wrong way. She'd made her decision. "If you can meet me at the park on our bench."

He chuckled. "Okay. One o'clock good?"

"Whatever works for you. If anything changes just give me a call."

"I will. See you tomorrow."

"My best to Lena."

"Thanks."

Zoie disconnected the call. She drew in a long breath. No turning back now. She lifted her laptop from the nightstand and placed it on her thighs. Mr. Rowan Graham could expect a call from her in the morning.

"I had dinner with my mother tonight. My biological mother," Kimberly said and waited for Nick's reaction.

He stopped wiping down the bar. "Say what?" His brows rose.

Kimberly slowly nodded her head. She fiddled with her empty martini glass. "Had a long talk with my sister, too, Zoie. I told her about what me and you talked about and she agreed to contact Rowan."

"Wait, I'm still processing the first bit of info." He grinned broadly. "You're serious?"

"Very."

"You had some kinda day. So . . . how was it? How were they?"

She sucked on her bottom lip. "Better than I could have ever expected. " She leaned forward and smiled up at him. "It felt . . . natural."

"I don't know what to say other than I'm happy for you, Kim. Seriously."

"I know we all have a long way to go, but it's a start."

"Of course. There's a lot of years to make up for."

"True." She lowered her voice then looked at him from beneath her lashes. "What time do you get off?"

"Midnight." He angled his head to the side. "Feel like some company?"

"I think I do." She slid off the barstool. "See you when you get there."

He winked. "Looking forward to it."

Walking back to her hotel, she actually began to feel some hope for her future and good inside for the first time in months. New Orleans had been home to her once, maybe it could be again. A new start. A new everything.

The morning arrived overcast. Gray clouds hung low in the sky, a prelude to a hot, rainy Louisiana day. Zoie dropped the curtain back in place. She didn't have a Plan B for meeting Jackson if it rained, hopefully it would come and go.

She checked the time. Barely nine. Would Rowan Graham be out the door on his way to work? What about the children? Did they miss their mother? What story did he give to explain her absence? She could easily imagine their hurt and confusion. She'd been them at one time, wondering and worrying where her father had gone and why did he'd stopped loving her. If she had anything to do with it, that bit of the family legacy wouldn't continue.

She walked to her closet and took out her teal and white striped sundress and white sandals. Even though her day would be an exercise in delivering bad news, she wanted to look nice delivering it.

After she dressed, she booted up her laptop and pulled up the article that she'd spent half the night revising. She reread it one last time before she called Rowan.

She tapped her fingers against the wood of her desk as the phone rang on the other end.

"Rowan Graham."

Her fingers froze. "Hello. This is Zoie Crawford."

"Who?"

"Your wife's sister," she said, enunciating each word.

Silence.

"I'm calling because I have some information that you might like to have before I release it to the press. I'm sure you know that's what I do." She waited a beat. "Check your email and when you're done reading, give me a call." She disconnected the call. Her heart thumped so hard in her chest that her hands shook.

She jumped up from her seat and began to pace, chewing on her thumbnail. What if he didn't call back? What if he didn't care about the article becoming public and called her bluff. But if he was really anything like the way Kim described, and if his treatment of her was any indication, he'd call. Men like Rowan Graham thrived on the image that they presented to their colleagues, to the world and would do whatever was necessary to maintain it. She'd wait. He'd call.

Her cell phone chirped. She snatched it up from the desk.

"Jackson, hi. Is everything okay?"

"I was hoping that maybe we could meet up here at the hospital instead of the park. Weather looks kind of iffy and . . . I don't want to be too far away from Lena. She had a pretty bad night."

"From her injuries?"

"Nightmares about the explosion."

"Oh, I'm sorry. So . . . you spent the night again?"

"Yeah, I didn't feel comfortable leaving and I'm glad I didn't. I know this is a lot, Z, but please understand."

"I understand," she said, her voice flat. She cleared her throat. "I'll come to the hospital about one. I'll meet you in the cafeteria."

"Thanks, Z. I'll see you then."

"Bye." Her eyes drifted closed. This only made what she needed to do that much easier and without guilt.

The phone vibrated in her hand. She looked at the screen and smiled. She pressed the talk icon. "Mr. Graham. I take it you had a chance to look at the article . . ."

Driving through the downpour, Zoie replayed her conversation with Rowan. To say that he was set back on his heels would be an understatement. She knew from his initial defiant tone that he was not accustomed to being cornered. The 'how dare yous' and 'who do you think you ares', underlined his every response, the superiority in his voice. He was the negotiator, the deal maker. She smiled. Not anymore. She'd given him forty-eight hours to decide if he was going to agree to Kimberly's terms or she would send her story to her editor in New York.

By the time she arrived at University Medical Center, the sky had fully opened, intent on washing away anything that wasn't nailed down.

Her umbrella was literally useless, turned inside out and dismantled within moments of her stepping out of her car. By the time she'd dashed across the parking lot and reached the sliding doors of the main entrance she was drenched from head to toe.

Shaking off the water like a wet pet, she squished across the lobby to the ladies' room in hopes of repairing some of the damage inflicted by mother nature. She grabbed a handful of paper towels from the dispenser, wiped away the water from her face and bare hair, and dried her hair as best she could. The usually straight pixie cut had morphed into a head full of soft curls. She turned on the hand dryer and did a combination of acrobatics to get her body beneath the blasts of air to hopefully get her clothing from wet to damp. She reapplied her lipstick and donned a light sweater that she kept in her bag to ward off the chill from the hospital's arctic AC, made worse by her wet clothes.

She took a last look in the mirror, satisfied that this was the best to be done under the circumstances, and walked out and headed for the cafeteria on the main floor.

Normally she'd turn her nose up at the thought of hospital food, but the hospital cafeteria rivaled some local restaurants and that included the meals served to patients—something she'd discovered when Nana Claudia had that first stroke a few years earlier. It was minor, the doctors had assured the family, a TMI, but Nana would need to change her diet and her lifestyle if she didn't want another one that could be debilitating or worse.

Nana Claudia sat in her hospital bed like the queen matriarch she was, surrounded by Sage, Hyacinth, Rose and Zoie. 'I'm damned near ninety,' she'd scoffed while she'd cut into a succulent hunk of meatloaf surrounded by thick mash potatoes and gravy and startling green broccoli, her favorite. 'Too old to change my ways now,' she'd said, and that if she had to come back at least the food was good. Zoie disputed the claim only to be told that one of these days she would be ninety and then she could do what she wanted, too.

Zoie smiled at the memory as she entered the sprawling cafeteria. Tables and banquettes were dotted with equal parts hospital staff and visitors. She was a few minutes early but was glad to see Jackson waving her over.

She stopped opposite him at the table. "Hi," she greeted, feeling oddly awkward.

He came around the table and kissed her cheek then helped her into her seat. Jackson dragged his chair closer to the table and sat. He reached across and took her hand. "Thanks for coming here."

"It all worked out. Imagine if we'd been in the park."

He chuckled lightly. "True."

"How is Lena?"

He drew in a breath and slowly exhaled. "Better. Resting." His brow knitted together in concern. "How are *you*? I know you must be working like crazy with all that's going on."

That was so like Jackson. No matter how difficult his circumstances were, he was always concerned about the other person. A twinge of sadness tugged at her heart.

"You're right. A lot is going on Jax." She paused a moment and linked her fingers together on the table. "Kimberly came to the house yesterday, met the family and stayed for dinner."

Jackson's eyes widened with surprise. "Sunday dinner!" His smile lit up his face. "That's a big step for the Bennett clan."

Zoie grinned. "I know right." She glanced down at her clasped hands then back at Jackson. They'd shared so many memories like Sunday dinners, sneaking him out of her bedroom in the early morning hours, picnics in the park, late night talks. Her throat clenched. "So Kimberly asked me to release the article to Rowan." She went on to explain the plan and Rowan's response.

"He's going to give up the kids?"

"Sounded like it."

"Hmm. Hope he does for everyone's sake. You know I was never a fan of you writing that piece in the first place."

Zoie inwardly cringed, recalling the tension and recriminations that bloomed between her and Jackson when she went full metal jacket to uncover everything she could on Kimberly Maitland, as if doing so would somehow put a salve on her own wounded soul. Ultimately, she'd never released the exposé, realizing the devastation it would cause, but the damage had already been done.

"I can't imagine what she must be going through," Jackson said, cutting into her soul searching.

His gaze drifted off and she wondered if he was thinking about almost losing his own child. "Jackson . . ." she said softly.

He blinked her back into focus. "So, is that what you wanted to talk to me about?"

"Actually, I wanted to talk about us."

"Us? O-kay." He shifted in his seat. "I'm listening."

"I've been thinking about you and Lena and the baby." She swallowed hard, her throat suddenly dry. "I thought I would be okay with it, but," she breathed a sigh, "I can't, or rather I shouldn't—"

"Zoie—"

She held up her hand. "Please hear me out. The other day when I stood outside of Lena's room and saw the two of you—how you were with each other. I knew we could never be that way. She loves you, Jax, and you love her. I could see it. The two of you need each other and your child needs you both."

"Z—"

"It's okay." She touched his hand, forced a smile. "We had our time, and I'll never forget it. But we need to move on."

He lowered his head. "You know I'll always love you." He looked up into her eyes.

"I know," she whispered. "And I'll still help out with the community garden, get it up and running—if you still want my help."

"Sure. I'd like that."

She pressed her hands on the table. "So, uh, I should be going. Let you get back to Lena." She stood, hoping to hold it together.

Jackson got up as well. "Lena agreed to the interview," he said absently.

Zoie nodded. "Thanks," she murmured. "I'll be in touch about when."

He came around to her and gathered her in his arms. It felt so right, as it always did. They held each other, letting the years of love and the memories flow back and forth between them.

Jackson eased back then tenderly kissed her forehead.

"Take care, Jackson." She turned and hurried away before he saw her cry.

On the drive home, she second-guessed her decision about walking away from Jackson. They had history. Maybe they could have worked through it somehow. But she knew deep in her soul that was not possible. *Move on, Zoie.*

She drove onto her street and slowed. The white car was parked across the street from her house. She pulled up behind it, got out but left her engine running. Whoever it was wouldn't get away this time. As she approached the driver's door opened and a man stepped out and turned toward her.

No!

He held up his hands—palms facing her. "Zoie—"

He can't know my name. Blood roared in her head.

He took a step toward her.

She stopped breathing.

"It's me, Zoie. It's your dad."

⇒⋗•⋖⇐

"You're lying!" Her heart banged in her chest.

He stepped closer. "Your favorite dress as a little girl was that yellow one with the blue and white flowers."

Her lids fluttered. A wave of nausea rolled through her stomach. She braced her hand against the side of the car to keep from falling.

Hank Crawford reached her an instant before her knees gave

out. He slid a supporting arm around her waist. "Here, sit." He eased her onto the front seat of his car and knelt on the sidewalk in front of her.

Zoie struggled to focus on the face in front of her, that was familiar and not at the same time.

"Breathe," he said gently, the voice taking her back.

"Daddy?" she whispered.

"Yes. It's me. I swear it is sweetheart."

She blinked rapidly to stem the cloud of tears that began to beg for release. "I don't understand. Where have you been?"

"I want to explain everything to you and your mother."

Her forehead furrowed. "It was you out here. I saw this car. Aunt Hy saw you. Why would you do that?" Her voice rose, gathering strength. "Why did you drive away that day that I spotted you? You left us! You left me," she cried, fury and confusion battling each other. "Real fathers don't do that."

"I had to leave Zoie," he said, his voice low and even. "I had no choice. The Maitlands made sure of that." His nostrils flared.

"What?"

Hank turned the full focus of his warm brandy-colored eyes on his daughter. *Eyes I could get drunk on* she'd often hear her mother say all those years ago, and in that instant when he looked at her the remnants of doubt were removed. She was that little girl again, bathed in the love and protection of her father. But since the day he left, she'd never felt quite that way ever again.

"The Maitlands arranged everything because I'd found out what they'd done."

She frowned in confusion. "What do you mean?"

"I knew what happened to Rose's daughter."

She gasped in shock.

"It's a lot to explain, and your mother deserves to hear this too."

She stared at him, trying to look beneath the veil of words for the lie. Disassembling words was what she did. She was a wordsmith. She wielded and molded words. She took them apart and put them back together. She understood their power. But these words that tumbled from his mouth, dipped in the sweet molasses of his drawl, she didn't understand. Her father knew the truth all this time?

She managed to get to her feet, pushed away his attempt at assistance. She swiped at her eyes with the back of her hand. "I don't know if she'll even let you in the house, and I wouldn't blame her," she said, the fire relit inside her. "You have no idea what your leaving did to her or to me!" She hurled the words at him. "You hurt us, your family, the people you were supposed to protect. And you show up here after all this time with some story," she yelled. "Why now? Why bother? Why not just stay the hell away?"

"I'm sick Zoie."

Her chest heaved, then caved, hit with the implication of all the things those words could mean. She really looked at him then, beyond the things that were familiar from his eyes, the caramel color of his skin, the waves of his hair—now shot through with gray, to see what was in front of her: the body that was maybe too thin for his height, cheekbones too sharp and a hollowness beneath his eyes.

All she could do was stare as the accumulation of her observations left her immobile.

"I'm staying at the Red Door on Pompano. I'll be there til the end of the week." He took out a piece of paper, wrote something on it and handed it to Zoie. "That's my number if she wants to see me."

She looked at the numbers. "How do I know that you won't just up and disappear again?"

"I won't."

"No. I don't believe you. You're here now. You explain now. To all of us." A rush of defiance pushed through her veins, stiffening her spine. He was not going to leave. Not this time. "Turn off your car," she demanded, "and give me your keys." She stood guard while he did as instructed, then placed the keys in her open palm. She lifted her chin toward the house. "You know where we live. Let's go." Walking next to this man she felt like law enforcement bringing in a prisoner instead of a daughter walking her father home.

The thumping of her heart shook her body as they crossed the street and up the walkway to the front door of Jessup Street.

Zoie walked onto the first step of the porch when she realized that Hank had stopped behind her. She spun around. His eyes were fixed on the front door, his generous mouth diminished to a barely visible line. His skin had a thin sheen of perspiration. She watched his chest heave in and out as if struggling for air. All of which could only be described as fear.

Her heart softened just enough to bring her to stand in front of him. "You came this far. You sat outside our door for weeks, watching and waiting for your chance to make things right." She paused. "This is it!"

Hank blinked several times before focusing on Zoie. He ran his tongue across his bottom lip, then slowly nodded. "All right, then."

She waited until he moved toward the porch then walked with him to the front, but before she could open the door it was pulled open from the other side.

Rose stood framed in the doorway. In one instant there was an expression of greeting and in between that split-second shocked disbelief. She gripped the side of the door. Her lips parted but no words came out.

Zoie hurried to her. "Mama." She put her arm around her mother's shoulder and they faced Hank Crawford together.

"Rose . . ."

Her chest rose and fell in an uneven rhythm.

"What's going on out here? Why ya'll standing in the door letting the flies in?" came Sage's voice from behind them. She looked past Zoie and Rose. "Dear Lord," she said on a breath of disbelief. She shoved Zoie and Rose aside and came up on Hank so fast that no one saw the slap coming that rocked him back on his feet. "I been waiting to do that for more than twenty years." She shook the sting off her hand.

Hank held his hand to his left cheek. "I deserved that."

Hyacinth ambled to the doorway, eased between the women. "Hi Hank. Where you been boy?"

Hyacinth's innocent question broke the rope of tension that held them all in place.

"Might as well come in," Rose finally said. "Say whatever you have to say."

Hank sat in an armchair on one side of the room, the women on the other. He folded his hands on his thighs and turned his attention to Rose.

"You remember how we met?" he began. "At that party in Harlem."

Rose's lips remained pinched closed.

He cleared his throat. "I worked in the registry office of the hospital, remember?"

Rose dragged in a shuddering breath.

"I was in charge of processing all the birth and death certificates. I used to make copies of the death certs for . . . friends that needed a new life."

Zoie gripped her mother's hand.

"I didn't know you'd had a baby at that hospital. Not back then, not til long after we were married." He shifted in his seat, ran a hand over his face as if to erase the past. "They paid me to forge a death certificate. A lot of money. So, I did it. Didn't think much of it. Wealthy white folks was always paying people off for one thing or another." He winced, gritted his teeth then continued. "But I always kept copies of everything—for insurance," he added as if that made it all right. "But that whole thing never really set right with me. Why would someone want to make up a death certificate for a baby?"

"We met maybe a year later. I'd forgotten all about what happened by then. I never made the connection. I got let go from the hospital shortly after we met. Was pretty hard to find a regular job and I didn't want to lose you because I couldn't offer you anything."

"That when the gambling started?" Sage's voice sliced through the air.

Hank's protruding Adam's apple bobbed. "You knew?"

Sage leaned forward. " 'Course I knew. Any man good looking as you was, throwing charm around like candy, always got a slick story and know how to tease a woman with just the right amount of laughter and compliments, got all the markings of a con man. No way you was dressing like you did, always a roll of money in your pocket on a supermarket manager job." She sat back.

Rose looked at her sister with alarm. "You knew all this, suspected?"

Sage lifted her chin. Her lip trembled. "I figured as much. But when you came back with some handsome man on your heels, we was still so mad that you got all those years to live it up in New York after what we knew happened." She blinked back tears and turned shining eyes on Rose. "I'm sorry, Rose. I should've said what I thought. But I made up in my mind that you got what you deserved."

"Sage," Rose whispered in pain. She pressed her hand to her chest. "Did you really hate me that much?"

"I was wrong. So wrong."

Rose sniffed back tears, turned her attention back to her prodigal husband. "I didn't see because I didn't want to see. How much did they pay you?"

"Three thousand dollars. It was a lot of money back then. But I ran through it like water. When you decided to move back here

I knew I needed a fresh start, loan sharks were after me, I was in debt up to my eyeballs."

"You married me to get away from loan sharks?"

"No, Rose. No." He shook his head. "I came here to NOLA to get away, yes, but I was already in love with you. You were the best thing that ever happened to me."

Rose turned her face away.

"I wouldn't lie to you about loving you, Rose."

"What does all of this have to do with the death certificate?" Zoie asked.

"When you were born, it was the most amazing day of my life. I wanted to give you and your mama the world. But I couldn't, not on a store manager's salary."

"So you went back to your old ways," Hyacinth chimed in clear as a bell.

Hank hung his head. "At first yes. And I was doing fine, til I started losing at the tables, on bets. My debt kept growing. I was getting threatened. I needed to do something, but I couldn't run the way I'd done back in New York. I had a family. And then one afternoon when we was sitting in the yard with Zoie, you told me what happened to you in the hospital. That you'd lost your first baby and you would move hell and high water to hold onto Zoie. It was the first time you'd talked about it."

Rose looked away.

"And those Sunday dinners with Nana Claudia." He smiled wistfully. "She always had a good story to tell. Mentioned working for the Maitlands a time or two. Name sort of rang a bell but I couldn't figure the Maitlands in New York. But then I did some reading up on them—on the family, the car accident that killed Kyle Maitland, the timing, you getting shipped off to New York."

"I never told you Kyle was the father!"

"You didn't have to, I figured it out." He wrung his hands together. "I was getting desperate. The creditors were threatening me, threatening to hurt me and my family. I dug through all my papers and found that fake certificate. I wasn't sure about all the facts, but I had enough and I knew that they had a little girl that matched up with the date on the certificate. I went to the Maitlands, threatened to expose what they'd done if they didn't pay me."

Rose covered her face with her hands. Zoie wrapped her tighter in her arms. The man that she'd dreamed about, idolized, fantasized about—the larger than life knight—was dissolving right in front of her eyes.

"Did they . . . pay you?" Sage asked.

Hank nodded.

Zoie jumped to her feet. "Then why the hell did you leave? Why?" She slammed her foot down. "Tell me!" Rage shook her body.

"They agreed to pay off my creditors and keep them gone if I agreed to go away and not come back. If I didn't, they were willing to take the chance with my story coming out. They would make sure that no one believed me, and I would have to take my chances with the people who were after me."

Zoie slowly lowered herself back onto the couch.

"I couldn't risk anything happening to either of you," he said looking from Rose to Zoie. "I couldn't, even if that meant giving you both up. I knew what the Maitland family was capable of."

A heavy silence engulfed the room. Hank's confession over the past hour, the dredging up of the painful past, rendered them all emotionally spent.

After several moments, Sage got to her feet. "I'm gonna set out some cobbler and sweet tea on the back porch. Come out when you're ready." She helped Hyacinth up and left them alone.

⇒•⇐

"Get the hell outta here," Miranda shouted into the phone. "We don't talk for a few days and all hell breaks loose. Damn. I need a drink."

Zoie burst out laughing. "You and me both."

"So you and Kimberly are on the same team. Who woulda thought. Humph."

"I know right. But I needed to do right by her, and I want to get to know her. If I've learned nothing else from being back here it's that family is what matters more than anything." She stretched out on her bed, tucked her hand behind her head and let her gaze follow the slender crack that ran along the ceiling. "There's more," she said on a breath.

"All ears."

Zoie spilled out the encounter with her father and the duplicity of the Maitland family that had all but torn her family apart.

"Oh my god, Zoie. Your dad!"

"Yeah, my dad," she said, still processing everything that had transpired. "Crazy."

"How are you with all that?"

"I don't even know." She sighed. "Part of me gets why he did things the way he did. He thought he was protecting us. But those fucking Maitlands. . . ." She clenched her teeth. "All the years I lost with my dad, the years my mom lost all because some privileged family didn't want their precious name muddied. And now he's sick. Told us that the doctors said maybe he has a year." Her voice broke. "It's so unfair! I finally get him back and . . ."

"I know. I know sis," she soothed. "I swear I wish there was something I could do."

"You are. You're listening." She paused a beat, sniffed back her frustration. "I'm just going to try to make the best of what time we have. Make up for what we lost."

"That's all you can do. I mean, maybe he could have done things differently but he's here now before it was really too late and the truth disappeared with him."

"Yeah," she sighed. "I have something to tell you."

"You mean there's more?" she teased.

"Actually, yeah. I . . . met someone."

"Met someone? Wait. What happened to Jackson?"

"Well, there's that story too . . ." She shared with her friend what she'd finally come to accept about her and Jackson—they'd reached the end of their long winding road. She'd help where she could to get the fresh vegetable market up and operational at his new development until it could function without her. It was important for all of them that she fade into the background so that Jackson and Lena could make things work. She cared enough about him to want him to be happy and she knew he would be with Lena. "He's gonna make a great dad," she said.

"Wow. Just wow. Look at you, all grown up and shit."

Zoie cracked up laughing. "I know right. Feels kinda good."

"So, tell me all about this new guy."

"Well, his name is Anthony LeRoux . . ."

The friends talked for another half hour, rehashing, adding new stuff and ending with a promise to see each other soon.

She swung her legs over the side of the bed, just as her phone rang. She smiled when the name flashed on the screen.

"Mr. LeRoux. How are you? Have an assignment for me?"

"Actually, I was hoping we could talk about how we can continue to work together. The piece you wrote on the University bombing was great journalism. My producer is going to make arrangements to get me to interview Ms. Banks. I want to thank you for that."

"Not a problem."

"I was, uh, wondering if you're free for drinks, maybe dinner. We could discuss some options."

She bit back a whoop of delight. "Um, yeah. Actually I am."

"I can pick you up or we can meet if you prefer."

She quickly debated the implications of him picking her up versus her meeting him. Option two gave her independence and mobility. "I can definitely meet you. Did you have someplace in mind?"

"You like authentic creole and good music?"

"I wouldn't be a NOLA girl at heart if I didn't."

"Perfect. Say eight at Fritzel's Jazz Club on Bourbon Street?"

"Great. I know the place."

"So I'll see you at eight. Meet you in front."

"See you then."

"Your sister came through," Nick said while he washed her back. The suds slid down the column of her spine.

"Yes. She really did."

"You think the two of you can have a real relationship?"

"I'd like that." She turned to him, pressed her hands against his chest. "I always wanted a sister, and now I have one," she said, the wonder of it lightening her voice. "And an extended family. I want you to meet them."

His eyes widened. "You do?"

She smiled. "Yeah, I do. My aunts and my mom make a mean Sunday dinner." She dragged the tip of her finger across his lips. "You're invited." Her eyes danced over his face.

"I'd like that." He used the bath sponge to bathe her breasts.

"What about your husband?"

She sighed. "He won't be for long, but the ball is in his court now. The choice is his—easy or ugly."

"You think he'll come through?"

"I have to believe that."

He leaned in and kissed her. She ran her fingers down the length of him. "Did I tell you how glad I am that you came into my life?"

"No." He groaned as her fingers encircled his erection. He kissed her again. "But I'd love to hear all about it."

CHAPTER 12

The Bennett house was filled with the aromas of Sunday fixings. Sage and Rose had gone all out to impress their guests.

Rose felt like a new bride preparing dinner for her husband. Since he'd returned, they'd spent all their time together talking, explaining, crying, apologizing, laughing and starting all over again. Whatever time they had left they intended to make the most of it.

The family had gathered in the backyard and the sound of their laughter rang through the warm air. Nana Claudia's garden and legacy spread out before them.

Zoie had invited Anthony and was relieved that her family didn't give him the third degree and that Aunt Hyacinth didn't bring up or mistake him for Jackson.

When Kimberly informed them that she'd invited 'a friend' and introduced Nick, the chorus of gray-green eyes widened with inquiry. There was no way that she planned to tell her aunts and her mother that she'd met him on a night of binge drinking, only that they'd met while she was out to dinner one evening. But maybe she'd tell her sister one day.

The six-foot backyard picnic table was lined from one end to the other with platters of food to satisfy every appetite. Fried chicken, ham, grilled salmon, string beans and collards straight from the garden, potato salad, rice and peas and of course mac and cheese. A second table held apple and peach pies, red velvet cake, corn bread, biscuits, a jug of sweet tea and another of lemonade.

"Do ya'll eat like this every Sunday?" Nick whispered in Kimberly's ear as he moved down the line to fill his plate.

She giggled. "Yep."

Hank sat down next to Rose. "You don't know how much I missed this."

Their eyes met, peeling away all the lost years.

"You're here now, that's all that matters."

Anthony pulled up a chair to the table. "You're a very lucky woman," he said to Zoie.

She angled her head in question.

"You have a great family. I hope you know that—warts, secrets and all."

She looked around at the smiling faces, listened to the playful scolding and the laughter. "Yeah. I do. Don't I?"

After dinner, the men carried the platters and pitchers into the house while the women put the leftovers away in plastic containers.

"Turn on some music," Hyacinth called out from her spot at the kitchen table.

"You feel like dancing, Auntie?" Kimberly teased.

"I sho' do!" She laughed.

"I'll see if I can do something about that," Zoie offered. She dried her hands on a kitchen towel and went into the living room. One thing she could admit, her family had a pretty decent selection of music, mostly blues and some R&B, all on vinyl. She opened the top of the record player and turned it on. She selected a Muddy Waters album and his signature song, "Got My Mojo Working."

"Good choice," Anthony said from his spot on the couch.

Nick and Hank concurred, saluting the DJ with a lift of their glasses of sweet tea.

"Well thank you gentlemen for your approval," she teased. On her way back to the kitchen the front doorbell rang.

"See who that is," Sage called out. "Probably the Reverend looking for dessert!"

Zoie turned back and went down the hall to the front door. She pulled the door open and froze. Her breath stuck in her chest.

"Is Kimberly Graham here? I'm her husband."

Rowan Graham was as she remembered him, handsome, polished, laser focused. Alexis and Alexandra stood silently on either side of him, the spitting image of Kimberly.

Zoie raised her chin. "So, you did show up." She bent over to the twins' eye level. "Hi. I'm your aunt Zoie. Your mommy's sister." She smiled at her nieces then slowly stood, searing Rowan with her gaze.

"Aunt Sage wants to know who—" Kimberly stopped short. Her hand flew to her mouth.

"Mommy!" the girls squealed in unison and tore away from their father's hold on them.

Kimberly dropped to her knees and took the full weight of their charge. She scooped them into her arms, pressing them against her chest, smothering them with kisses and cooing words of love. Tears of joy slid from her eyes. "My babies," she said over and over. "My babies." She lifted her eyes to look at Rowan who still stood in the threshold. Slowly she rose. The girls were locked around her waist. She kept a protective hand on each shoulder.

"Can we talk?" Rowan said.

Zoie stood her ground, her arms folded, ready for whatever.

"It's okay, Zoie."

"Are you sure?"

She nodded.

Zoie cut Rowan a look of victory. "Come on girls," she said, her smile bright, her tone light and cheery, "let me introduce you to the rest of your family while your mom and dad talk."

"Mom?" they chorused in question. Their eyes were wide in a combination of confusion and fear and excitement.

"It's okay. I promise. Go with your aunt Zoie. It's okay."

Zoie mouthed her thanks and took them by the hand. She threw a last warning look over her shoulder at Rowan then walked with the girls to the kitchen.

Kimberly slowly walked toward Rowan, a melee of emotions spinning through her. In those few steps the life they'd built and shared popped like flashbulb lights behind her eyes, bright, sudden and sharp. Admittedly, there were more good times than bad. They'd had their share of differences, but in the end they always made up, made love and made the bad go away. She stopped in front of him. But not this time.

"How did you know where to find me?"

"Gail called me."

Inwardly she smiled. "Thank you for bringing the girls."

His blue eyes darkened, they took in the space around her and Kimberly could see his unease, his distaste. He settled back on her. "We can work this out, Kim."

"Really?" she asked incredulously. "Work what out exactly? How not to be black?"

He flinched. "You forget all this," he waved his hand, "come back home and things could go back to the way they were."

Her stomach clenched. She blinked back a hot rush of tears that pooled and simmered in her eyes. "I can only blame you but so much. There was no way for you to know me, because I didn't know myself," she said, her voice laden with sad conviction. "My entire life was orchestrated by a single drop of blood, a flash of color." The tears she'd held slipped down her cheeks. "That belief of the 'other,' of being less than, has ruined communities, families, influenced governments. I'm that other, Rowan! That person that can be treated differently simply because of the DNA that runs through my veins.

"Sure, I could go back to who I was, and no one would be the wiser." Her brows rose, widening her eyes. "We could say that after years of marriage we decided to part ways. I could pick up my old life as if nothing ever happened." She shook her head. "But I won't. I won't continue to live a lie, not even to make my life easier or to ease your embarrassment. My life has been one long lie, but it ends now." She drew in a long breath. "I guess what hurts the most, Rowan, in all of this is that even as I found out who I truly am, I found out who you are as well. I'll have my attorney send the papers. Sign them, Rowan."

His face reddened. His shoulders stiffened. "This is what you want?" he asked, clearly in disbelief. "To live like some peasant after the life I provided for you. The life that you've always lived. Is it?"

"That's really what you think 'this' is, don't you Rowan?" She snorted a laugh. "And that is the real problem." She took a step back and put her hand on the handle of the door. "My family is having dessert. I've got to go. I'll make sure the girls stay in touch. Unlike what you did to me." She looked at him one last time. "Goodbye Rowan." She shut the door.

<hr />

"You okay?" Zoie asked Kimberly later as they stood side by side on the back porch.

She drew in a long steadying breath. "Yes, I actually am." She waved to Nick who was playing catch with the twins after they'd finally peeled themselves off her.

"He's a hot one," Zoie said and nudged Kimberly in the side.

Her cheeks heated. "Yes, he is kinda hot. And you look like you hit the jackpot yourself," she tossed back, with a lift of her chin in Anthony's direction.

"Yes, I definitely will not mind being his leading lady," she said giggling.

On the other side of the yard beneath the willow tree, Hank sat with his arm around Rose while her head rested on his shoulder, and Anthony charmed Sage and Hyacinth who were tickled to have a 'real TV star' in their home.

"One marriage lost and another one found," Kimberly said soberly.

"Wow. Yeah. You're right." She sighed. "I'm sorry things went down the way they did—but I'm glad how they turned out. For everyone's sake."

"So am I." Kimberly sighed. "What are we going to do about those pesky grandparents of mine? They can't walk off into the sunset after all the damage they've caused."

Zoie put her arm around her sister's waist and looked toward the sun setting above the arc of treetops. "If there is one thing that I finally figured out since I've been home it's that nothing is more important than family." She looked at Kimberly. "Your grandparents came from a period of time that is better left behind, with a different set of values and rules. But no good will come from trying to settle scores. Trust me, I know first-hand."

Kimberly pressed her lips together in a tight smile. "You're right. Whatever their motives were they did take care of me, gave me a life filled with opportunity."

Zoie nodded in agreement.

They were quiet for a time, enjoying the tableau of family and friends.

"Since it looks like I'll be staying in NOLA I'm going to need some place to live for me and the girls," she casually announced. "I can't stay in a hotel forever." She slid Zoie a sidelong glance. "Would you help me look?"

Zoie beamed. "You're going to stay?"

Kimberly nodded eagerly.

"Of course I'll help you look. We can start tomorrow."

"And then maybe we can take the girls to see their grand-parents," she said softly.

She looked into Kimberly's eyes. "Absolutely."

Kimberly rested her head on Zoie's. "I always wanted a sister," she whispered.

"Yeah me, too."

THE OTHER SISTER

Donna Hill

ABOUT THIS GUIDE

The suggested questions are included to
enhance your group's reading of
Donna Hill's *The Other Sister*.

Discussion Questions

1. Every family has its secrets, both big and small. How does keeping secrets help or hurt the dynamics of a family?

2. The Maitland family had a sordid legacy. Based on the history of race and race relations in America, what are your feelings and impressions on what Lou Ellen Maitland did to hide the family scandal?

3. Understanding what Zoie's grandmother Claudia did with regard to Rose and her pregnancy, do you agree with her behavior and her reasoning for going along with the Maitlands?

4. What were your initial impressions of Kimberly Maitland-Graham?

5. What did you think of Zoie's relationship with her mother?

6. Discuss Kimberly and Lou Ellen's relationship. How did that relationship help to shape Kimberly?

7. Kimberly has a rude awakening when it came to her true heritage. She began to see the world through a new lens. What are some of the things she discovered about herself and society?

8. How much did the loss of having her father in her life impact who Zoie became?

9. Would you ever be able to continue in a relationship with a man who was having a child with another woman? Why or why not?

10. The history behind how blacks became 'bi-racial' or 'mixed,' especially in the south has many ugly implications. How did those old beliefs and prejudices play out in the lives of the Maitlands and the Bennett/Crawford families?

11. On one hand Kimberly seems to have accepted her new reality. However, she never goes public with the information. Do you think she ever will? Does she need to or will she simply make a 'new' life in New Orleans?

12. Was Kimberly justified in wanting to keep the truth out of the public eye? Why or why not? What was she really trying to protect?

13. Zoie's strength—her tenacity—is also her weakness. How does her tenacious personality adversely affect her life and relationships?

14. Kimberly had a one-night drunken affair. Do you think she was wrong? Why or why not?

15. What was a moment, event or conversation that really hit home for you and why is that?

16. What question would you ask Kimberly? Zoie?

17. What would you have liked to see happen in the story that didn't happen?

18. Does this story of family feel like it could be real? Why or why not?

19. How do you see Kimberly and Zoie becoming true sisters? How do you envision their future together?

20. If Nana Claudia—who put this all in motion—could be resurrected what would you ask her?

Don't miss the prequel to *The Other Sister*

A House Divided

Journalist Zoie Crawford had to leave New Orleans to finally make her own life. Her grandmother, Claudia, inspired her to follow her dreams—just as her mother, Rose, held on too tight. But with Claudia's passing, Zoie reluctantly returns home, where the past is written in the lonely corners of the bayou and the New South's supercharged corridors of power. And there she discovers a stunning, painstakingly kept secret—one that could skyrocket her career but destroy another woman's—and change both their vastly different lives, for better or for much worse.

On sale now

Enjoy the following excerpt from *A House Divided* . . .

PROLOGUE

Zoie closed her grandmother's cedar trunk and ran her hand lovingly across the smooth finish. What a wise woman her grandmother had been.

She rose from her knees and crossed the creaking wood floorboards to gaze out of the attic window and onto the future that was now truly hers. The sound of laughter from below floated upward to meet her. She smiled in acceptance. Her grandmother knew the firestorm that her will would evoke, what it would do to her three daughters, and to Zoie.

Loss may have forced Zoie to return here, but love and commitment allowed her to stay. She understood that now. Understood that everything she'd been searching for had been right in front of her.

CHAPTER 1

Come home. Come home.

The words tumbled over themselves in Zoie Crawford's head. Her mother, Rose, had mastered the singular ability to weave her words into a mantle of guilt that she ceremoniously draped over Zoie's shoulders. The weight of it, heaped on her over the years, eventually forced Zoie to flee her home in New Orleans to build a new independent, guiltless life in New York. A life free of the overbearing, the clinging, the neediness, and the possessiveness that threatened to swallow her whole.

Not now. Not an option. Not even for Nana Claudia. Too much was at stake, and she knew her grandmother would understand, even if her mother didn't. Yes, her grandmother was in declining health. Yes, she was pushing ninety. Yes, she had been the mother to her that Rose had never been. But the world was still reeling from the horror of the Twin Towers crumbling and the devastating loss of thousands of lives. Her immediate responsibility was to dig through the debris of misinformation and present her findings. Her readers, the world, deserved nothing less than her best. It was her Nana who always told her, "You is a little black girl in a white man's world. You gon' haveta work ten times harder to get halfway to the finish line." Zoie lived by those words. Those words got her out of bed every morning. As a result, she was a rising star in journalism, and her focus remained on getting the story and the coveted prize. Her coverage of 9/11 had Pulitzer written all over it, and she couldn't do her job from the family home in New Orleans. She dropped her cell phone into her purse.

She'd call her grandmother later and listen for herself whether there was any truth to her mother's clarion call or whether it was simply another ploy to manipulate her emotions.

Zoie strode into the hub of the newsroom and instantly felt the familiar orgasmic rush that fueled her. She'd long since given up trying to explain why she was so hellbent on pulling back the curtain to reveal the Wizard of Oz. Her zeal and single-mindedness had estranged her from her family and contributed to the demise of her relationship with Brian Forde. Then there was Jackson Fuller—but that . . . was different. Yet her tenacity jettisoned her career, taking her from being a beat reporter to a senior correspondent. She took great solace in that fact and forged a new family in her co-workers. They understood her passion and commitment. That was the balm that soothed the raw places in her soul, the places she shared with no one other than her one friend, Miranda Howard—even though they often bumped heads over the importance of having more than work to keep one warm at night.

"Zoie! I need to see you," Mark Livingston bellowed over the cacophony of chirping phones, slamming doors, and a chorus of voices. He stood in the frame of his office door with his usual harried expression. For Mark, everything was code orange.

"Be right there," Zoie called out over the bent heads of her colleagues. She dropped her purse, coat, and laptop on her desk and wound her way around the bullpen to Mark's office.

"Close the door and have a seat," he said without preamble.

Zoie stepped into the claustrophobic space of her publisher, quietly shut the door, and was quickly sucked into the abyss of paper and the towers of files that occupied the four corners of the room. She lifted a box from the one chair, placed it on the floor, and sat down.

The organized chaos of Mark Livingston belied his brilliance. He had a nose for news and the ability to recognize that fever in others. His reputation for integrity and excellence was renowned in the field. He'd spent ten years with the *Washington Post* and the *New York Times* before pooling all of his resources and launching the *National Recorder*. In the fifteen years since its launch, it had stood toe to toe with the *Post*, the *Times*, and the *Wall Street Journal*.

When Zoie graduated from Columbia University's School of Journalism, she bounced around for two years before landing, five years earlier, a freelance spot with the *Recorder*, which soon became more of a staff post than freelance. But Zoie was firm in keeping her "freelance" title. It allowed her to maintain a sense of independence. Mark took her under his wing. He mentored her, groomed her, tested her skills, fed her the passion they both shared, and treated her like the child he never had. She was his protégé, and would be his heir apparent when he retired. She'd come a long way under his tutelage, but she would never be satisfied. She could always be better.

Mark lowered his long body onto his mud-brown leather chair, which had long ago seen better days. He linked his pink and white fingers together. The overhead light reflected off the bald patch on his head, projecting an illusion of a halo.

"What's up, Mark?" She crossed her legs at the ankle.

Mark leaned back. His disarming green eyes zoomed in on her. "I know you've been knee-deep in the Twin Tower series," he said, quickly adding, "and you're doing one helluva job," nodding his head while he spoke as if to reaffirm his own affirmation. He cleared his throat, and Zoie instinctively held her breath. "I have another angle that I want you to follow. I want you to turn your notes and your contacts over to Brian."

It took a moment for what he'd said to register. Zoie's eyes narrowed in shock an instant before fury exploded. She leapt up from her seat.

"Are you freaking kidding me, Brian? Oh, hell no. I worked this series." She jabbed her chest with her finger for emphasis and began to pace the tiny space. "No." She vigorously shook her head and folded her arms in defiance, then swung toward Mark. "No!"

Zoie planted her palms on the quarter inch of available desk space. "This is my story," she said again, in a singularly deliberate tone. "I've worked inhuman hours, turned in stories that no other paper has done." Her voice rose with emotion. "This is what you groomed me for, and you want me to turn it over to Brian Forde. Why in God's name would I ever agree to that?"

"Have I ever steered you wrong?" he calmly asked.

Zoie tried to focus on her breathing and not the numbness that began to rise from the soles of her feet. Her heart raced, and she had to rapidly blink to stave off the hot tears that threatened to expose that part of her she kept hidden.

"You'll continue to receive a co-writer byline."

Her nostrils flared.

Mark flipped open a folder and turned it to face her. "Kimberly Maitland-Graham."

Zoie couldn't focus. What the fuck was he talking about? She shoved it back. "What about her?"

"She's running for New York State Senate against the Democratic incumbent and she has a groundswell of support. Especially now. She comes from money and is being propped up as a star in her party. If she wins, it will be a major coup and shakeup up in Albany."

Now he had her attention.

"I want you on this from the beginning. I want her life, her policies, her stump speeches, everything she's ever written, and every job she's ever held. I want interviews with her staff and friends, the works."

"Are we positioning the paper as her supporter? Since when have we backed a Republican?"

"We aren't." He leaned forward. His green eyes darkened. "That's why I want you to cover her. No one else on the team has the tenacity to turn over every stone to get to the truth."

"What truth?"

"Who she really is, not this picture-perfect brand that her people are creating. I know there's something there. I feel it in my gut, and you're going to find it." He pushed his face forward. "If she wins, she'll tip the balance in the State Senate."

Zoie's thoughts swirled. Excitement bubbled in her veins. Her reporting could very well help set the narrative of the state's politics.

"But it must be balanced."

"Of course." Zoie reached for the file and slid it toward her.

"I don't want this to come off as some kind of witch hunt. Facts, facts, facts," he reiterated with a slap of his palm on the desk. "I've already gotten you assigned to her press pool." He opened his desk drawer and took out her credentials. "You'll have full access."

Zoie glanced at the laminated tags. "How'd you know I'd agree?"

Mark grinned, deepening the lines around his eyes. "When have you ever turned down anything this big?"

Zoie bit back a smile. "You know me too well."

"This is it, Zoie. This is the story that will get you that Pulitzer."

"And Brian is on board with this whole co-byline thing?"

Mark nodded. "Listen, I want you on this like yesterday."

Zoie pushed out a breath and stood. "Okay." She snatched up the folder and press tags. *Come home.* A flash of guilt knotted her stomach. "I'll get started." She turned to leave.

"You won't regret this."

Zoie opened the door.

"Send Brian in, will you?"

Her step halted for a moment. "Sure."

⟶⟵

Brian Forde was smart, driven, an excellent journalist, and an expert lover. One would think they'd be a perfect match. That's what Zoie thought, too. But it was those very qualities that imploded their very tempestuous relationship. They were too much alike, and the fire that flamed between them burned them both. Their fights were epic, their voracious work ethic combustible, and after six months, their monumental lovemaking couldn't overcome the very qualities that made them so damned good at what they did.

Zoie stopped beside Brian's desk. His total focus was on his computer screen. His earbuds blocked out the office noise. If she pegged it right, he was listening to John Coltrane, his go-to guy whenever he was deep into a story. The hand of melancholy tried to grab hold of her, but she shoved it aside.

She tapped him lightly on the shoulder. His head snapped up as he simultaneously snatched the buds out of his ears. His initial expression was pure annoyance at being disturbed until his focus settled on Zoie.

"Oh, hey." He swung his chair around to face her and took her in with a single eye sweep.

Brian had the uncanny ability to look at her as if she were naked. Zoie cleared her throat. "Mark wants to see you."

He folded his arms. "You cool with the co-byline?"

Her lips thinned. She found a smile. "I'm good. I've done the bulk of the work."

He slowly stood, forcing her gaze to follow the rise of his hard-packed body until she found herself looking into his eyes. Her pulse quickened. She swallowed and took a half step back.

"I'll keep you in the loop," he said.

The deep timbre of his voice swung like a metronome in her stomach. "Great." She turned away, headed to her cubicle, and realized that her heart was pounding.

———◆———

"This could be big. It *is* big," Zoie said while she sipped on her margarita.

Miranda crunched on a nacho loaded with guacamole and

cheddar cheese. "Hmm," she mumbled and chewed. "So you don't have a problem handing your work over to Brian?"

"Of course I do. But this assignment is bigger and has teeth."

Miranda turned her focus from their shared plate of nachos and directed her full attention on Zoie.

"Since when have you been about destroying someone, especially another woman?"

"You're being dramatic."

"Am I?" She stared until Zoie shifted in her seat.

"This is not about destroying. It's about uncovering. There's a difference. This woman's win could very well shift the balance of political power in Albany. Should she be there? What are her beliefs, her policies, her allies, and her vision? Those are the things I want to find out and things the voting public needs to know."

Miranda reached for another nacho. "Okay. As long as you're clear. I know how you can get when you sink your teeth into something. This poor woman has no idea what she's in for."

Zoie chuckled, then sipped her drink. "Got a call from Rose."

"Is everything okay?"

Zoie waved her hand in dismissal. "You know my mother—always the alarmist. She left a message saying that Nana wasn't well and that I need to come home."

"When are you leaving?"

"I can't. Not now."

"Why the hell not? It's your grandmother."

"I know that. But—"

"Don't tell me it's that fucking job, Z."

Zoie glanced away and focused on the dissolving foam in her glass. Bit by bit, the white froth became consumed by liquid until the foam was gone.

"There's more to life than work."

"We've had this conversation, Randi."

"Apparently, I was talking to myself." She tsked in disgust. "I don't believe you."

Zoie jerked forward. The tips of her fingers clenched the table.

"And why not, Randi?" she challenged. "What has home ever done for me? A mother who tried to suck the life out of me, and two aunts who can't decide whom they dislike most—me, my mother, or each other. And Nana . . ." Her taut expression eased. She pushed out a breath. "There's only so much one person can do in a den of vipers."

"Zoie! That's your family," Miranda said, her voice rising.

Zoie slowly shook her head. "You come from this big ole happy family that actually enjoys being around each other. My family portrait is next to the diagnosis of dysfunctional." She finished off her drink, then craned her neck in search of the waitress.

"It's been almost ten years, Z." She reached across the table. "People change, mellow with age," she added with a soft smile. She squeezed Zoie's fingers.

Zoie's throat clenched. "But the hurts, the slights, the suffocation—I had some time to let all that scab over. Ya know." She looked into the eyes of her friend. "Going back is like picking the scab. I don't think I'm healed underneath." A tear slid down her cheek. She sniffed hard.

"Listen to me." Miranda leaned across the table so that their heads almost touched. "You've lived in the biggest, baddest city in the world. You pushed yourself through grad school, landed a job in your field, and made a name for yourself in the industry. No one can take that from you—not your overbearing mother or the wicked aunties. Go see your Nana," she said softly.

Zoie dabbed the corner of her eye with the knuckle of her finger.

The waitress stopped at their table as if cued from the wings of the stage, ready to take their orders, giving Zoie a momentary reprieve.

As usual, Miranda had the waitress explain each item and how it was prepared. The infuriating habit had lost its punch with Zoie ages ago. Zoie would generally bury her head in her menu until Miranda was finished and then smile apologetically to the wait staff on her dear friend's behalf.

She and Miranda met in college. Zoie majored in journalism, and Miranda went after a business degree, which she parlayed into a plum position with the Port Authority, and now she oversaw operations at Kennedy and LaGuardia airports.

Miranda was right, Zoie thought, as Miranda prattled on. She'd put plenty of time and distance between herself and her family. She was stronger now.

"And for you, ma'am?" the cool-as-a-cucumber waitress asked.

"Oh, yes, sorry," she stuttered, jerked from her musing. "Umm, I'll have the roasted chicken and grilled vegetables . . . and another margarita."

"Right away." She scooped up the menus and moved away as stealthily as she'd appeared.

Zoie nursed the ice from her glass.

"How *are* things between you and Brian?"

Zoie blinked several times. How did they segue to Brian? That was one of Miranda's other talents—changing subjects without warning. "There's nothing 'between us,'" she said, making air quotes. "Our working relationship is fine, if that's what you mean."

"I still think you could have worked things out." She snapped a white linen napkin open and spread it ceremoniously on her lap.

"Why does it have to be me who has to work things out?" she asked two octaves above her normal range. "What about him?"

Miranda's hazel eyes darted around the room. "Because you're the pain-in-the-ass stubborn one, that's why."

"With friends like you, Randi . . . I swear."

"Would you rather I be the kind of friend who kisses your ass even when you're wrong?"

"Yes, damnit!

They burst out in laughter.

"You're crazy," Miranda said over her chuckles.

The waitress returned with their drinks. "Enjoy," she said and hurried off.

Zoie lifted her glass. "To truth."

Miranda tapped her glass against Zoie's. "That's all there is."

Twelve hours had passed since she'd listened to her mother's message. With work, the shock of her new assignment, and her standing after-work meet-up with Miranda, she'd been able to relegate the words to the back of her mind and tamp down the guilt that niggled at her conscience. She simply had not had the time. That's what she told herself.

Now, however, in the aloneness of her one-bedroom condo, there was no escape. Rose's words echoed, that sinking feeling resurfaced, and the fear that she'd successfully ignored demanded her attention.

A glass of wine first. A shower next. Yes, wine and a shower. Then she would call. Nothing was going to change.

She almost felt like herself by the time she'd finished off her wine and let the waters beat against her skin. Down the drain her worries went, along with her anxieties. She was fortified now.

Inhaling a breath of resolve, she sat on the side of her bed and picked up her cell phone from the nightstand. She swiped the screen and tapped in her password. Her heart thundered. *Three messages from her mother.* She didn't want to listen to the chastising, the questioning, the guilt trip that Rose would surely send her on.

Zoie tapped in the number to the family home in New Orleans, held her breath, and waited.

"Hello . . ."

The sound of her mother's voice drew her all the way back to the days that she longed to forget, but never could.

"Mom, you left me several messages. I'm sorry I was—"

"She's gone."

The jigsaw puzzle of words made no sense. They didn't fit together.

"What are you saying? What do you mean? Gone where?"

"About an hour ago," her mother said, her voice flat and empty as if siphoned of whatever emotion she had left. "I suppose if you're not too busy you can come home for the services."

"Mom . . . Nana . . ."

"I have to go. The reverend is here."

Click.

She couldn't breathe; her heart raced and her thoughts spun. A rush of raw anguish rose up from the depths of her soul and escaped. The keen of a wounded animal vibrated in the room, bounced off walls, and slammed back into her, knocking her to her knees.

Pain became a swirling vortex that stole her breath, shredded her heart, and whipped her around until she was weak and spent.

Come home.

"Oh God, oh God, what have I done? Nana! . . ."

She curled into a ball on the floor and wept.

Connect with